CW00958536

Sword For H

Book 1 in the Border Knight Series

By

Griff Hosker

Contents

Published by Sword Books Ltd 2017

SWORD
BOOKS

Prologue

Arsuf, Outremer- 1191

The day my father died was the worst day of my life and, at the same time, the best. I lost a true hero of England and a father whom I adored and I was knighted by King Richard of England. You remember such days in great detail. Every action, every moment is etched into your soul and you never forget any of it. It was the day I lost everything. It was the day I had to begin my life over.

My father was the third Earl of Cleveland. He had been born in the Holy Land where my grandfather, William of Aqua Bella, had been a crusader. My grandmother was Jewish. She had always been worried about what the Normans at court might think of her and so she had stayed in my grandfather's castle in Stockton until the day she died. She had loved that green and verdant valley that had been such a contrast to her home in the east. My grandfather had died fighting the Scots. My grandmother had followed him soon after. They had been buried in a tomb within the church of Stockton Castle. It was our family church and our entire family were buried there. When my mother had died giving birth to what would have been my sister, Matilda, my father who was broken-hearted, took the cross and followed King Richard to the Crusades. He took it as a sign that he ought to do something to honour her memory. He took with him the knights from the valley. They were his oathsworn. They were the best of the best.

I remember every moment of that fateful day. My name, Thomas of Stockton, would be forever associated with that great victory over the Seljuk Turk and Ayyubid warriors. My father, Sir Samuel, had been with King Richard when we had followed the wild Hospitaller's charge. My father's conroi was always close to the king. My family had been defenders of the royal family since the time of the first King Henry. As his squire, I had been behind my father with his standard. The Turks were fierce warriors. My grandfather had told us of his battles with them and neither my father nor myself underestimated their skills. My father had not brought men at arms with him. He had left those to guard our home and the valley. The legendary archers who had been raised by my great grandfather, known as the Warlord, also remained to protect our people from the ravages of the Scots. Instead, we had brought the knights from the valley. On that day as my father led his knights across the coastal plain to follow King Richard's

2

banner I was a young squire and my journey to become a knight had barely begun.

I remember every vivid detail of that charge. Richard of Hartburn rode on my father's right; as he always did. Roger of Norton, a doughty warrior with arms like young oaks, rode on his left. William of Elton and Ralph of Thornaby flanked those. I was the eldest of the squires and I rode in the centre of the rest. My father's war horse, Storm Bringer, dwarfed my palfrey, Skuld, but I would not swap them. My horse was descended from a line that went back to my grandfather and the eldest was always named Skuld. I knew that I would need every ounce of my palfrey's skill. We were riding against Turks. Their horse archers were deadly and we rarely charged them. Later, long after the battle was over, when scarred and battered knights, much more senior than I, discussed the battle they said that had not Garnier de Nablus, the Master of the Hospitallers lost his head and charged recklessly then we would have retired to Arsuf and the battle might not have been won. I was there and I was not certain. I was just a lowly squire clinging on to a banner with a yellow gryphon on a blue background.

We charged after our lord. King Richard was a leader that all men would follow. Guy de Lusignan, the King of Jerusalem was just a figurehead. Even the French warriors followed Richard. My father led his household knights as close to the king as he could manage. It meant risking death for every Turk and Ayyubid was trying to kill our king. It was a point of honour for my father.

A battle never unfolds the way you expect it to. Before you charge you assume that all the lines will be straight; the ground will be flat and every stroke you take will be successful. It is rarely like that. My father had taught me well and I saw that, although he stayed as close to the king and his knights as possible, he kept as straight a line with his knights as he could. Inevitably, however, he ended up slightly ahead of Sir Richard and Sir Roger.

All that I could see were the knights just beyond my father. I saw arrows strike them. Often that did not stop a knight. With their surcoat, mail and gambeson, they had good protection. Their horses, on the other hand, could and did die. Although I was riding close to my father I had my wits about me. When I saw him lift his horse's head and stand in the saddle then I knew he was leaping over something. A good knight, my grandfather had told me, always anticipates. I pulled Skuld's reins up but, in truth, she was a clever horse and she was already leaping over the dying horse and pinioned knight. Aubrey of Chateau Galliard would never return home. His skull had been crushed by one of the King's household horses.

When I saw swords raised I knew that the Hospitallers and the King were engaged! That was a miracle for the archers had not managed to flee. My father stood in his stirrups and pointed to our right. The enemy could attack the king on his unguarded flank. My father jerked his reins over and we followed him. He

3

had seen a gap and ahead of us were horse archers. Even better was the sight of over a hundred of them who had dismounted. They were packed so closely together that many of their bows had no target. He lowered his lance and spurred Storm Bringer. Arrows were sent in their direction and I saw one hit my father's left shoulder but he never faltered. Another hit Storm Bringer but he was a war horse and he ploughed on. One clanked off my helmet and made my ears ring but I did not deviate from the path carved by the Earl of Cleveland. I was his son and the blood of the Warlord coursed through my veins. The first Ayyubid and Turk to die were struck by spears and lances in the head and chest. Others were trampled to death. I both felt and heard the sickening crunch as Skuld's hooves crushed a Turkish skull. Horses might try to avoid stepping on men. When the ground is a sea of them then they cannot.

My father's lance drove through the first Ayyubid horse archer and knocked him from his saddle. I drew my sword, holding my reins and the standard in my left hand; it meant that I had no shield. Had an archer aimed at me then I had little protection. The range was so close that even my mail would not have stopped it. My father allowed the Ayyubid to slide from the lance. His war horse was biting and snapping at the Turkish horses. He had been wounded and was angry. As my father skewered a second horse archer his other household knights slew their foes and we carved a hole deep into the flank of the horse archers. They tried to flee. Their horses were small and swift and could normally outrun our war horses. They were stopped by their sheer weight of numbers.

When their spears were shattered our knights drew their swords. Had my father held out his hand then I would have given him the spear which I held with the standard. He drew his sword and would not need a spear. We were close and either a sword or a mace were the best weapons. The Seljuk Turks and the Ayyubid we fought had light, almost delicate weapons. Our swords were heavy and they were long, even when they were blunted they were still a formidable weapon. Being hit with one was like being struck by an iron bar! I saw one warrior hit by my father. His helmet and head were split and the sword drove deep into his neck. Sir Richard and Sir Roger were laying about them with their swords so that there was nothing for me to do. My father had often said that the standard with the gryphon upon it put fear into the hearts of our foes and just by being there I was helping to win battles. The banner had been carried in the Holy Land before by my grandfather.

I was aware that we had galloped more than a mile. In the heat of the Holy Land and carrying mail, that was a long way for a war horse and I saw that Storm Bringer was lathered. King Richard was also aware of the danger of exhausting horses and I heard his horn as he sounded the halt. My father stopped when we were just forty paces from the king. He turned to me and raised the face mask on his helmet. He was smiling.

"I see you are still there, my son."

4

I nodded and showed him my sword, "Aye but I have yet to strike a blow in anger."

He pointed to the banner. "That is a weapon which kills but shows no blood."

Suddenly there came a wail from ahead. Sir Richard shouted, "Fools! Sir James d'Avesnes has led his Flemish too far! They are being slaughtered."

Skuld whinnied and raised her head. She had the ability to sense danger and I had learned not to ignore it. I looked to my right, "Lord! Ayyubid! It is the Sultan's bodyguard!"

I saw seven hundred horsemen hurtling towards us. They were led by Saladin's nephew, Taqi al-Din. My father did not falter. Despite the fact that he and his horse were wounded he raised his sword and shouted, "King Richard, God and for England!" He led his household knights, other knights from the north and the sergeant at arms who followed us in a charge to stop the horsemen or to slow them down, at least.

The men who charged us were not horse archers. These were armed as we were. They had spears and mail. Their helmets, bayda or egg helmets, had a full mail coif hanging down so that they looked to have a mailed head. They wore a cuirass beneath their flowing robes. With a lance and a curved sword, they had a shield that looked like ours. These were the best that the Seljuk Turks had.

Our line was no longer as tight as it had been. My father wished to break up the enemy formation. Behind me, I could hear orders being given as King Richard reformed his line so that he could charge the enemy. He needed time and we were buying it for him! I glanced behind and saw that other English knights had joined us. My father's banner was well known. He was a respected leader. In a perfect world, my father would have had two squires, at the very least, and one would have carried a spare lance for the earl. Robin had died. It had been an inglorious death. He had been bitten by a snake and died. I was the only squire left and I carried the standard. The spare spear was next to the standard.

Although our foes did not ride such large horses their mounts were the equal of ours and it would be a hard-fought battle. Neither side slowed although they were travelling faster than we were. Their horses were fresher and carried less weight. I lowered the standard slightly. It was not that I was tired but it was a weapon I could use. As I did so the spear slipped from my grasp. I cursed myself. A good squire would have had a weapon ready for his knight. I drew my sword and held it slightly below and behind me. One advantage I had over the enemy was that I was at least a head taller than any of them. My grandfather had taught me to use every advantage I could!

We crashed together and the sound was like a thousand blacksmiths all hammering on their anvils at the same time. I could no longer watch my father. I had to watch the Seljuk Turk who aimed his spear at me. Skuld was so good that I could just use my knees to guide her. That saved me. I dropped the reins and swept the standard to my left as the lance came towards my unprotected side. My standard was a large and a clumsy weapon but it had a banner. The lance became entangled in the cloth and I stood in my stirrups and brought my sword, which had been hidden below my saddle, up and over. The Seljuk was almost past me as my sword connected. My height and my swing hacked across his back. His cuirass was on the front and my sword bit through to his backbone. He tumbled from his saddle. I had no opportunity for self-congratulation for another spear was jabbed towards me. I did the only thing I could do. I swept the blade backhand and deflected the blade.

I saw that my father was surrounded by enemies. Even as I jerked Skuld's reins around to get to him Sir Richard rode to his aid. As he speared a Seljuk in the back he was, in turn, speared through the side. The head emerged from the other side and he tumbled from his horse. My father had one less enemy but he also had one less knight to protect him. I dug my heels into Skuld and she leapt into the gap vacated by Sir Richard whose lifeless eyes stared up at me, his helmet having fallen from him. I swung the standard somewhat clumsily at the nearest Seljuk. It merely clattered off his helmet but it stopped him from attacking my father. Instead, he turned and swung his lighter sword at me. I countered with my own sword. I expected his to bend but it did not. They used good steel. My advantage was my height and my strength. He was more experienced and better suited for this combat. He was not as restricted as I was. He only had a cuirass on his front. I pulled back my left arm and rammed the pointed head of the standard towards his face. Even though it was covered in mail his head jerked back and I stood and brought down my sword with all the strength that I could muster. I smashed into his helmet and the mail which covered his face. He fell backwards over his horse's rump. My blow must have rendered him unconscious.

As he fell I saw, to my dismay, that my father and I were the only two Englishmen left on their horses. His knights lay where they had fallen. I saw one dead squire. I turned in time to almost hurl my standard to block the sword that would have sliced into my father's right side. As it was, a spearman ran up and rammed his spear into my father's leg and, worse, into Storm Bringer's side. As Storm Bringer reared and my father fought to control his horse one of the Sultan's Askari's thrust his spear into my father's side. He fell from his horse. I saw him manage to roll to the side but there was a great deal of blood. I rammed the standard into the ground and leapt off Skuld. Storm Bringer, mortally wounded, galloped through the enemy biting and kicking as he went. He bought me time to get to my father. He tried to stand but I could see that he was spent.

"Lie still father, I will protect you." I planted the standard on one side of his body and held my sword with the other. If we were to die then we would die together. I could not abandon his body to be butchered by these Ayyubid warriors. I looked for the next warrior.

6

Sword For Hire

My father's horse had not got far and now lay dying. The Ayyubid were reforming to come at me again. I sensed a movement to my right and saw William, Sir Richard's squire crawling towards me. He was wounded but he held his sword. He hauled himself up the standard and stood behind me. I gave him what I hoped was a brave smile but, in reality, I was scared. Six horsemen galloped at us. They wanted the banner and they wanted my father's body. The head of the Earl of Cleveland would make a great prize.

I counted on the fact that the horses would not ride over us. There was room to our left and right. If we stood our ground then we would have just three lances to contend with. The others would get nowhere near us. They did not come at us full tilt. They came at a measured pace. I saw their spears pulled back ready to strike. The ones on the outside of them had dropped back. They would attack us once the others had tried their attack. The standard was all. I could not see their eyes nor could they see ours. It was like the games of dare we squires played. Who would blink first? Without the luxury of seeing eyes, you had to rely on your own courage. That day I saw what I could do.

Just as the first Ayyubid pulled back his arm I heard my father's voice, "Fight them, my son! You are of the Warlord's blood!" They were the last words he spoke to me. They stayed with me to my dying day.

As I deflected the first lance a second one was thrust at me. William managed to flick it away with his sword. He was leaning against the standard for support. The horse from the first rider was so close that I could feel its breath. I swung my sword and it bit into the horse's chest. Its head came down and the Ayyubid flew from the saddle. The third horseman veered to avoid the dying horse and his lance missed me but stuck in William's leg. As I glanced down I saw that the spear which had been deflected by William was now sticking from my father's chest. He was dead and I was alone in the world! As William slumped to the ground I picked up one of the lances which had fallen to the bloody ground. Bracing it against my left foot I held it before me and kept my sword ready. I would sell my life dearly.

The remaining Ayyubid were more cautious. It was as though the rest of the battle was being fought elsewhere. This was now a battle between me and these Ayyubid bodyguards. They were trying to surround me. They wanted the banner. I used the standard and my father's body to guard my back. I would force them to come at me. One of them, more reckless, or possibly angrier than the others spurred his horse at me. There was no point in flinching. If I flinched then I died. I would face my death and see it coming. I began to swing my sword. He was moving so quickly that he found it hard to react. His eyes must have gone to the sword and he failed to see the lance. It went under his shield and up into his body. I was forced back to the standard but the Ayyubid was pierced through to his spine. His weight broke the lance and he fell before me. It was another barrier.

Two of them rode at me next and they came on two sides. With just my sword I could not possibly hope to deflect two lances. I was a dead man. One was slightly ahead of the other and I chose him to be the one I would take to the grave with me. I held my sword in two hands. I watched him pull back his lance. A lance is a long and heavy object. I saw the head waving up and down. I had to ignore the point and concentrate on the one strike I would have. At the last moment, when it seemed certain that the lance would strike me, I stepped to the side and swung my sword with all the remaining strength I had. His horse had avoided both me and the standard. I struck the leg of the Ayyubid warrior and chopped through it and into the horse.

The last two warriors roared a challenge and came at me. I turned warily to face them and then, to my great joy and delight, saw them lanced by the household knights of King Richard.

The King reined in next to me, "You are a true warrior!" He saluted me with his sword. "I will return after the battle. You deserve honour."

I was spent and had no words. All that I could do was to give a half bow. I sheathed my sword and turned to William. I tore the surcoat from one of the Ayyubid warriors and used it to bind the leg above the wound. William was still conscious. "They are all dead, Tom! All!"

William was a couple of years younger than me and had not been a squire as long as I had. "But we are alive. Lie still while I tend to my father."

His helmet had fallen from his head and he lay, looking at peace. He had been born in this land and he had died here. Perhaps that was why he was smiling. I took the lance from his body and hurled it away. I gently lowered his ventail so that I could see his face clearly. His eyes were closed and he had a half-smile upon his lips. He must have been in great pain when he had died. How could he have been smiling? I laid him out so that his legs were straight and placed his sword down his body with his hands folded over it. Then I stood. The battle had moved away from us. Dying men were moaning. Wounded horses were thrashing their legs in pain. I ignored them all as I spoke to my father.

"Father, I tried to do that which a squire should do and protect you. I failed. But I swear now that I will return to England one day and I will protect our valley as you have done; as did grandfather and as did his father. You said I have the blood of the Warlord in my veins. I will try to live up to that." That done I took my cloak and laid it over his body so that it was covered.

I went over the field to seek out the other knights. Perhaps they lived. All had fought bravely but they had been assailed by too many men. They were all dead. From the cuts and wounds, it had taken many strokes to end their lives. I found the bodies of Tristan and Peter, Sir Roger and Sir William's squires. Of Raymond, Sir Ralph's squire, there was no sign. I went to the dead Ayyubid. These warriors were mercenaries and well paid. William had no lord now. I searched their bodies and took their purses. It might help William to get home.

The alternative was for him to find a new lord. I suddenly realised that I had no lord to follow. Perhaps I would need the coin to get home too.

I turned around as Skuld neighed and walked towards me. I was relieved. I had thought that she had been hurt too. She nuzzled me and I stroked her mane. I was not entirely alone. I had Skuld.

The priests arrived. They were the healers who saw to the wounded. If a warrior was too hurt to live then a sergeant at arms would be asked to give him a warrior's death. Their vows had to be adapted out here in this merciless land. I watched as they began to dress William's leg. I had just checked that Skuld had no wounds when I saw a column of men approaching. It was King Richard.

He and his knights dismounted. He took off his helmet. He spoke loudly so that all men could hear, "Once again the men of the Valley of the Tees have come to my aid. Your grandfather did so often enough with my father. Now they are dead." He took out his sword. "I cannot bring them back but I can reward a squire who deserves to be a knight. Kneel!" I did so. He touched me on both shoulders with his sword. One of his knights had taken the spurs from my father. He handed them to the king as King Richard said, "Rise, Sir Thomas of Stockton, serve me as your father did." He handed me my father's spurs. I was now a knight. I looked at the spurs and then at my father. I would give it all up if he were only alive. I was alone.

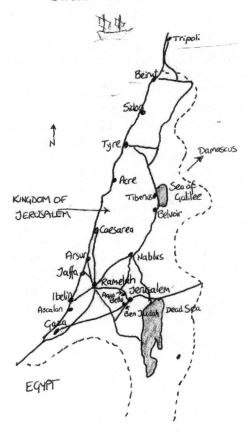

The Holy Land

Chapter 1

Acre 1193

It was more than a year since I had been knighted. I had wished to go back to England but the King had said that he needed knights such as me. I do not think that was true. I think he wanted the banner. I was one of the youngest knights and I had but one squire, William. I did not even own a war horse. I had captured three horses from the Ayyubid warriors I had slain but I had no war horse. King Richard liked my banner to follow his. The gryphon was known. It was feared. Despite the fact that there were no longer any knights save me he kept up the illusion. William had taken three months to heal. In that time, we had learned how to be a knight and a squire in the mighty fortress of Acre. It was crowded but we were both accorded respect for our actions that day in Arsuf. The king kept us close. At the time, I was flattered but now, in hindsight, I see that he enjoyed the reflected glory of what we did. The glory was his by association.

One advantage of being so close to the king was the fact that I had a better idea of what was going on. He was tiring of a war he could not win. He had argued with Leopold of Austria and sent him home. He browbeat and bullied the other leaders and there was dissension in the camp. He had promised to recapture Jerusalem but he would fail. He knew that. He was looking for a way out of this war that would leave him with some honour. I knew, from the secret negotiations that he was seeking some sort of honourable peace with Saladin. That suited me. I would be able to go home. However, events were being set in place which would prevent that.

William and I were housed in the citadel that was Acre. Fought over for a century it was a formidable fortress. The only fighting we had to do was an occasional foray into Saladin's land. Gone were the protective patrols for pilgrims. Now King Richard sent us out to harry the Seljuk Turks and to gather booty and treasure. I think that my grandfather would have been appalled. I had been unable to give William more than a third of the treasure I had collected. My fortune went with the death of my father. He had been earl. There was no mention of the title coming to me. Each time I asked I was told that I would have to wait until we returned to England. My father had used the money lenders to fund our knights. It went back to the time of my grandfather. He had used the money lenders to move money from the Holy Land. There was money in England but, without my father's contacts, I was virtually penniless. I was reliant upon the goodwill of King Richard. He was not a generous king.

I knew that King Richard was not in Acre. He had left with his closest advisers. There were, however, many Templars and there was the King of Jerusalem. He was a king with no kingdom. Jerusalem had been taken but their king still harboured dreams of retaining the city. It had been incredibly wealthy. I did not like him. He never ventured forth to fight in battle. I think that King Richard shared my view for he rarely spoke to him outside of the councils of war.

One evening, after a month in which we had not ridden forth, I was summoned, along with other knights to the Great Hall. I expected an announcement from King Richard that we would be returning home. I could not afford to travel home without his help. King Richard, however, was not there. He had still to return from this mysterious meeting. It was the King of Jerusalem, Guy de Lusignan who spoke to us. He had achieved the crown through dubious means and he was not the most pleasant of men. If we were working for him then the task would not be an honourable one.

There were twenty knights gathered. Most were English but I saw one who was not. He looked to be Swedish from his mail. The Scandinavian knights tended to wear slightly more old-fashioned mail and helmets. He sat next to me. I was alone. The other knights had clamoured to be close to my father but I had no influence. I did not even have a spare suit of mail.

The knight smiled, "Can I sit down, young Cleveland?" His voice was accented but his words were clear.

I gave a wry smile back, "I have no title, sir. I am plain Sir Thomas of Stockton. Any other title will have to wait until I return to England and the king can decide if I warrant the title."

"I am Jarl Birger Persson. I am from Sweden."

"You are even further away from home than we are. I have not seen many of your countrymen here."

"We have our own crusade against the Estonians, Slavs and the Karelians. They are barbarians and even worse than the followers of Islam!"

"Then why are you here?"

"Bishop Albert sent me here fetch back a piece of the true cross. He believes it will help us." He shrugged, "I have been here some time and seen little evidence that anything from this crusade brings luck."

There was a trade in objects which purported to be from the time of Jesus. Most were fakes. Until Jerusalem fell there were plenty to be found. Since then the priests were constantly trying to find them.

"Just take a piece of wood home and say it is the true cross. I am not certain how anyone would know the difference!"

Birger Persson laughed and clapped me on the back, "I like you Englishman! You are incredibly cynical for one so young!"

"Perhaps it is this land."

"I knew your father. Not well but I knew him to be an honourable man. He would not like your cynicism."

"I have seen little noble about this war. I saw my father and his knights die to protect a king who does not seem concerned about the sacrifice. It is almost as though that was to be expected. Men will give their lives for the Lionheart!"

I saw Birger Persson open his mouth to speak but the King of Jerusalem stood, "King Richard has asked me to speak with you. He has a task for you that is both dangerous and necessary. It requires knights who are noble in both heart and mind."

Birger said, out of the side of his mouth, "And poor knights such as you see here who will do what they are ordered for they cannot afford to do else."

The King frowned at the mumbled conversation. He continued. "However, you will be paid for your services. King Richard has observed that all of you in this hall have a need for coin. Before the Turks took Jerusalem, much treasure was rescued and taken to the Hospitaller's refuge a few miles from Jerusalem. Unfortunately, the knights who were supposed to bring it to safety were killed. Now that the refuge has fallen the treasure would appear to be lost."

I shook my head. If the treasure was lost then what was this meeting about? This would be another waste of knights who could be fighting for something more than coin.

"Word has come to us that the Turks have not discovered where it is hidden. There is a chance that it is still there. You will find it and return it here."

I looked around. Now that I had a chance to look at them I saw that Jarl Birger was correct. All of us were poor knights. We were desperate men. Without sponsors, we eked out a living. We were expendable!

The King pointed to his right and a knight entered. "Robert of Blois will lead you. He is a kinsman and a great warrior."

It was not Robert who had my attention. Behind him came four squires. They were all dressed in his livery. One of them was Raymond of Thornaby. He had been Sir Ralph's squire. I had thought him killed at Arsuf. Now he looked not only alive but prosperous. His hair was groomed and, compared with William and me, well fed. He saw me. I did not expect his reaction. He grinned. His lord was dead but I was the son of the Earl. I would have to speak with him.

I had never met him but I quickly realised that I did not like Robert of Blois. He was a broad and powerfully built knight but he had a hawk shaped nose. However, it was his voice that grated on me. It was hectoring. The King left and the knight from Blois spoke. "I have been charged with returning the treasure. That is my only concern. You are a means for me to do so. The fewer of you who survive the greater the pot of coins we will share! When we return I expect to be

13

rewarded with a castle of my own. If you impress me then I may well have a position there for you." He allowed that to sink in. "This refuge is at a place called Aqua Bella and we leave tomorrow before dawn."

It was as though someone had walked on my grave. Aqua Bella had been my grandfather's home. My father had been born there. It was many miles inside Saladin's Caliphate. Robert of Blois and Raymond of Thornaby were forgotten as I tried to remember all the stories my grandfather had told me about Aqua Bella. Knights moved and Robert of Blois and his squires left.

Jarl Birger said, when I had been silent for so long and everyone else had left us, "Something troubles you, my young friend. I mean apart from the fact that we appear to be led by a man who would slit our throats while we slept."

"My grandfather was master of Aqua Bella when he was in the Second Crusade. My father lived there too."

"The Vikings of my land from whom I am descended told me that there were spirits who plotted and planned, who spun and trapped. They would believe that this was meant to be." He laughed, "Of course I am Christian and do not believe such superstitions." He tapped my gryphon, "However, I should tell you that another reason that I sat by you was because of this. The house of Folkung is a powerful and important family in Sweden. They are descended from Folke the Fat. The head of the family is now a jarl called, Birger Brosa. He is a cousin. They come from the town in which I was born, Stock Holm. The ruler of that town is related to Folke the Fat. The family have a battle flag. It is called the Folkunga Vapnet. It is a yellow gryphon on a blue background."

I looked down and rubbed my hand over the mythical beast. My grandfather told me how he had chosen the design when he had come to the Holy Land and now there was another connection.

Jarl Birger said, "I like you, Englishman. You have an honesty I find refreshing. I think that we will need to watch each other's backs on his little expedition. What say we make a pact to be brothers in arms until this is over?"

I was grateful. For the first time since my father and his oathsworn had died, I was not alone. I took his arm in a warrior's grip. "Aye Jarl Birger for I agree with you. There may be as many enemies inside this camp as without."

I found William. He had recovered well from his wound. However, if we ever returned to England I did not know how he would cope. His wound ached in the cold and wet. Here it was not a problem. In England, he might be in constant pain. I told him of our task and also of Raymond.

"I never liked him, lord. He bullied us. He would not try that with you for you were the son of the earl but he made our lives a misery."

"I did not know. You should have said something."

Shaking his head, he said, "That is not honourable in a knight. The others are free now but when I see him…"

"You will say nothing. You will smile as though all is well."

14

"Lord?"

"There was something about his look which I did not like. You had heard of Aqua Bella before we came, had you not?"

"Of course. All knew the tale of your grandfather and how he had made a fortune when he was lord of Aqua Bella."

"And Raymond knows that too. I see now why we were chosen. They think we might know how to find the treasure however once we have it then we are no longer needed."

"Do you know how to find it, lord?"

"Not really but I remember my grandfather describing it to me. As we ride I will try to recall the details. We will take Skuld and one of the horses we captured. Leave the others here in the stables. They will be safe enough. As for our weapons and clothes; we have few enough of them. We will take them."

William was practical. "And food, lord?"

It was my turn to smile. "Oh, I think we will be fed. At least until they have the treasure and then we watch our backs." I then told him of Jarl Birger. "Get to know his squire. There may be just four of us against the world!"

We gathered before Acre while there was still the chill of night upon the air. Robert of Blois and his squires were the last to arrive. I saw that they had with them four sergeants at arms leading sumpters. We had food. Robert of Blois said, "It will take us three days to reach our destination. We will take it in turns to be the vanguard. I will lead for the first part of the journey."

As we headed south down the coast road Jarl Birger turned and said, "The safest part of the journey for our illustrious leader. I would hazard a guess that when we reach the high ground and the places where there may be an ambush then it will be one or the other of us who have that dubious honour!"

I laughed, "Now who is being the cynic?"

We rode hard while it was dark. I did not think that Robert of Blois would wish us to fail before we even reached Aqua Bella. We would avoid the castles which the Muslims had captured. Thanks to our victory at Arsuf, Saladin was still rebuilding his army. He wished to drive us from the land he had captured but he had his borders to guard too. He had his own eastern borders threatened by barbarians from the east. Getting there might not be the problem. Getting out would.

When dawn broke the heat began to build. We found a grove of trees beneath which we could shelter during the heat of the day. There was a stream and the horses were given grain. They were vital. A knight who was on foot was dead. We had avoided all contact with any of those who lived in this land but as I drank from my water skin I saw shepherds on the hills. A column of Franks would be reported. We would not be unusual. The garrison from Acre often sent patrols out to seek battle with the enemy. I think that Guy of Lusignan had picked our number to deter enemy attacks. We could defend ourselves against the Turkish patrols.

As we rode, later in the afternoon, Birger said, "I do not think that King Richard has ordered us to go on this treasure hunt. He is in negotiations with Saladin's men. He is not even in Acre. I think our King of Jerusalem is looking to enrich himself before the peace is signed."

"You mean King Richard will forego the capture of Jerusalem?" Jarl Birger nodded. "But he swore that he would capture it."

"And he has failed. I believe the best that he can hope is that he will secure the coast for those who remain. As for me, as soon as I am paid for this I intend to take ship for home. You should come with me. You could earn money as a sword for hire. Men talk of your courage defending your father. You would become a rich man."

"No, Jarl Birger. I have a manor at home. I, too, will take ship but mine will end its voyage at Stockton. I have much to rebuild. I know not how my valley fares. Like you, for me, this is a means to an end. I sup with the devil for the good of my people."

I saw Robert of Blois had one of his squires ahead of the column. He was looking for a site at which to camp. It was getting towards dark and I smelled the smoke of a cooking fire. Suddenly Robert of Blois raised his sword and shouted, "Charge!"

I had spied no enemies. There had not been the sudden flurry of arrows which normally preceded an attack by horse archers but Birger and I drew our swords, our spears were on our spare horses, and leaving our squires we galloped after our leader. We had been at the rear of the column. When we reached the huddle of huts that were on either side of the road I saw the villagers lying on the ground. Even as we rode up Robert of Blois took the head of a woman fleeing with a babe in arms. There was a sickening crunch as the baby's head hit the ground. He had slaughtered a whole village.

Sheathing his sword, he smiled, "Food is cooked. Have the squires dispose of the bodies."

One of the other knights, who also had a bloody sword said, "How? The ground is hard."

"Cover them with rocks! I do not want my sleep disturbed by rats feasting on flesh!" He looked up as he saw the two of us with clean swords, "And our little virgins can stand a watch today! As they have not raised their swords in anger they can keep watch while we sleep."

I was about to object when Birger, sheathing his sword, said quietly, "Peace. Our time will come. We will share the shift. Let us lay these innocents to rest."

While the other knights laughed, Birger and I toiled with the squires to cover, as best we could, the dead with stones. The mother and her dead baby were the hardest to bury. The woman had seen no more than fifteen summers and the babe was less than a month old. The squires of Robert of Blois did not help us. They saw to their lord's needs. I had not had the opportunity to speak with the squire of the valley, Raymond of Thornaby. I had determined that I would, at some point.

It had been a poor village. Blois' squires had searched for coins but found but a pathetic few. The food also reflected their poverty. It was a porridge made from grains and cooked in a mutton stock. A few vegetables and dried fruits enlivened it. Many of the other knights complained about the lack of drink. Birger shook his head, "They are Muslim! They do not drink wine! Do these knights know nothing?"

I had been examining the other knights. They looked to be desperate men. I suspected that their sponsors had died and, like me, they were desperate to return to England. Unlike me, they were willing to do anything to facilitate that!

I took the first shift. William joined me. After making sure that our horses were well watered and fed we went to a rock that stood higher than the tallest hut. After taking off my spurs we were able to scramble to the top. I had been taught to scout by Masood, my grandfather's scout who had been raised in these parts. He had shown me how to move as little as possible and yet to gather as much information as I could. He showed me how to use my nose and ears as well as my eyes. William had none of those skills yet nor had I had the opportunity to teach him. We remained silent and listened to the sounds of the night.

There were creatures out there. This land was hot and most creatures that hunted did so at night. The animals which died did so silently. There would be a flurry of wings or a scrabble of claws and then silence. I was mindful of Robin's death and we had been careful, as we climbed the rock, to watch for reptiles.

I knew that the massacre of the villagers was a mistake. It would bring down the wrath of the warriors in these parts. It might take a day or so to discover that they had been killed but they would find our trail. I could differentiate between a Turk and Frank from their tracks and their horses. The Ayyubid were even better at tracking than I was. When we returned there would be an ambush. It had been so unnecessary. Had we left the villagers alone they would have forgotten us. We had been seen already by shepherds. Fearful of Franks they would probably have shared their food with us. My grandfather had told me of knights such as Robert of Blois. One, de Waller, had slaughtered my grandmother's family. The slaughter of the villagers was the last straw. I would find a way home, even if I had to ride the whole way!

I woke Birger when I deemed it to be the middle of the watch. I rolled up in my cloak and I was asleep instantly. A lesson my father had taught me was to sleep when I could.

Robert of Blois had obviously decided to punish us. I knew not why. We had been at the rear of the column by his orders. We could not have helped him slaughter the villagers even had we wanted to. He sent us and our squires to be the vanguard. "Ride a thousand paces ahead. If there are horse archers then you should flush them out." Once again, I saw a grin from Raymond. We were bait!

I turned to William and Petr, Birger's squire, "Stay ten paces behind us. Skuld has good ears. If we are attacked then ride back to the column."

"But lord…"

"Obey me, William. We trust to God and our own senses."

Jarl Birger chuckled as we rode south, "You are young in years, Thomas, but old in experience. You have said what I would have and I am ten years your elder."

I shrugged, "From when I could barely ride I rode abroad with my father. I learned to sniff out Scottish ambushes. I will not fall foul of an Ayyubid arrow!"

We found an olive grove during the midmorning and Birger decided we would rest there. "If our captain likes it not I care not. He will be glad enough of our spears and swords if we are attacked."

In the event, nothing was said. We watered at the small stream. One advantage of being first was that we could fill our skins and let our horses drink before the rest had muddied the water. After the sun had passed its zenith we rode again. It was still unbearably hot but Skuld had become acclimatised and I had ensured that she drank plenty of water.

As we rode I scanned ahead and to the side. I did not make the mistake of moving my head quickly. I used my eyes to sweep the horizon. I sought out things that should either be there or not be there. I expected birds and animals to fly and to scatter when we approached. I did not expect it two hundred paces from us. I listened for bird song. The absence of it would cause worry. I looked for horse droppings on the trail. A good warrior would pick them up to hide his trail but I noticed that Robert of Blois had not bothered to do so. He was leaving a trail that a blind man could follow.

Birger must have noted what I was doing, "You should reconsider coming to Sweden with me. A man with your talents would do well."

I had no intention of deserting my father's valley a second time but I humoured him by asking him about his home, "This Jarl Birger Brosa, is he a kinsman?"

"His title is The Jarl Birger Brosa. It means he is the chief lord in Sweden. He is second only to the King. He is a second cousin but most of the families are related. His forebear gained power but did not seek to be king. I think that was wise. They escaped the plots and battles between Denmark, Norway and Sweden. They hold the balance of power."

"And these enemies they fight. Why do they fight them? Is it for land and conquest?"

He shook his head but he was smiling, "What a cynic you are! But you are right. They say it is because the Estonians and those Rus who live in the area around Novgorod are not Christians. That is just an excuse. The only place we can expand is east. The Danes do the same by their borders. They use the Teutonic Knights much as the Templars are used here. Bishop Albert intends to create an order of knights to drive the pagans hence or convert them. When I return with a piece of the true cross then the Order of the Brothers of the Sword will be created."

"And you will be one?"

"I will. Not the master but a senior one. I have experience of this Crusade. The land in Estonia is easier for fighting. You are never thirsty!"

I spied, ahead, a village. It was even smaller than the one de Blois had raided the day before. Turning to Birger I said, "I cannot let these be slaughtered. Stop and examine your horse as though it has a stone. I will go and warn them."

"A cynic with a conscience! You are an enigma wrapped in a riddle. My people would love you!"

I spurred Skuld. The villagers stopped when they heard her hooves. I saw the men fingering weapons. I took off my helmet. Masood, before he had died, had taught me the language. Since I had been in the Holy Land my skills had improved, "If you wish to save your lives then ride into the hills. The lord who leads us is a cruel man. I beg you to leave and save your lives."

An older man with a beard and a long scar running down a lifeless eye spoke to me. "So that you may take what little we have? We have done nothing wrong."

"I know. Take what you will but go quickly, I beg of you."

An old matriarch looked up at me, "I see honesty in his eyes. He speaks true. Let us go for we know how cruel the Franks can be." She looked up at me, "May Allah reward your kindness, Frank!"

They moved quickly. I dismounted and when Birger and the others rode in I said, "They fled when I approached."

"Why did you not stop them?" Robert of Blois' voice was angry.

I smiled, "I took an oath when I became a knight. I do not kill women and children!"

He dismounted and came over to try to face me down. I stared into his eyes and did not flinch. He was a bully and my father had taught me how to deal with bullies. He decided not to force the issue. I suspect he was not certain he would win, "Then as punishment you shall do a duty again tonight!"

Birger dismounted, "No we shall not! Choose others."

"I am captain and I decide!"

"And what will you do if we refuse?" He pointed to the hills, "The ones who fled will tell the Ayyubid horsemen of our presence. Can you afford to be without four warriors? For," his voice became low and threatening, "if you begin something then you had better kill us for we will take many of you with us."

It was Robert of Blois who blinked first, "This is not over. When we return to Acre I will have you punished."

Birger laughed, "If we get back to Acre alive then I will accept any punishment dealt by King Richard. However, I do not think you answer to King Richard, do you?"

And I nodded, "We have seen through you, Robert of Blois!"

I saw that his words had struck home. For the first time, Robert of Blois looked nervous. Birger had been right. This was nothing to do with King Richard. We should have turned around there and then and returned to Acre but we did not. Many months later when I thought back to that moment when we chose to go on I wondered if this was meant to be. Certainly, that was the moment when there were four of us against all of the rest. We were in hostile lands surrounded by enemies we had brought with us.

Chapter 2

The rest all pointedly ate together. We were being ostracized. As the four of us sat around the fire in the hut that we had been forced to use, William kept looking nervously out of the opening that passed for a door. "What if they try to slit our throats in the night?"

Birger chewed the tough piece of meat. He spat out some gristle, "They will not, at least not until your lord has been of some use to them. They need him. His grandfather lived in Aqua Bella. I think that the squire, Raymond, has made himself useful to Robert of Blois. He has told him that you know where the treasure might have been hidden. We are safe until then. After?"

Depressingly Birger was right. "Now when they have the treasure we had best watch out. The daggers will no longer be in men's eyes but their hands!" I stood, "However, to be safe I will bring an extra pair of eyes." I went outside and brought in Skuld. Birger laughed. I shrugged, "If anyone tries to enter then he will let us know. I will make up for the sleep I lost last night."

When I awoke, we were all safe. Birger came back having made water. He was laughing to himself, "What amuses you, Swede?"

"While we had a goodnight's sleep, they had ten men watching us and our horses. They thought we either meant to do them harm or flee."

"How do you know?"

"They are not as good as we are at keeping watch and I heard them. They are worried about you, Thomas and you are right. They mean to shorten our lives!" I took satisfaction that we had had a small victory.

"I think, my friend that you were right the other day. None know of this save the King of Jerusalem and Robert of Blois. We are treasure hunters and we are dispensable. The only survivors will be Robert and his squires. The quip about not sharing the treasure was not a quip; it was a prophecy!"

We had less than a day to go to reach our destination and this time we were relegated to the rear with the horses and baggage. I do not know if Robert of Blois feared that we would join with those inside the fortified hall or not. It suited us.

We were now deep into the territory controlled by Saladin. There were many trails and small tracks which crisscrossed this land. We had not stayed on the main road. My grandfather had told me that he and his men at arms when they were protecting pilgrims, had often used the smaller trails. Robert of Blois must have had a map from the Hospitallers for we had rarely been on the road. I knew that, by now, men would be hunting us. The dead villagers and the reports from their shepherds would have let them know that Franks were deep into their land. They would have no idea that we were heading for Aqua Bella. I had no idea what they thought our purpose to be but they would hunt us until they found us.

We laid up in the heat of noon but we left earlier than we had, hitherto. Our leader was keen to reach Aqua Bella. There was now a noticeable air of apprehension. The other knights and squires had made a cacophony of noise whilst on the road but now, as we were so close, they were looking over their shoulders. We stopped in the early afternoon. We had rejoined the road and it twisted up to higher ground. Robert of Blois led us to a dell.

"We wait here until dark. The hall is just half a mile away. We tether the horses here." He jabbed a finger at Birger and me. "Your squires can guard them."

I did not like that but we could do nothing about it. I would speak with them before we left. I suspected that the intention was to leave us in Aqua Bella, dead and then return to kill our squires.

"Leave your shields, spears and cloaks here. They will encumber us. Some of us will have to scale the walls. I will point to those who should climb. They will have to slay the sentries and let us in. Get some rest. Once we have the treasure then we ride back as quickly as we can. I would do it in two days."

Birger shook his head, "That will kill the horses."

"Better the horses than us!" Robert of Blois was a ruthless and ambitious man.

The four of us sat apart again. "William, Petr, I fear they mean us harm. When we return, if we return, then I will whistle three times. If you do not hear the whistle, mount the horses and ride for home. It will mean that we are dead."

"Then do not go with them!" pleaded William.

Birger shook his head, "Your lord thinks of you. You would be used to pressure him to do as they wish. This way keeps them off balance. They do not know what we intend. We will go along with their plot. I think your lord and I can come up with a way out of this. If we cannot outwit a monster like Blois then we do not deserve to be called knights!"

We rested but I did not sleep. I was apprehensive. Despite what my friend had said this could be my last night on earth. There was a certain irony to the fact that my father had been born within these walls and I might die within them. I wished that I had tried to return home as soon as my father had died. I had believed King Richard's words. Now I saw them to be a falsehood. He cared for glory and not for his knights. My father and his oathsworn had given their lives for King Richard; it had been a waste! The king was grateful in the immediate aftermath but he had done nothing for the people the dead had left behind. I had been so caught up in being a knight that I, too, had forgotten. The valley was open to raiders and worse. This journey to Aqua Bella was necessary for it had reminded me of my duty. I just had to survive so that I could get home.

"It is time!"

I was roughly shaken by one of the other knights. Despite myself, I must have dozed off, albeit briefly. I prepared myself. I drank some water and then I used some of the dust to cover my face, hands and surcoat. William looked puzzled, "An old scout told me this trick. It is dark at night but your face can be seen as well as your hands." I slid my sword in and out of its scabbard and then made sure my dagger was in my belt in the small of my back. I undid my mail mittens and let them hang. I took off my spurs and handed them to William. Then I gave him my helmet.

"Will you not need it?"

"It restricts my view. If danger threatens I will raise my coif."

Jarl Birger nodded, "A good idea."

As we joined the others I saw that they still wore their helmets. It was a mistake but I said nothing. Using hand signals Robert of Blois led us up the side of the gully and we rejoined the road. He knew what he was doing. The road was as safe as the rough ground for we would hear any who approached. He waved us to the rock wall on our left as we neared a bend. I saw why when we turned. Aqua Bella was just four hundred paces from us.

I looked up and saw the rough-cut stone. My grandfather had told me that they had cut the stone out of the hillside to make the walls and battlements. Robert of Blois tapped me and Birger on the shoulder and pointed upwards. He did the same with Raymond and another of his squires. He selected four other younger knights and squires and pointed further down the wall. I looked at Birger and shrugged. He held out his arm towards mine and we clasped them.

There were large gaps in between the stones. They were old and the mortar had dried and crumbled. I reached up as high as I could go and put my fingers into the crevasse between the stones. I found that they were deeper than I had thought. I reached up my right leg; it was stronger and I managed to put my toe in a crevasse. I sprang up and raised my left leg a little higher than my right one. I felt like a spider. I ignored the others. I concentrated on scaling the wall. I repeated the moves. Each time I did so I made sure that I had three limbs attached to the walls. I was moving faster than I had expected. I glanced up and saw that there were crenulations just above my head. The next time I reached up I would be grabbing the top. I took stock and gathered my breath. As I did so I saw that Jarl Birger was just below me but the others were much lower. Their helmets were not helping them even those with just a nasal restricted what they could see. They had poor vision.

I readied myself and sprang up to grab the top stone. Bringing my left leg up I rolled through the gap. I landed on my back. Turning I saw that the fighting platform was empty. I realised then that Birger and I had been given the highest part to climb. To my left was a tower. I heard voices above me within the tower. That was where they had the sentries. It explained why no one had looked over the walls to spy on us. I raised myself and peered over. Birger was close. I hissed and held out my right arm. He grasped it with his left and, as I pulled, he threw his right arm up to grab the top. He nodded his thanks as he stood. I slipped my mailed mitts over the back of my hands. Then I donned my coif. My head would have some protection.

We were just moving down the fighting platform when there was a scream followed by a metallic clang and a crack. I peered over the top and saw that one of the knights had fallen. Even as I looked another two fell. The climb needed confidence. The death of one had undermined them. Above me, I heard strident voices and then the sound of a bell. Drawing our swords, we ran down the fighting platform to the ladder which led down to the courtyard. They could still bar the door to the tower but if we could reach the main gate and open it we had a chance.

An arrow smacked into the wall next to me. I did not look up. I knew they were in the tower. Speed was all that was important. It was dark and if we moved quickly then they would not see us! I heard shouts from my left as we descended the ladder. The door to the tower opened. They were sending men to stop us. Even as I turned and drew my sword I heard another shout from without the walls. Another of our men had died. We had now lost four.

I turned, just in time to deflect the spear which was rammed at my middle. I drew my dagger and, stepping into the Turk, rammed it up and under his ribs. I shouted over my shoulder, "Get the main gate! I will hold them off!" It was obvious that no one else was coming over the top. Those in the tower had a clear line of sight. I heard another cry and a body pitched from the walls and landed next to me. It was one of Robert of Blois' squires.

More Turks spilt from the doorway. We had no idea how many men were in the garrison. Four men ran towards me. My grandfather had told me that when you were outnumbered the best thing you could do was to close with the enemy. They would not expect it and their weapons might become entangled. The first two obliged me by running at me with spears. I used my dagger and sword to deflect them. They were long weapons and hard to control. Once I was between them I cross my hands and stabbed the one to my left with my sword whilst slashing the other with my dagger. Even if I had not killed them I had hurt them. More men poured out of the tower but they ignored me. They ran to the gate. I heard a shout behind as the huge gates were opened and our men rushed in.

Birger Persson shouted, "Hold on Thomas! I am coming!"

The next two guards had swords and one had mail. They moved apart so that they could approach me from two different sides. Rather than letting them decide when they would attack me, I ran at the one without mail and, flicking his sword aside with my own, I rammed my dagger into his side. The mailed warrior stabbed me in the back with his sword. It would have been a mortal blow but I was turning and his tip caught in my surcoat. Even so, it pierced my mail links and scored a line down my side. The Turks liked to use the point of the sword. We preferred the edge. Ignoring the pain, I spun around with my sword held horizontally. He had a mail coif upon his head but my sword, the sword of my Uncle Wulfric, hacked through the mail and into his neck. I think my blow broke his neck but it mattered not for the edge was so sharp that it tore through his flesh and into his artery. Blood gushed.

I glanced behind. There was a battle going on at the gate and no one stood between me and the tower. I ran for the open door. As I entered the well-lit chamber I saw that two warriors stood before me. One was a lord. He had donned his mail. The other looked to be younger and might have been whatever the Ayyubid used for squires. I knew that I was overmatched. This was a warrior. It would be like fighting my father and I had never bested him.

He was angry and he shouted, "Death to all infidels! Death to the enemies of Allah."

He launched himself at me. His squire also ran at me from the lord's left. The lord had a long sword, it was as long as mine and it was tapered to a sharp point. He rammed it at my middle. My move was not honourable. I was fighting for survival. I used my dagger to fend away the lord's sword. Our guards locked. I would kill his squire first. His squire's sword scraped over the back of my hand. Without the mitts, it would have been sliced open. My sword skewered him. I saw, as his body fell that he was little older than William.

My distraction almost cost me my life. The lord grabbed me by the throat. Luckily most of what he grabbed was ventail. I pulled my head back and butted him in the face. He was a tough warrior. His nose erupted in a bloody mass but he did not let go. I had no room to swing my sword and so I held it vertically and drove it down into his foot. The blow was so hard that the tip of my sword struck the stone floor. He gave a roar of pain and his grip slackened. In that heartbeat, I changed my grip on my sword and pushed it up under his arm. The tip came out below his ear. The light went from his eyes and his body slid from my sword to the ground.

Behind me I heard a noise, Birger rushed in. "Thank God you are alive." He looked at the Turk. "He was a big one." He saw that I was panting. The exertion and the choking had almost done for me. "I will check the tower. They are finishing off those within."

I was using the dead lord's raiments to clean my blades when I saw that he had a purse attached. I took it and saw that it contained gold. I slipped it into my pouch. I would split it with Birger. I needed funds to get me home and God had sent me the means. I would not ignore the gift. I took the sword too. It was a fine weapon. William's sword was not the best quality. I would give it to him.

Birger descended. "There are none in the tower. They emptied it to oust us."

"How did it go outside?"

"The Turks fought well. Sir Robert has fewer men to slit our throats now!"

When we left the tower, I saw what he meant. Ten of our men had died. Two squires lay dead and all of the sergeants at arms. Robert of Blois now had just twelve men. We had four. If it came to a battle I do not think that our leader would relish the fight. I saw Raymond hacking at a dead Turk. I shook my head it was pointless. Birger said, "The Turk slew his friend. He is now the only squire."

Robert of Blois was covered in blood and, from the way he held his left arm, some of it was his. He just nodded at us. I suppose that was our thanks for scaling the walls. He said, "Move the bodies and find the treasure!" He looked at us, "Is it inside?"

Birger said, "I did not see it. We can search more thoroughly if you wish. I was looking for more foes!"

"I will fetch our squires and the horses."

Our captain shook his head, "Leave them! I want the treasure!"

"And I want our squires and horses here and safe. Your horse may not mean much to you but mine does." I thought he would object further but he moved out of my way. I headed down the road. When I neared the gully, I whistled three times. "Come, William! We have won! Fetch the horses."

I wandered down and helped them to tether the horses. We now had spares and that might just prove to be our salvation. We would be able to change horses. We might reach Acre in two days! If the Turks did not catch us first.

Petr asked, "And my jarl?"

"He lives although the Turks took a heavy toll of the others."

It took longer to bring the horses than I had expected and it was dawn before we made the gate. We had to bang on the door for it was barred. That made sense. I did not like our captain but it had been a sensible precaution. The stable was clearly visible. The doors had been opened by our men searching for the treasure. The sun would soon be up and we led the animals inside. There was both feed and water. Just as important, there were six good horses.

I could hear both banging and the tearing up of floors. Robert of Blois came out of the tower. His face was effused with rage! "Where is the treasure?" He jabbed a finger at me. "You, this was your grandfather's hall! Where is it?"

I stared at Raymond and this time he could not hold my stare. I had been correct. My inclusion was the fault of Raymond of Thornaby. I would make sure that he paid for his treachery.

"He did speak to me but he did not say if there was a place to hide treasure." I looked at the open doors. "What lies within?"

Birger came over. He held a flagon of wine. "One holds wine and oil. The second is the stable and the third is the living quarters of the guards. We have searched them all. There is coin but there are no chests of treasure."

I looked at Robert of Blois. You did not say how much treasure there was."

He reluctantly answered me, "Ten chests. If they were here then we would have found them. They must have been moved. We have searched all three rock-hewn chambers."

It was as he spoke that my grandfather's words came to me. I closed my eyes. I pictured him by the window in his solar. Old and grey with the wine next to him he spoke again. I heard the words. *'There were four large doors leading off from the courtyard one was a huge barrel-vaulted chamber which had been hewn into the rock. That was where we lived. One was the stables and the other two were for storage. We had great quantities of oil and wine. I miss my old home but I fear that it is now in the hands of the enemy.'*

I stood back. The sun had just peered over the wall and when I looked at the wall before me, in the light of day, I saw that the stone was new. It was not weathered. Birger said, "What is it? Have you see a ghost?"

"Find me an axe or a hammer." I had their complete attention now.

Robert of Blois waved an impatient hand and the others fled to find me what I need. He came over to me. "What do you see?"

"It is what I don't see that is of the most interest!" I enjoyed his confusion. One of the knights, Sir Guillaume, rushed out with a large axe. It reminded me of the Danish war axe Uncle Wulfric had had over his fire in his hall at Thornaby. I turned it so that the flat side of the axe would strike the wall. I hit at the juncture of two stones. The wall moved. I swung again. Perhaps I mistimed for the axe head hit the stone in the middle and the whole stone moved inwards. I hit the stone next to it and suddenly both stones flew inwards.

Robert of Blois saw what I was doing, "Everyone! Beat down this wall!"

It did not take long. The mortar was but a couple of years old and had been hurriedly applied by warriors who feared the Turks who were chasing them. The sun suddenly flashed above the wall and illuminated the interior of the chamber. The chests were there.

Robert of Blois clapped me about the shoulder, "You have done it!"

Even as he said it I wondered if I had just signed my own death warrant. Perhaps I could have pretended that the treasure was not there and they might have left. I could not go back and undo that which I had done. I dropped the axe and walked backwards.

Birger and our squires came to me, "How did you know?"

"My grandfather said that there were four chambers cut into the stone. I counted three. This is not over. They no longer need us."

Birger said, "They do. They have enough horses to carry the treasure but they do not have enough men. They will try to kill us but it will be closer to Acre."

I had my doubts but we could do nothing about it. I did not wish to fight over treasure but I would fight for my squire and my new friend. For the next few hours, there was peace and harmony. We emptied the chests and loaded the treasure into sacks which we hung from the horses. We had more than enough horses now and each horse had two sacks attached. We would all lead two horses. A spare and one with treasure. We left in the late afternoon. The horses were rested. We had eaten. It was true that we had not slept over much but the Turks would be seeking us.

We four were at the rear of the column. I knew that, if we were attacked, then we would be abandoned. We made good time. We rode hard and did not stop until night fell. This time we were not in a village. I thought that was a good thing. We were at a point where the road crossed a stream. We had food we had taken from Aqua Bella. We had water and we could sleep on the ground. All might have been well had not Raymond and some of the other knights not taken wine from the manor.

The four of us had our beds apart from the rest. We had our horses tethered close to us and had our own fire. The horses with the treasure were still close by us. Robert of Blois was worried that if they were all together then they were a temptation for someone to steal. I wondered about the manor Guy of Lusignan had offered him. We had a fortune here. Such a man as Robert of Blois might be tempted to abscond with it all. He had enough to buy himself a kingdom.

I was weary and, despite my misgivings, I was too tired to stay awake. It was Skuld who woke me. She tapped my leg with her foreleg and I was awake in an instant. I sensed movement close by. I could smell the wine. I could smell the sweat and I could smell fear. I risked opening one eye briefly. I saw Raymond approaching me. He was ten paces from me. Behind him were five others. All had daggers in their hands. They were coming to slit our throats. I had my own dagger in my hand. I had fallen asleep clutching it. Now that I knew where he was I could estimate his approach. I smell his breath and I listened as he breathed. I heard his foot scrape along the ground. I knew where he was.

I opened one eye and reaching out with my left hand grabbed the hand with the dagger. Its tip was touching my throat. His eyes widened in fear. "So, Raymond, you snake! Not content with fleeing your lord during a battle, you sell me out to this butcher. You have made a mistake and it will cost you your life." I rammed the dagger into his heart.

Even as he was dying I pushed his body from me and lunged towards the two men approaching Birger. I shouted, "Treachery!" My dagger went into the ear of one as Birger awoke and gutted the other a heartbeat before his own throat was cut. William awoke and he managed to roll away from the knife in the night. I threw myself at his would-be killer. I knocked him over. His dagger rose, ready to plunge into me. My hand came up and so did my head. I cracked him on the chin and, as he rolled backwards, drove my dagger up into his groin.

I grabbed my sword and stood. William had his dagger ready. Robert of Blois and his handful of men faced us. "Do we end it here? Are you men enough to face us or will you wait until we sleep?"

I saw the debate in his eyes. They had treasure. He spat at me, "You can die here! Let us ride and leave these to the Turks."

They ran. They must have prepared in advance for their horses were saddled and the sumpters with the treasure, tethered. They galloped off into the night. I looked at William, "Are your hurt?"

"No lord and once again I owe you a life. Soon I will need to be a cat to repay you."

"Thank Skuld, she woke me."

I saw that Birger was kneeling next to his squire. "Thomas, he has been wounded."

I saw that he had had his left arm laid open. Birger had tied a piece of rope above the wound. If we did not do something then the squire would die.

"William, fetch me a brand from the fire." I looked at Birger. I have seen this done but never attempted it."

"Do it!"

As soon as the brand was in my hands I wasted no time. I plunged it onto the savage cut. Petr screamed and then, mercifully, passed out.

Birger grabbed my hand, "And now I owe you a life. Petr is my young brother. What is mine is yours."

I nodded. I felt numbed by the events which appeared to have overwhelmed us. "It seems we are alone." I nodded to Petr. "We cannot leave until he wakes. William, search the bodies for coin and weapons. I have a sword for you from the Turk but we may need all that they have and more."

He said, cheerfully, "Aye lord! I am alive and I could have been dead! I am happy!"

I shook my head. I was surrounded by madmen. We were deep behind enemy lines. We had a wounded man and yet my two comrades were happy.

I fed and watered the horses. I found that Robert of Blois had left two horses. They might prove the difference between life and death. Petr slept and William brought the purses of the dead. All of them had taken from the sacks we had packed. I had expected as much. I shared the coins out between the four of us and the horses we led. I was a realist. If four of us made Acre then that would be a miracle. We all had to get home. This way I gave each man a fighting chance.

The sun had been up for some hours when Petr awoke. He looked up at his brother and grinned, "Then I am not dead?"

"No, but we are far from safety. Can you ride?"

"I can try."

William said, "I will watch him, lord. You will make sure we get home and I will watch my friend."

They believed I could do it but I was not so certain.

When we left I rode in the van and Birger took the rear. I had said that life was more important than the sack of treasure we carried. If enemies came then we would flee and just take a spare horse with us. We had enough coin to take passage to Nissa. If we had to we would ride across France.

Chapter 3

We did not get to travel far that first day. Petr was in pain and we had no wine for him. That had all been taken by Blois' men. We went steadily and we went warily. I relied on Skuld's ears and sense of danger more than anything else. We did not use the road. Blois and his men could ambush us. More than that, I had seen signs, on the road, that the Turks had men riding it. In this land, anyone that we met would be an enemy. I used the sun as a guide. I used none of the trails from our outward journey. We had to head north and west. My grandfather had told me a tale of how he had escorted my grandmother to her father. In order to avoid an enemy, he had ridden a camel trail used by merchants. It was to the east of the road. We had ridden along it until dark. We found a watering hole. There were some dried, almost desiccated lumps of camel dung there. It confirmed that we were on the right path.

There was some scrubby grazing for the horses and we still had some grain we had taken from Aqua Bella. While Birger saw to Petr and William prepared food I examined the horses. Two were not in the best of condition. When I looked at them closely I saw that both had injured hooves. I would not risk them. When we left, I would free them. They would find water themselves and, hopefully, recover. We could not afford to be burdened with lame horses.

We ate cold rations. I did not want to attract enemies. We would have no fire. That meant we were eaten alive by flies and biting insects. "I have been thinking, Birger. The last place we need to go to is Acre." He looked at me with questions in his eyes but he said nothing. I explained, "If Robert of Blois gets there first then who knows what tale he will tell."

Birger nodded, "And where would we go?"

"Since the battle of Arsuf, we have many ports along the coast in our hands. There is Ashdod, Ascalon, Caesarea Maritima and Jaffa. They are all closer than Acre. We could be there not long after dark."

"We would have to change horses."

"We now have those two spare ones."

I saw that William and Petr looked relieved that we might have a shorter journey. Birger said, quietly, "And the coins we took from Aqua Bella, what of them?"

Sword For Hire

I had thought this through. "If King Richard had sent us then I would feel honour bound to deliver the treasure to him. We were duped and used. I say that we keep the treasure. I have heard a phrase, I think it is Viking, weregeld. Call it that!"

Birger nodded, "I have not heard that word for some time. You are right it is Viking. It means blood money. It is money paid for a life that was taken. But this treasure cannot be used for that. None have died. We head to a port and then we see if we can return the coin to King Richard. That would be the honourable thing to do. We have the coin we took from the dead. That might buy passage to France and then we could ride through France."

I nodded but I did not agree with Birger. King Richard had betrayed me. My father's sacrifice had been forgotten but Birger was older and wiser than I. I would go along with him.

The three of us took it in turns to watch. I had the last one. Birger woke me. "It is quiet but…"

"But you have a feeling of danger."

He smiled, his teeth white in the dark, "Aye, how did you know?"

"My grandfather's scout, Masood, told me that a man ignored the hidden voice inside him at his peril. He said it was the dead watching over the living. We are Christians and so we should not believe that."

"Yet you do. You are the most interesting Englishman I have ever met. I should have liked to have known this family of yours."

"I am the last." Just saying it made my spirits slump. I was the last and was I worthy enough to carry on the name?

As I took my watch I realised that I was not the last. There was my Aunt Ruth. She lived. Her husband had died in the border fighting and she had no children. She lived in a rambling hall at Wulfestun. With a handful of men and other widows from the wars, they were a tiny community. My father used to visit her once a week. I wondered if she was still alive. She had always been fond of me. Perhaps that was because she had no children of her own. Another reason, perhaps, was that my mother had never been a well woman. Four babies had been born dead or died in the womb and Matilda had killed her. My aunt had often come to care for me. She had tried to be as a mother to me. Strange, I could remember Aunt Ruth's face but not my own mother. When we returned to England, if we managed to return to England, then I would have to speak with her. She ought to know how her brother had died. They had been close.

I woke the others before dawn. Petr was stiff but he looked to have slept. We rode in the same formation. Leaving the two horses behind we rearranged the coins so that all of us had some in our bags. We used the pack horses for our spare weapons, our food and our water. I wondered if we might be able to reach friendly territory before dark. Our plan to change horses was now in tatters. The two lame horses had seen to that. In my head, I had a picture of a map my

32

grandfather had had in his solar. If we headed south then we would reach Ashdod and Ascalon. If we kept heading due west it would be Caesarea Maritima and north and east would take us to Jaffa.

We came to a trail that crossed ours. We could go southwest or northwest on the trail we crossed or we could head due west. Due west was the shortest and I chose that route. Birger went along with my decision.

The vultures which took flight as we approached the gully told me that we were entering a valley of death. The eyeless heads on the spears told me who had died. It was Robert of Blois and his men. Their emasculated and tortured naked bodies littered the ground.

William averted his eyes. Birger said, "Should we bury them? It is the Christian thing to do."

Skuld snorted and, as I glanced to the hills to our right I glimpsed a movement. "Keep moving, we are being watched. Keep your hands from your weapons."

We had just left the charnel house when a line of riders appeared before us. They were Seljuk Turks. There were ten of them and six had their bows with an arrow ready to end our lives. I showed my palms and said, "We mean no harm. We are travellers heading home. Let us pass."

The leader rode up to me and pointed behind me, "You are Franks like these butchers of women and children. Are you also cowards that you will not fight us like men?"

"It would not be a fight that we would win. Your arrows would pluck us from our horses. We are not like those you slew. We have killed no women and children."

He frowned. I had spoken truly. He had looked in my eyes. Had he seen the truth there? He turned and shouted something. Four men, not warriors, came from behind a large rock. I saw that one was an older man. He had a scar across a lifeless eye. I had seen him before.

He pointed at me and said, "He is the one. He told us to flee."

The leader looked back at me. He nodded and waved his arm. "You speak true. I saw it in your eyes and this man has confirmed your story. I will spare your life."

"Thank you."

"On one condition."

I nodded, "Ask."

"That you leave this land and return to whatever land that spawned you devils. Swear on your cross that you will do this and you shall live."

I took out my sword and held it by the blade, "I swear, by Almighty God that I will leave this land and never return."

He nodded and looked pointedly at the others. I was not certain how much of the words they had understood. I turned and said, "Swear on your swords that you will leave this land. If you do so then we live!"

They did as I asked. The warrior nodded, "Now go and soon this land will be free from the Frankish fist!"

As we rode toward the road I was aware that we were turning our backs on the Turks. If they chose then they could slaughter us. I had to trust that they would keep their word. Despite what others heard I had always found that the Turk if he said something, kept to it. Some of our own people like King Richard, Guy de Lusignan and Robert of Blois did not.

We reached the outskirts of Caesarea Maritima after dark. We had made better time than I had hoped because we were on the road. It was a much shorter road than the one we had taken. As we passed through the streets we noticed a buzz of excitement. Spying an inn, we stopped and discovered that they had stables and a room. The four of us would have to share but that was no hardship. We had endured much already. We made certain that the horses would be well cared for, especially Skuld and then we went in to the inn.

"Do you have food?"

"Aye, we do."

We ordered food and then I asked, "There appears to be great excitement in the town; why is that so?"

"Have you not heard? Where have you been? The news is all over the land."

"What news?"

"King Richard of England has signed a treaty with Saladin. We are safe! We have the ports and the land around them! Your leader is a great man!"

I felt relief. I could go home. My task had been completed. "Where is the King now? Acre?"

"The word is that he has left this land to return to Normandy!" The inn keeper, a one-armed Frank said, "Of course, I do not know how he will do so. The King of France has closed his ports to any Norman or Englishman. There is bad blood." He shrugged, "We have peace! I will fetch your wine and your food."

"Well, that gives us a problem. How do we get home?"

Birger said, "We could always get a ship which was neither Norman nor English."

I smiled, sadly, "You could for you are Swedish. We are English. We will have to take another path."

"We will not abandon you. Had it not been for you then we would both lie dead along with Robert of Blois. We will find another way."

The food and the wine came. It was the first hot food in a long time and we wolfed it down. Perhaps it was the food or the wine or a combination of both but Birger suddenly said, "What if we take a ship to Genoa? They are good sailors and their ports are not controlled by the French. We could head up through the Holy Roman Empire. We could part at Brugge. I could take a ship home to the Stock Holm and you return to Stockton."

I nodded. It would be a hard journey. We would have to travel through and over the Alps. We would need to buy horses. Accommodation would not be cheap. Thanks to Richard's treatment of Leopold of Austria we would not be welcomed in much of that land. I was now grateful that we had chosen to save the treasure for us. It was pure luck that we had done so. King Richard had gone. The treasure was never intended for him. I had a feeling that the King of Jerusalem was seeking the treasure not for his kingdom but for his purse.

The next day we went to the harbour to find a ship. There were none to be had. When the peace was signed then many soldiers had chosen that moment to leave. We would have to wait. We took the opportunity of equipping ourselves for the journey home. We all had coins and there were too many to remain hidden. We converted some of them into goods. William and Petr bought themselves new suits of mail. I had mine repaired. We bought William a helmet like mine. We had new surcoats made. War and the ride to Aqua Bella had taken their toll. We had new cloaks made. I bought spices. They were light and yet they were valuable. We could trade those on the way home. We bought silver and gold necklaces. They were lighter than the gold we paid but would increase in value in the Empire. And then we all bought supplies. We bought preserved fruit and meats as well as cheese. I had no doubt that there would be food available on whichever ship we took but it would cost us. As the passage would be expensive too I doubted that we would have more than half of our treasure left when we eventually reached England.

We visited the port every day for a week. Ships arrived but they were going in the wrong direction. We had no wish to go to Constantinople. There Crusaders were treated badly. The Greeks had not forgotten how they had been treated by the First Crusade. We saw the same people each day. They were mainly soldiers who wish to return home. I wondered how some would pay for their passage. They looked to be poorly dressed. What I noticed was that the ones who held their heads the highest were the ones whose swords were still sharp and shone with daily cleaning.

We began to talk with some of them. We found we had much in common. They were men at arms but they were also real warriors. The ones who spoke each day all had similar stories to tell. Their lord had brought them on Crusade. Each had lost their lord in one of the many battles. Some had been in the Holy Land for more than ten years. Henry of Bath's lord had married a Turk. They had had a castle that had been attacked and Henry had been the only one to escape. That had been ten years since and he had eked out a living as a hired sword since then. The departure of King Richard had decided him. He would go home.

"The thing is, my lord, that all I know is being a soldier. When I followed my lord, I had seen fourteen summers. The only trade I know is fighting."

Phillip of Poitiers had been in the Holy Land for the same length of time as I had. He had served under James D'Avesnes. He had been moving from lord to

lord since Arsuf. Henry Youngblood and David of Wales had followed King
Richard. Both were bitter about being abandoned. David of Wales was an archer,
"It is not right my lord. The King promised much and then we were abandoned. I
should have left with my fellows after Arsuf but I stayed for I thought that the
king had not finished. And now I am left here and left penniless."

Robert of La Flèche had a connection to me. He came from the manor which
had belonged to my great grandfather. Long ago a knight of Stockton had been
lord of the manor there. I believed it was still a fief of my family. It had since
passed to an Angevin, a descendant of Sir Leofric but Jean was descended from a
man at arms, Robert of Derby, who had also served my great grandfather. He and
Phillip of Poitiers had followed the standard of Geoffrey, Count of Brittany. The
Count himself did not journey to the Holy Land and the knight whom Robert
followed had not been an honourable lord. Wounded and left by his lord he had
had the hardest of lives. He had been forced to work in stables to find food. It had
taken him three years to recover from the wound and he was bitter about his
treatment. He, alone out of all of the ones we spoke to did not have a weapon.

We took to sharing our food with them. All of the ones who waited for a ship
slept rough. It was fortunate that the weather was not cold. "How will you pay
for a ship home?"

Henry Youngblood had shrugged when I asked the question, "I will ask to
work my passage. There are many pirates in these waters and many of the cities
fight with other cities. It is said that the Genoese and Pisans fight a war at sea. I
have never fought on a wooden ship but it cannot be much different from fighting
on land. Besides if it gets me to England then I will be happy."

I looked into each of their faces. They were the nutty brown of men who had
lived here for some time. They had knotted muscles and yet their waist told that
they had not eaten well. "And what will you do in England?"

Hugh of Bath said, "What we know, lord. We will fight. For myself, I will
choose a lord who is worthy of my service."

Birger was curious, "And how will you judge them?"

David of Wales smiled, "We have all learned many things over here, lord. We
have learned to find brothers in arms." He swept a hand around the five of them.
"We know who to trust. We have learned to judge a lord by his actions. None of
us will leap into bed with a knight because he offers a fine surcoat and a purse
full of coins. We have all seen brave lords, with barely a silver penny to their
name, but they fought and died bravely. They are the sort of lord we will follow."

It was two days later when a ship arrived that offered hope. It flew the
standard of Pisa. Birger had proved himself to be the best negotiator. He went
aboard as the passengers and the cargo was disembarked. He was aboard some
time. As soon as he walked back to the quay some of the other men at arms who
had been waiting for passage clambered to be aboard. A huge sailor barred their
way.

I nodded towards him, "That does not look hopeful."

Birger said, "He is unwilling to take impoverished warriors." I saw the five who had been sharing the quay with us. Birger's words were like a death knell. "However, he is willing to take two lords and their retinue." He glanced at the five men. None heard his words for they were in the depths of despair.

"And horses?"

"He is unwilling to take horses."

"I will not leave Skuld. We would not be alive but for her."

Robert La Flèche said, "We will look after her lord. You have shown kindness to us and it is the last we can do to repay you."

I turned to Birger, "Go back aboard and tell the captain that we will pay well for the passage of two lords and their seven men and one horse. I will not negotiate the horse!" he nodded and returned to the ship.

The five looked up, "You would take us, lord?"

"Let us say that I feel that someone owes you. I will pay. I just ask that you stay with me to England. After that, you may leave as you choose."

They all nodded.

"And, of course, you will have to wear my surcoat for I feel this Pisan will be suspicious otherwise. As soon as Jarl Birger returns we will have your blue surcoats made. They will not have the gryphon but it should suffice."

David of Wales spoke for them all, "Lord we swear that we will be your men. You can trust us!"

I looked into their eyes, each of them in turn, and I knew that they spoke true, "Aye, I know."

Birger's smiling face told me all that I needed to know, "He will take us and Skuld but the pirate is robbing us."

"Just so long as we leave this land then I am happy."

We were going home.

The Road to England

Chapter 4

The ship was larger than I expected. It was the type known as a cog. There were cabins at the stern beneath the steering mechanism. There was also a hold. Skuld was lowered into it by means of a sling and a crane. I made sure that she had plenty of feed. We shared one cabin. The crew used canvas slung between beams for beds and we did the same. It was crowded but we only slept there. The rest of the time we were on deck. We were lucky. In the month we were at sea, we only had rain for five days in total. A bigger problem was the unrelenting sun. One of the coolest places to be was the hold with Skuld and the cargo. I suspected we had paid too much and the captain did not need a cargo. He was a clever man for he brought spices which did not take up much space and yet would yield him an enormous profit. We all took it in turns to be with Skuld. It was no hardship and she was the best-groomed horse I had ever seen.

Birger made the suggestion that we keep moving while on the ship. He had the two of us walking around the ship when we were on deck. It amused the crew and it proved interesting for the new men who wore my blue surcoats. They were already showing the benefits of regular meals. I had bought Robert of La Flèche a sword and helmet. His whole demeanour changed. A warrior without a sword was nothing. The five of them spoke of war and of the battles in which they had fought. William and Petr listened to them. The five soldiers had not been mounted men. They had fought on foot. They had trudged behind the horses and had eaten their dust. Often, they had been abandoned when the knights and mounted sergeants had charged off after Seljuk Turks. I saw a change in my squire. He now understood the ordinary soldier. They fought for coin and their lord. Treated well and they would die for him.

One evening when the wind had dropped and we were barely making way we sat at the prow trying to get some breeze to cool us down. The captain, who seemed to know these things, told us that there would be a storm. He said that the air was heavy. I believed him. Petr and Birger were cooling Skuld down with sea water and I was staring north. I was looking beyond the coast of Sicily. I was looking for home.

David of Wales suddenly asked, "Lord, where will you go when we land in England?"

"My father was Earl of Cleveland. There is no one to take over the manor of Stockton. I shall take over my father's duty."

Robert asked me, "Will you not become earl in his stead?"

It was a question Birger had asked too. I shook my head, "It is the King's decision. I dare say when he returns to Normandy I can petition for the title."

Henry Youngblood was a thoughtful man. I had often seen him speaking with the new Arrivals in Caesarea to garner news, "Prince John rules England for his brother. He does not rule from London but the land around Derbyshire and Nottinghamshire. That is close to Stockton is it not, lord? Could you not ask him?"

He was right of course. I could ride to the Prince's castle in under two days. "Perhaps but the king is on his way home too. He may even be in Normandy now. When we travel from Pisa we will have to avoid France but we can travel to Normandy and see him then."

"And us lord, what of us?"

I looked at David of Wales. He was a typical archer. He had a chest like a barrel and arms like oaks. My father had told me that outside of the men of Sherwood, the Welsh made the best archers. "As I said in Caesarea when we get to England then you will have fulfilled your obligation to me."

It was the Welshman who looked at his comrades and seeing them nod asked, "And if we wish to serve you in England, lord?"

"I would be honoured but, as I said, I know not what the king has in mind. Stockton is a powerful castle and an important manor. He may choose to give it to another."

That did not seem to worry them. "That does not matter. If I was to speak truthfully, and for the others, I would say that what we have seen of you, lord, we like. You do not speak to us as villeins but as warriors."

"You have not seen me fight!"

David grinned and pointed to Phillip of Poitiers, "But he has. He was at Arsuf and he told us of the young squire who stood with his standard and a sword defending a wounded squire and his dead father. We need to know no more."

Phillip nodded, "Aye lord. I could not believe what I saw. Your father's standard rode against the finest cavalry the Turks had left. He went with a handful of men and if you are from his stock then you will be a worthy lord. He died but in his death, he gained much honour. That day did not see much to be joyous about but the sight of you standing with the standard defying the Ayyubid will live long in my memory."

After that talk, the mood changed amongst the men. They joined us as Birger and I marched around the decks. They began to practise with their weapons. They asked me about shields and weapons for they had little left between them. They had a sword and a helmet. That was about it. They talked of Skuld and what horses they had ridden when they had been warriors. They had fought on foot in the Holy Land but they had all ridden. In Skuld, they recognised a special horse. As we sailed north we began to become one.

Perhaps some spirit had made the change I know not but, as we passed through the straits of Messina and saw the Genoese ship, all of us would soon be tested as warriors. I recognised the cross of St. George which flew from her mast. Unlike us, she had two castles, one close to the bow and one at the stern. She was a warship. In comparison, we were a sheep to her wolf. Fate had made us take a Pisan ship rather than a Genoese. We had known they were at war and now we were to pay the price.

The captain shouted, "She means to take us, lord. Will you defend us?"

I looked at Birger who nodded, "Aye captain." Turning to the men I said, "Now we have an opportunity to see each other's mettle. Get your weapons and meet me at the stern on the aft castle."

"Aye, lord!"

Petr and William hurried to the hold to fetch our shields and our mail. We had not worn it since we had left the Holy land; there had been no need.

Birger asked as we climbed the steps, "Have you ever fought aboard a ship before?" I shook my head, "I have. Keep your feet wide apart and avoid over swinging. The motion of the ships is something you need to use and not fight."

When we reached the captain he said, "She is bigger than we are." Even I could see that. "She has crossbowmen at the top of the mast. Unless I miss my guess, there will be twenty men at arms aboard her."

"Knights?"

"Probably not. Does that make a difference?"

"Let us hope so."

The Genoese ship was closing with us. She was much bigger and had more canvas as well as the wind. Our captain was a good seaman but they were inexorably catching us. Our squires and men arrived. While David of Wales strung his bow, the others helped us to don our mail. I was acutely aware that, beneath their surcoats, my men wore just a leather jerkin. None had shields yet. They had swords and they had knives and daggers. They would have to do. By the time we were ready, the Genoese was ten ship's lengths behind us.

I pointed to the mast head, "David, they have a pair of crossbows at the top of the mast. Can you deal with them?"

He spat over the side and grinned, "Lord I hate crossbow men worse than Scotsmen! They are as good as dead."

"I leave it to you to decide when to strike." Turning to the other four I said, "We four have mail. I intend to tackle any who try to board us. I want you four to watch our backs. If one of us falls then take our place. If we can kill or disable ten of their men we stand a chance."

Phillip of Poitiers said, "We stand more of a chance, lord. We are English and they are not!"

David of Wales was pulling back his bow to stretch his muscles. Without looking up he said, "And I am Welsh, Norman! We are hard to beat too!"

I saw that the Genoese had closed to within four lengths of us. They intended to use their castle at the bow to launch their attack. That suited us for it was smaller than our aft castle. Although slightly higher, they could only send over three men at a time. We would outnumber them. I said, "Shields!" The four of us brought our shields up. Soon we would be the target of the crossbows. I could see those deadly weapons peering over the top of the wooden box atop the mast.

Suddenly I heard the thrum of a bow string as David sent an arrow aft. It thudded into the wooden box behind which they sheltered. His strike must have worried them and they released. One struck our stern and the other hit our mast. My men jeered. David was laughing, "Now they have to reload. They will be a bigger target!"

I saw what he meant. The two crossbowmen had been able to release their bolts while crouching behind the wood. Now they had to stand and put their foot in the stirrup in order to pull back the cord. The arrow from my Welshman's bow flew straight and true. His first one had allowed him to see the effect of the pitch of both ships. His second arrow struck one of them and he tumbled, screaming to land on the deck. They were just three lengths away and we heard the crack as his body hit the deck. The second man looked towards us. The last thing he saw was David's arrow as it struck him and pinned his head to the mast. My men and the crew cheered. It was a fine strike.

"Well done! Now see how many more you can hit."

"I only have seventeen arrows left lord."

"Then make them count."

"Aye, lord!"

"We have seen what our archer can do, now let us see what we can do. I am sorry Birger but the cry today is God, King Richard and England!"

He laughed, "I care not. Until I reach Sweden I have no home!"

The Genoese was a length and a half astern of us. I saw the men at arms waiting to attack us. They had open-faced helmets. They wore no mail but they had leather jerkins studded with metal. Their shields were intended to be used aboard a ship for they were smaller than ours. David sent an arrow into the face of one Genoese. He fell into the sea. The others raised their shields. That was good for it meant they could not see. Someone else would have to order them across. A seaman began to whirl a grappling hook and David sent one into his chest. The range was so close that my archer could not miss.

The captain looked astern, "He will try to ram us next."

I saw that his bow was higher than our stern, "David, do not let them get a grappling hook aboard us."

I saw that some of the crew were ready with axes. They would also cut the ropes should they attempt to grapple us. The bow sprit towered over us and three

41

men leapt. Birger and I had already rammed our swords into the air. William and Petr were a little slower. My sword slid up and into the thigh of the man at arms who jumped. His scream reminded me of the pigs when they were castrated on Peter the Pig's farm at the Oxbridge! Birger was not so lucky. He impaled his man but the dying man landed on the Swedish jarl. Hugh of Bath picked up the dead man's shield and stepped into the breach.

William had only wounded his man. The Genoese rose and Robert of La Flèche rammed his new sword into the side of the man at arms. He tore the shield from the dead man and stood next to Petr. We had five men abreast now. Birger pushed the dead man at arms from him and struggled to his feet. He had been winded.

The three dead men had bought time and space so that four leapt down and we were forced back a little. They landed without a wall of swords facing them. I stepped forward, aware of Birger's advice. Planting my left foot before me I did not swing over hand but lunged upwards with my sword. My opponent's shield came around to block it. It only half blocked it and my sword scored a hit along his thigh. As he winced I hit him hard with my shield and he toppled backwards. His fall caught the next man who tried to jump aboard and he lay prostrate at my feet. I changed the grip on my sword and rammed it into the back of his neck. It was too hard and my sword stuck in the planks. A Genoese, seeing his opportunity, lunged at me. Henry Youngblood's sword swept down and bit into his neck.

I saw another sailor fall to one of David's arrows. One of the Pisan crew threw a hatchet at a man at arms who was about to leap aboard. It caught him on the head and he fell backwards. Birger was now fully recovered and he launched himself at the nearest man at arms. There were two Genoese left on our ship. David was sending his arrows into any who tried to clamber aboard us. When the last two were butchered by Robert, William, Petr and Hugh the Genoese began to back off. They had lost enough. David had accounted for eight men and there were eight men at arms who lay dead on our ship.

The crew and my men cheered as the Genoese changed course. They had been hurt more than they had expected. The captain said, "Throw their bodies to the fishes!"

I shouted, "Hold! Take their weapons, mail and shields from them first eh?"

We had a rich haul. I allowed my men to keep the coin they found. They took what they needed from the dead. Robert said, "We have our shields now lord. All that we need is paint and we will look like your retinue!"

They went below decks to see if they could find any. The captain handed over the steering to his first mate. He led me to the stern and said, quietly, "I am indebted, lord. We would have perished but for you. I will return half of your gold."

"Thank you. captain. You are a generous man!" I knew then that he had overcharged us. He had thought us to be desperate men. The tables were turned and he had become the desperate man. He was grateful.

We went to the bows to clean our weapons and to sharpen our swords on our whetstones. I told Birger of the captain's offer. He said, "We are probably still paying too much."

"I know but I would not change things. Did you see my men? They fought as one! I have men whom I can lead!"

When we reached Pisa, I knew that it would take some time for Skuld to recover. We also needed to buy horses for my new men to ride and sumpters to carry our goods. The captain showed his gratitude by recommending an inn that would not rob us. It was his brother. To be fair they did not charge excessive prices. We took over the whole inn and that suited me. It meant we could see if there was any danger to us. We were in a strange country and we had money. I knew human nature. There were thieves and vagabonds everywhere.

Birger and I sought horses. We both knew that which we needed. A good palfrey was all that was required. Sadly, the men of Pisa knew ships. They did not know horses. We spent three days searching. It was not time wasted for Skuld recovered from the month at sea. Petr and William exercised her each day. David of Wales found someone who could supply him with willow and goose feathers. He had almost run out of arrows. He would not do so again. He also found a smith. It cost me coin but the smith made the arrow heads which David wanted.

"Knight killers, lord, that is what we need! With these arrows then mail will not stop me killing your enemies!"

It was the blacksmith who pointed us in the right direction. We trekked four miles from Pisa and found a horse farm. I could not speak his language but I knew that he knew horses. He caressed them and spoke to them as though they were human. We bought twenty. It did not cost us as much as it would have done in the Holy Land and we had a long way to travel. I expected to lose at least a quarter in the Alps.

It was almost September when we headed north. Even as we left Pisa, the mountains loomed ahead of us. Had the French not closed their ports to us we could have reached England a whole ten days quicker. We were meant to take this journey. We had borne the heat of the Holy Land and now we would be tempered by the ice of the mountains.

In one respect, we were aided by the Romans. When they had ruled their vast Empire, they had built good roads to aid their armies as they marched to conquer and control their provinces. They had also built places for their important people to stay. Many still existed. Not as grand as in the great days of Rome they offered stables and beds. We also found monasteries. There our tanned skin and stories of the Holy Land gained us entry, food and a bed for the night.

Sword For Hire

We had skirted Genoa. The last thing we wanted was for our shields to be recognised by the sailors from the ship we had fought. Turin was the last walled city before we began the tortuous ascent of the mountains. Had we delayed our journey by even a few days we might not have made it. The snows began. It was just a flurry at first. We reached the area known as Luciaria and managed to take shelter there while a storm raged. The people were welcoming. When we had been in Savoy we had been able to speak with the people but here they spoke German. Birger did the talking for us.

There William discovered that his wound did suffer in the cold and the damp. He ached. He began to use drink to help him to sleep. Birger shook his head, "No, Master William. For there lies madness." He went to his bag. He had a flask containing oil. When he opened the stopper, it had a strong smell. "We have a berry on some of our trees at home. We call it the muscle berry. Women crush the fruits and distil this salve. If you rub it, sparingly, on your wound it will ease the ache. Just use it before you sleep and only when in the cold and wet."

I laughed. "That could be any time in England."

The salve worked.

Delayed for a day while the snowstorm raged we heard the unwelcome news that King Richard had been taken by the Austrians and was being held for ransom. I could not believe that the King had allowed himself to be taken. The selfish part of me wondered how that might affect me. My new men were also unhappy at the thought that our king was now a prisoner.

"Austria isn't far away, lord. Could we try to rescue him?"

I looked at David of Wales. The question was an honest one but showed that he had no idea of what was involved. "Austria is close but there are many castles. How would we know which one he was in? He will be guarded and there are only nine of us. It is best we get to England. Perhaps there is an army already gathering to free him!"

Birger shook his head, "No my friend, Austria is but one part of this Empire. Emperor Henry must have been consulted before Duke Leopold took the King. An army, no matter how big, could not hope to march through the Empire. Your country, I fear, will have to pay for the return of its king."

When we left Luciaria it was with heavy hearts. As our horses struggled through the snow we huddled beneath our thick cloaks. They had proved a wise investment. We rode in silence. The confidence we had felt when we left Pisa was now evaporated. We were only halfway along our route and there would be no welcoming king in Normandy to confirm my manor.

Gradually the roads improved. The real snow of winter had yet to begin. In fact, when the sun came out and shone on the snow-covered peaks and icy blue lakes of Swabia the land could be seen to be beautiful. We stayed in inns which catered for travellers such as we. The horses were stabled and, although we slept in small, corded rooms, we were warm and we were fed.

44

Sword For Hire

When we reached the Rhine, we were forced to sell four of the horses. They had suffered in the mountains. We sold them to a horse trader. We were paid a pittance of their true value but he offered us valuable information. We discovered that we could pay to be carried downstream on barges. He assured us that they would take us all the way to the coast. Birger was a good judge of character and he believed the man.

Leaving our squires with the men and the horses we rode down to the place on the Rhine where the barges were moored. Many of the bargemen were willing to take passengers but few would take horses. I was not going to leave Skuld behind. The one who would take horses was not the cheapest. However, as Birger pointed out, we could sell most of the other horses and that would offset the higher cost. We just retained Skuld and three other horses. The horse trader gave us a better price for the fit horses. He allowed us to use the horses to transport our baggage to the barges and then took them off our hands.

Unlike the ship from Caesarea Palatinae, the journey on the barge was stately and smooth. The sail was used when the wind was in our favour. Otherwise, the captain appeared happy to allow the current to take us. We stopped regularly to take on more cargo and to offload goods. It was probably the same pace as we might have managed on horses but this was both safer and easier on our mounts.

Our barge journey finished at Nijmegen. The birthplace of the Emperor was the largest place we had seen since Turin. A bustling port we sought passage on larger ships. This would be where we parted. Birger found his ship first. There were more ships trading in the Baltic than in the seas around England.

"Thomas, we have been through much together. I do not think our journey will end here. Let us not say farewell. We both know where the other can be found. If you ever need help from me then you know where to send word and I will do the same for you. I have an estate at Sigtuna. It is not far from the Stock Holm. If you ever get to my land then seek me out."

I clasped his forearm, "And I too believe that our friendship will endure. I cannot see clearly what the future holds for us but I think our destinies are tied together."

My new men were also sad to be losing Birger and Petr. They had both been good company on the journey home. Men who have fought and bled together, as we had, are bonded. They are like brothers.

It took another four days before we found a ship. It was going to a place I had not heard of, Hull. It was on the Humber. The captain was going there to pick up wool from the monks of Meaux Abbey. Travelling empty, he was more than glad to take us and our two horses. The idea of seven armed men was appealing for the German Sea was not a safe place. There were still pirates. We headed home.

England and the Bishop of Durham

Chapter 5

Compared with the journey thus far the short trip to England did not last long. The seas were colder and the skies greyer but it took but three days. There was little in Hull save for the hall which was used to store the wool which the monks of Meaux sent abroad. We had to walk. We headed north and east. I was anxious to get home but we had to move at the speed of the five men who marched with us. We had to use our two horses to carry our goods. The sooner we could buy horses the better.

Beverley was less than ten miles away but it took the better part of half an afternoon for us to get close to it. Luckily, we passed a horse farm just four miles south of the burgeoning market town. They only had sumpters but that would do and I bought ten of them. We reached the market town in the late afternoon. We found accommodation in an inn and it was there that we discovered that this was not the land we had left. Beverley was far enough from my home for me to be unknown but I learned that life in my father's valley had changed.

When the inn keeper heard where I lived and discovered who I was he said, "Aye it is a pity that the Earl of Cleveland died. He kept us safe here from the ravages of the Scots." He had lowered his voice, "I wouldn't say this to another, lord, but Prince John seems more concerned with making money than keeping our borders safe. Taxes were high enough but now he is trying to raise a ransom for King Richard! There is only so much money in people's purses. First, we paid taxes for a crusade and now we pay taxes for a king."

William and I ate with our men. They looked unhappy with the inn keeper's words. Henry Youngblood said, "Aye the people paid money but we left many good men over there. They paid with their lives!"

I nodded but I was distracted. If the Scots were now raiding south of the Tees what had happened to the castle? For almost a hundred years that had guarded the crossing of the river. My great grandfather had denied the Scots access to the south. I know that my father's death had caused a problem but surely there were enough lords who were left to defend the town.

When my men began to become agitated I said, "These people are not warriors, Henry. They are farmers and innkeepers. This is their world. They have no more idea of what went on in the Holy Land than you have of life in a nunnery!"

That made them all smile and the evening ended a little better.

We had eighty miles to go and I chose the shortest route. I decided to avoid York and head through Malton and then Helmsley. There was a castle at Helmsley. I would try to stay there for the night.

We saw more animals than people as we headed north. This was sheep and horse country. Those that we met greeted us with smiles. It was obvious that we were crusaders. In addition, we were mailed and armed. They would not risk angering such men as we. We reached Helmsley in the late afternoon. This was a mighty castle and the equal of Stockton. The lord of the manor had been Sir Aubrey de Vere. He had been a friend of my father's. When I said my name, I was welcomed. The knight remembered me and my father.

William and I ate with the lord and his family as well as his household knights. The food was good and the company excellent but the news they delivered cut to my very soul. After we had answered all of the questions about the Holy Land, the battle of Arsuf and my father's death, I asked about Stockton.

The silence which greeted my question and the embarrassed looks should have been warning enough. I persisted, "Come, my lord, tell me of my father's manor. We heard in Beverley that the Scots have been raiding again."

The knight, who had been of an age with my father, sighed, "Prince John took advantage of the death of your father to return Stockton and all of the manors thereto to the Bishop of Durham. The bishop had been demanding their return for some years. It is still the same bishop that your grandfather bested. Hugh de Puiset does not forgive nor forget. Your grandfather's power and influence meant that the bishop's complaints fell on deaf ears. Your father was equally strong. King Richard had no time for Bishop de Puiset. He listened to your grandfather. Prince John, now he is a different matter." He paused. His wife gave a shake of her head. Sir Aubrey said, "I will speak no more about motives for I do not know the truth of it but I have my suspicions."

I detected an undercurrent. "And the people who served my father what of them? The families of the knights who died, where are they?"

Sir Aubrey looked uncomfortable, "I have to say I know not. We did not discover what had happened for some time. The family of Sir Richard of Hartburn came here. His wife had family in Anjou. Her father had a manor there. She and her family were returning to her mother. It was she who told us what had happened. I sent my son to discover what had happened to the rest."

He gestured and his son, Sir Roger, continued, "All the families of the dead lords had left the valley. There had been Scottish raids on some of the smaller manors. Cattle were taken. I think some were killed. I know many who had family elsewhere returned to them. They might have stayed but the bishop has given the manors to his own knights. We took on some of the men at arms who had served your father. They are here in the castle." He sighed, "We heard that some became outlaws."

"I thank you for that. They were good people. Then tomorrow we head for Stockton and I will try to discover what happened to my father's things. The manor may have been given to the bishop but all else belongs to me!"

"Would you like me to send my men to escort you? You have but six men behind you."

"Thank you but no. I would not embroil you and your family in my problems. I will use peaceful means first. I plan on visiting Prince John to make a direct plea. Where is he?"

"I believe he is in the estates he has claimed in Derbyshire. He is spending money to make Bolsover and Peveril castles stronger!" There was a warning in his words that I was not to take on the Prince.

As we headed north the next day William was pensive and my new men were silent. William had no family. His mother and father had died of the plague when he was seven years old. My father had brought him up until he became a squire. He knew the castle and its people well. "Surely some must be left at home. They cannot all have left."

I was not certain. Although Sir Aubrey had not elaborated I knew there were many things he was not telling me. Prince John was a dangerous man. I had known that before I left England with my father. My grandfather had always said that he was the one son of his friend King Henry who had not a noble bone in his body. His other sons had all trained with my grandfather. Prince John had been the only one not to have met with grandfather's approval. I know, from what my father said, that King Henry did not have much time for him. He was famously known as Lackland as he was the only one of Henry's sons not to be given any. John was his mother's favourite. He was the youngest. She had indulged him and kept him far from his father. The results of that could now be seen.

We closed with Thornaby in the late afternoon. The castle was gone! All that remained was the hall. Sir Edward had built the castle and Sir Wulfric had made it stronger. Ralph of Thornaby had been a bachelor but he had plans for it. Now the walls were gone. I saw other stone buildings close by. They had reused the stone. My heart was filled with dread as we dropped to the valley of the Tees. The towers and turrets of Stockton Castle, the strongest castle in the whole valley, were gone. I could see men still toiling to dismantle the walls. The two large halls stood. The other buildings: the stables, kitchens, granary, they were still there. I saw that the wall around the town was now no longer wood. They had reused the stone. For that I was grateful.

I was recognised by the ferryman, Alan. His great grandfather had built the ferry. "My lord you have come home! We did not know if you had perished with the other knights. We had no word!"

"It is good to see you, Alan. Will you take us across?"

He nodded, "I have to tell you, though, lord, the bishop has doubled the rates for crossing the river."

"Your family no longer controls it?"

We were halfway across and he shook his head. "When the new lord came the bishop came with him. He said this was his river and he would determine the prices. He said that this was the price the people had to pay for protection from the Scots."

"Yet the Scots have raided!"

He shrugged, "We are just poor men, lord, what do we know? The priests tell us that we cannot argue with the bishop. He is God's and the King's representative." We were nearing the north shore, "Stockton is not the prosperous place it was in your father's time, lord. More coin goes out than comes in."

We stepped ashore and that was a low point for me. The gatehouse and the walls were gone. My home was now a mean and bare place. We led our horses towards the hall. No matter what I thought of the lord I had to speak with him. After that… for the first time, in a long time, I did not know.

I was met halfway to the hall by two men at arms. I did not recognise either of them. They were polite. That was understandable for the seven of us had the look of veterans. We were toughened, armed men. We had the looks which told others not to argue with us. "My lord, what is your business here?"

"If you recognise my shield and surcoat then you know what my business is. Stockton is my home. It was my father's castle."

They looked at each other. One said, "If you would wait here, lord we will seek counsel from our lord."

I shook my head, "I will not stand like a beggar before my father's hall." Handing Skuld's reins to Hugh I strode towards the hall. William gave his reins to Robert and then spoke to David. He followed me.

The two men did not know what to do. They delayed and in that delay, I was already twenty steps closer to the hall. The door opened and a sergeant at arms stood there with a drawn sword. I did not pause but growled, "Sergeant, sheath that sword now or use it! I am Sir Thomas of Stockton. I do not respond well to threats." My hand was on my sword.

A voice from inside said, "Ralph, sheath your weapon and allow in Sir Thomas."

I saw the sergeant at arms hesitate and glare at me. Then he obeyed. As he stood to let me pass I said quietly, "You should thank your lord, for he has saved your life." I nodded behind me. There was an arrow aimed at him. David of Wales was less than forty paces from the sergeant at arms.

The knight who greeted me was older than I had expected and he wore the tunic of a Hospitaller. "Sir Thomas, come in and you can tell your archer that none of you will be harmed. I have seen too many useless deaths."

I turned to William, "Tell the men to watch the horses but remain alert." The knight looked vaguely familiar, "Do I know you? Your face…"

He smiled, "You may have seen me. I was at Arsuf and followed Garnier de Nablus in that reckless charge. It was where I was hamstrung. I am Sir Richard D'Aubigny and I am the lord of the manor of Stockton." He gestured with his arm, "I beg you to sit and I will explain."

I did so. I stared around at the familiar tapestries. Old Alice had sat with the young women and they had sewn the scene with the battling warrior. This had been my hall. I had grown up inside its walls. I had played on the fighting platform. I had sat in the solar on my grandfather's knee. Now the solar and the fighting platform, along with the walls and towers were gone.

"After I was wounded I was sent to the valley to tell them of the loss of your father. When I arrived, I discovered that the news had already reached the Bishop of Durham. Prince John was in the Palatinate visiting with him. Prince John decreed that no sanction had been granted to build the castles of Stockton, Yarm and Thornaby. He said that your great grandfather was a Warlord and had not sought permission from the lawful king."

"But he had the permission of Empress Matilda!"

"Looking back always gives us a clear view of what we should have done. Prince John did not recognise that for there was nothing written down. Your great grandfather should have sought King Henry's permission to build. He should have had it placed on record. Prince John could then not have done as he did and ordered the destruction of the walls."

"But the Scots!"

"I know." He poured me some wine, "Drink. You are upset but I have to tell you that I am not your enemy."

"Yet you are lord of the manor."

"I am a hostage to fortune. I was appointed because of Arsuf. I have no connections and I am not a threat to either the Bishop of Durham or Prince John. I can never have children and when I die then Hugh de Puiset can appoint someone who is more amenable to his orders. I am a stop gap."

I drank some of the wine. He was right, he was not my enemy. He could have closed his door on me. "I am sorry for my attitude but…"

"You have every right to be angry. I was there the day you were knighted. If I had had a son I would have had him to be as you. You deserve this manor."

"And yet I do not have it."

"If you can persuade the bishop to give it to you then I will leave. I have no desire to be lord of any manor. I stay only to help the people."

"But the bishop hated my grandfather and father. I will receive short shrift there."

"Then you should try the Prince."

"I will do so."

"You will stay here tonight? Your men can sleep in the other hall." I hesitated. "Pride is a sin, Sir Thomas. Bend your neck a little."

I nodded, "And my father's things, where are they?"

"I have them in storage for you. Nothing has been touched." He leaned forward, "Nothing. All of his chests are still there."

I stood, "I will speak with my men and then visit the church. I would visit my grandfather's grave."

He put his arm on mine and looked, suddenly, much older, "I will come with you."

"Why do you need to? I know where the church is. I was there when my mother was buried and my grandfather and grandmother are buried there!"

"Nonetheless I will come." There was a tone in his voice. He reminded me of my grandfather. It was the same tone Grandfather William had used when he had told me that Old Aiden, the scout had died.

As we left the hall William and my men looked up. "We are staying the night. Stable the horses. The men will be housed in the other hall."

"Yes lord."

I did not recognise the priest who scurried out of the way as we approached the church. Father James had been the priest my father had appointed. Of course, the bishop would want his own man here. Was this why Sir Richard had insisted upon accompanying me? He did not know how I would react to a new priest in my great grandfather's church.

When I stepped inside I saw that was not the reason. My father had had two niches built, one on the left and one on the right. The one on the right was my great grandfather's grave. It had his effigy carved in fine stone. On the left was the grave of my grandfather and grandmother. They too had their effigies carved in stone save that my grandmother's effigy was not there.

I whirled around. Sir Richard held up his hands, "It was not my doing. The bishop came and said that your grandmother was not Christian. He ordered the stone removed and her bones cast into the river. I am sorry. I was not here when he did so. Your priest, Father James, objected and he was sent hence. The bishop, it seems, has old scores to settle with your grandfather. He could not do so in life but now that he is dead…"

I was angry and I wanted to hurt someone. This Hospitaller was not to blame. My anger would have to cool and, when I had my vengeance, it would be in cold blood. I walked down to the next niche. It was the one with the newest stone. It was the grave of my mother. On the floor was the grave of my great grandmother, Adela. Kneeling before my mother's tomb I took out my sword and holding it like a cross said, "I swear that I will have vengeance for the wrong that was done, my grandmother. I will not rest until Hugh de Puiset has paid."

When I stood Sir Richard said, "I know that knights such as we set great store by oaths but I wish you had not sworn that one. It will cost you your life."

"Sir Richard, what have I now? My home has gone. The warriors I left England with are dead save one. My father's warriors are scattered to the four winds. My family are all dead and the Bishop of Durham has desecrated my grandmother's grave. You fought in the Holy Land. You know the horror that was there. I came home to find peace or a sort of peace. If I cannot have peace then I will have war. A whirlwind has been unleashed. The most dangerous of enemies is one with nothing to lose. What else can I lose?"

His silence was eloquent. He did not speak until we reached his hall, "Come, I will take you to your father's chests. I also have his horses. He did not take his war horses to the Holy Land. I had the beasts cared for. There is his stallion, Gonfanon and two breeding mares. They are fine horses and worth a small manor! There are good palfreys and sumpters. I know not where you go but you will have horses to carry your goods."

I smiled for the knight was trying to do what was right, "You are a good man and the people of Stockton are lucky."

"I try. I am not certain how long God will grant me on this earth but I too have taken an oath to be the best lord of the manor that I can be. I can do little about the privations heaped upon the people but I can ensure that I do all I can to ease them."

He took me to a locked door. It led down to the cellars which my great grandfather had built. He took a brand from the wall and, as we descended the stairs, he lit the sconces in the wall. There were many chests.

"I had your father's people pack clothes in one chest, weapons in another, papers in a third. There is another chest of your mother's things and two more chests with items which they said belonged to your grandfather and great grandfather. Their mail is in the chests. Their swords, I believe, were buried with them." He pointed to one chest which was smaller than the rest. "That is your father's treasury." He smiled, "The bishop wondered where it was. I believe he wished to have it himself."

I nodded. I found that tears were springing to my eyes. My family had thought that we would be here forever. Now their legacy was boxed in chests. I forced out a question to steady myself, "Where is his steward, old John son of William?"

"Ah, old John. I liked him. Once he saw I meant well he helped me. It was he who showed me the secret place where your father had hidden his treasure. He told me tales of your great grandfather and grandfather. You have a lineage of which you can be proud. Old John died last winter. I think he simply could not live alone in the hall without the Warlord's housekeeper, Alice. He had been fond of her. She lived to a ripe old age. I had never heard of any living until they were eighty. He thought you would not return. To me, he gave up on life."

I had regained control of myself. I remembered, fondly, the old woman Sir Richard spoke of. She was as much a part of the castle as the solar my grandfather used. I turned, "Have you a wagon I could use or carts?"

"Surely there will be one. There were some when I came here. I will leave you while I search them out." He handed me a key. "Here is the key. Lock it when you leave. I trust my people but…"

I spent some time examining the contents. I took, from my great grandfather's chest, a dagger. It was beautifully worked and had a wolf beautifully carved in the handle. There was a single blue stone. I had never seen it for I had never met the Warlord but my father had spoken of it. From my grandfather's chest, I took the two seals I remembered hanging around his neck. One was the seal to Aqua Bella. Having been there it had a special significance for me and I took the signet ring given to him by King Henry. He had been one of the inner circle of knights who advised King Henry. The only other who was left was William Marshal, the Earl of Pembroke. I slipped it onto my finger.

I locked the door. Before I rejoined Sir Richard I went to the hall where my men had gone. There were four other warriors in the hall. I said, "I would speak alone with my men."

They nodded, "Aye lord. Come on lads." The one who spoke paused, "You might not remember me, lord. I am Edward. My father was old Edgar who used to care for your grandfather's hawks after Old Aiden died. I was a young lad when you and the earl went to war. We are all sorry for what went on. If I can do anything…"

I nodded, "I will speak with you before I leave. I do remember you."

When I was alone I said, "When you swore an oath to me in the Holy Land it was with the expectation that I would have a castle to return to. That is not the case. I have come back to nothing and I can offer you nothing. I release you all from the oath you took. More than that I will give you all a hundred silver coins each for the service you have done me. I know not what the future holds for me. I cannot ask you to risk your future."

They looked at each other. David of Wales always seemed to be their spokesman, "Are you saying you want rid of us, lord? Have we offended you?"

I was confused. "No, of course not. Were you not listening? I have nothing! There is not only no title, but there is also no manor! Your future will be a bleak one. I will be a sword for hire. It will be like the Holy Land all over again!"

He said, quietly, "Have you ever broken an oath, lord?"

"Of course not!"

"Then are we lesser men? We know what has happened to you and we will not abandon you. You did not abandon us and yet you barely knew us. We will face this uncertain future with you. Isn't that right, lads?"

There was a chorus of 'Ayes'.

"And we have been speaking with Edward and others. Your family are good people. They have saved this valley more times than enough. They deserve to be remembered. If we can keep you alive then they will be remembered."

William was awaiting me outside the hall. "I am sorry for what they did to your grandmother, lord. It is not right. Justice must be done."

"I am not certain that justice lives in this land any longer." I put my hand on his shoulder, "William, I will say the same to you as I said to the men. You have followed me since that day at Arsuf. I release you now from any obligation to follow me. I have a debatable future. I cannot promise that you will ever be knighted. Sir Richard has no squire and he seems an honourable man. If I ask him I am certain that he will take you on as a squire."

He smiled, "Sir Thomas, I care not if I never become a knight. Our destinies are bound together. I will follow you. We may have a poor future but I guarantee that it will be interesting. I am your man, until death!"

And so, I began a new life with just six men to follow me. They say that seven is a lucky number. I prayed so.

Chapter 6

The next morning, I rose early. I had not slept well. The food had been excellent, the wine had flowed and Sir Richard had been as courteous a host as one could wish but I had much on my mind. I went from the hall to the river. My grandmother's bones were now in the river. For once I was glad that my father was dead. It would have broken his heart to have heard what had happened to his mother. Then I remembered Aunt Ruth. She would not know of this. Even though she lived but a few miles away Wulfestun was a quiet place. She was a recluse. My father and I had visited her before we went on crusade and they had parted well but neither expected to see the other again for a long time.

I turned and headed back to the hall. I would have to do one more duty before I left to confront Prince John. I was about to re-enter the hall when Edward son of Edgar appeared. "Sir Thomas, I hoped to catch you alone. I need to speak with you." He sounded worried.

"Of course."

We went back to the river. The wall had guarded the hall against the river but now the foundations that remained made a bench. We sat.

He took a deep breath and then began to talk. His voice was urgent. "When the bishop came some of the men who served your father objected to what the bishop was doing. They tried to stop his desecration of the tomb. Men died. Men on both sides. Your father's men were brave but they were outnumbered. The bishop declared them outlaws."

"And you, Edward son of Edgar?"

He hung his head, "I am sorry to say I did nothing. I could do nothing for I was not here. Sir Richard had sent me to pick up his chests from Herterpol. When I returned I saw the heads of the dead on the walls of Stockton and the others had gone. They had been declared outlaws. I am sorry."

"No Edward. That was unfair of me. You could have done nothing alone. Where did the men go?"

"Jack, son of Harold Will's son, led them to the forests to the west of Norton. There were seven archers left and five of the men at arms."

"Thank you for that Edward. I am grateful." I reached into my purse for a coin.

He shook his head, "No, Sir Thomas. I tell you this because I wish to do right by you for the sake of my father and my uncle. I would follow you."

"I have no future."

"Lord, I know. I spoke with your new men last night and they told me what you said. I am just a lowly warrior but I can see that this land is not the one your grandfather fought to make safe. How could I sleep at night knowing that I had done nothing? I have no family. I will follow you if you will have me."

"And what of Sir Richard? I would not have you betray him."

"Nor will I. I am a man and I will ask him if I may follow you."

"If he agrees then so be it." He nodded and strode off to speak with the Hospitaller.

I found Will. "Have our horses saddled. We ride."

He did not question me. I went to my chamber for my cloak and helmet. I saw Sir Richard, "I beg a favour. I would visit with my aunt in Wulfestun. I promise that I will leave by tomorrow."

He smiled, "Stay as long as you like. I am enjoying your company."

I shook my head, "What I have planned means that I must stay a short time lest you become implicated too. You are a good man and I would not have you hurt on my account."

"You are a refreshing knight, Sir Thomas. You have values and you have honour." He spread his arm in a circle, "The lords appointed by the bishop to the manors around here would not know one end of a spur from the other but they know how to take the last groat from a tenant. If the Scots ever come then God help them!"

I returned him the key, "I would have my chests loaded onto the carts you said I could borrow. My men will pack them."

He took the key, "And then where will you go?"

I pointed south, "I must speak with Prince John. If he is a good leader then he will honour the memory of my father and return the manor to me." The look Sir Richard gave me told me that I was dreaming.

My aunt's home had been given to her by the Warlord himself. The farm had been abandoned after a raid by the Scots when my grandfather had been a child. He had built her a fine hall. Sitting in the middle of a huge forest it was as isolated as one could be and yet Stockton and its market were but a few miles away. As we made our way through the forest of oak, elm and ash I remembered coming hunting with my father and grandfather. I even recognised some of the trails which led into the heart of the woodland. The green way we followed had had some stones laid. It was not cobbled but, in the heart of a wet winter, the road could be trodden.

The hall was quite simple in design. Made of wood and lath it was just one-storey high but it had two wings. I remembered when my Aunt had come here. I was just a child but even then, I could hear her clear and crisp orders as she made sure that the builders did exactly what she had wanted. My father always said that Ruth was a man in a woman's body. She did not suffer fools. Had she been a mother then she would have been a good one for she was always kind to me and yet I could never get away with anything. As the only child who had survived childbirth, I was given a great deal of attention from my widowed aunt.

As we dismounted she came from her hall. She was grey but her eyes were as sharp as ever. She embraced me and did not say a word. I felt dampness on my cheek. I waited until she relaxed her grip. It took some time for her to compose herself. "My young hero! They told me how you stood over my brother's body!" Shaking her head, she said, "Foolish! You might have been killed! Your father would not have wanted that but I am pleased that you are alive. And a knight! It is good that you are home. Come, bring your squire indoors. We have much to talk about." She linked my arm. I had always remembered her as being taller but I towered over her now. She said as we entered, "You have come without baggage. I am guessing that you will not be staying the night."

I felt awful. I was being rude, "I am sorry, I did not..."

"Do not worry, Thomas. We will have plenty of time to talk and you have things on your mind."

"How do...."

She laughed, "I am no witch but I know you. You are like my brother. He was the same. You are both deep. When we were children I would chatter all the time but Samuel would watch and listen. Once he had made his mind up there was no dissuading him. That foolish crusade was an example. I wish he had stayed but then he would not have been Samuel, would he? He was like our father."

Her women appeared with bread, ham cheese and beer. They were all of an age with her. She smiled, "Like me, they lost their husbands and also their sons to the Scots. We are a little community here. Like nuns but without the interminable praying and bending the knee. We are much more practical; we make things! Now sit and tell me all."

I did so as she poured beer for William and me. When we paused she insisted that we eat something and then asked us to continue. I reached the point where we took horses at Hull and I stopped. "And then we were back in England."

"Aqua Bella eh? Strange that you went there. I do not remember it at all. I was a suckling babe when we left but Samuel would have remembered it. Of course, my father spoke of it often. I envied you two. Your talks in the solar... You were born to be a warrior and he saw himself in you. He loved you, Thomas. It was a pity that your mother was denied more children. Both Samuel and my father would have liked that."

"And you?"

"Of course, I would, but that was not meant to be. God decided that I would be barren and use other skills. I have another purpose." She stared at me. "And is that it? Have I had all of your news?"

I felt her eyes boring into me. Was she reading my mind? "No, Aunt, there is something else but it is terrible to speak."

She put her hand on mine, "Then I will save you the pain. I know what they did to my mother's grave."

"You know, how?"

"We are not isolated here. My women go into Stockton to trade and to get that which we cannot produce. And there are townsfolk who come to see me. I knew within the hour what that evil man did. He was afraid of my father during his life and could never best him."

"I have sworn an oath to have vengeance."

She stood and jabbed a sword-like finger at me, "No! It would cost you your life! He is not worth it! He will be punished in the afterlife. You have a life! Live it!"

I said nothing. I would not argue with her but I would not be foresworn. The bishop would die by my hand.

She sat and drank some wine, "So what are your plans?"

"I will go to Bolsover Castle and speak with Prince John."

She shook her head and snorted, "A waste of time and your breath. My father knew him to be a weak and pathetic excuse for a man. His brother, Richard, is a mad man and hot-headed but at least he has honour. Prince John should have been drowned at birth. At least that is what my father always said. However, you are like my brother, you will do things the honourable way. You had best be careful on the road. It is almost as bad now as when the civil war was on. The Warlord would be turning in his grave at some of the things which are going on."

"I will be careful. I have men."

"Six I believe."

"Possibly seven." I stared at her, "How did you know?"

"I told you I know everything which goes on in Stockton. I know that Sir Richard is a good man but the others are as venal as Prince John and Puiset! You need more men." She said it simply. "More ale?"

I realised that I had finished it. "Yes, please." She disappeared. William grinned, "I have never seen anyone like your aunt, lord!"

I nodded, "She is special. I hope she stays safe."

She came back with a jug of ale. "Did you find your father's things?"

I nodded, "And grandfather's and his father's."

"What do you intend?"

"I cannot leave them in Stockton. Could I leave them here, in your care?"

She looked relieved, "Of course, for that means you would have to return and I would get to see you again!"

"I will return, I promise."

"If you have just six or even seven men to guard you then that is unlikely."

"When I was coming home I hoped that some of my father's men might still be around but I heard that many of them died trying to stop the desecration of my grandmother's tomb and the rest are outlaws living in the forest."

She shook her head, "They live in the forest but they are not outlaws. They live in my forest and they guard travellers on the roads. They are here." She smiled, "I may not be a man and I may not be a warrior but I share the same blood as my brother and I do not abandon oathsworn." She clapped her hands and the door opened.

I looked up as the twelve of them came in. They looked as I remembered them save one or two had greybeards now. I had grown up with some of them for they had followed their fathers as I had followed mine. Most were descended from the archers and men at arms who had served my grandfather and, in one case, my great grandfather. Some had chosen to have children late in life when the valley became a little more peaceful.

I recognised them all. The men at arms: Jack son of Harold, Alf Smithson, Rafe son of Roger, Ridley the Giant and Walter son of Wilson. The archers, powerful men with thick arms and broad chests: Will the son of Robin, Thomas son of Tom, Gruffyd son of Tomas, Mordaf son of Tomas, Garth son of Garth, Dick One Arrow and Cedric Warbow. The two sons of Tomas were twins and I could still not differentiate between them. Ridley the Giant was the son of a Varangian who had come all the way from Constantinople to serve my grandfather. Each had his own story and now they stood before me.

"I am sorry that you suffered and neither my father nor myself were here to help you. Thank you for what you tried to do for my grandmother."

Alf Smithson had always been the one who would speak up, he was the eldest. The son of the smith who had made so many swords and so much armour he, alone out of Alf's sons, had chosen the way of the sword. He shook his head, "No, lord. We failed your family. We were charged with protecting the castle. We hesitated for these were priests and a man does not kill a priest."

Jack son of Harold was like his father. He was a wild man in a fight and he growled, "If I had that bishop before me now I would show him that I have changed. If a priest can do as they did then he deserves to die."

There was a murmur of approval.

My aunt said, "My nephew goes to speak with Prince John to try to get back his lands."

Rafe son of Roger shook his head, "I fear it would do little good, my lady. The Prince wants the coin that this valley generates. It is not a surprise that the people are poorer since the Prince and his bishop took over the manors. They are bleeding the people dry. They will never give it back peacefully. It would have to be taken by force."

I looked at them. This was insurrection and treason that they spoke. "You would be outlaws?"

Rafe shrugged, "We are outlaws now, lord. If we are found we will be hanged. The Bishop of Durham drove us hence."

Alf looked at the others. They nodded. "If you would have us, lord, we will follow your banner. It may lead to death but it will be an honourable death. Your blood is that of the Warlord. All men die but it is the manner that determines how they are remembered. We would rather die with you doing something honourable rather than eke out a life as outlaws."

My aunt shook her head, "Let us talk of living and not dying. Nephew, will you take them?"

"Of course, I would be honoured."

"Then what would you do after you have visited Prince John?" She held up her hand, "Think before you speak, Thomas. I know what is in your heart. If you do harm to the bishop then you will be hunted down and killed."

She was right. You cannot undo an oath. Once sworn you must follow it else it eats at your heart and you die from within. I had sworn to kill him and he would die but I could not drag these men to a death for such a creature.

I nodded, "We are warriors all. I know of a war where we could hire our swords out. It is an honourable war for it is against the enemies of Christ, barbarians."

My aunt was intrigued, "The Holy Land again?"

I smiled, "No, Aunt, another war and I will not speak of it yet for Prince John may yet choose to be the kind of man his father hoped he would be."

She shook her head, "I met him and knew him when he was a child. He was a nasty little boy. Rafe is right. He is a mean little man but I have more hope than when you arrived."

"Then we will return to Stockton. I have chests to fetch here. I will return on the morrow and then we can set off on this quest. It may be doomed to failure but the Warlord fought the whole country for Empress Matilda and her son. We will do the same for this valley."

Ruth smiled, "You remind me of my father. You will do, nephew, you will do."

As we rode back to Stockton William said, "Lord, forgive me for speaking out of turn but you intend to kill the bishop do you not?"

"I do but keep that to yourself."

"How do we kill him and escape with our lives?"

"I have yet to work that out but we have a long journey to Bolsover and then the same journey back to Durham. The road is a good place for a man to think. At least I have hope now. When I saw the desecrated grave, I was as low as a man could be. Those twelve men have revived my belief."

When we reached the hall, I saw that my men were waiting and that Edward son of Edgar was with them. They were wearing surcoats with the gryphon on. Henry Youngblood said, "When we loaded the chests we found these, lord. There are another ten. I hope we have not offended you by wearing them."

"No, and we will be leaving soon. Have our horses saddled. I will speak with Sir Richard. William, take charge and do not speak with the men at arms from the castle. I trust Sir Richard but not the others. I fear they may be the bishop's spies. If you are asked where we go then say nothing. If it means being rude then do so. We are now in a land of enemies."

Sir Richard awaited me. He nodded, "You did not stay overnight."

"No, and I beg a word in private, beyond any ears!"

"Then let us walk to St. John's Well. Since the wall was demolished I find it a peaceful place and it is deserted at this time of day."

The remains of the curtain wall could be seen and then the river. We sat on the stone of the well, "I am leaving and taking my chests. I tell you this for I know you to be an honourable man. I will leave my chests with my aunt. She is a strong-willed lady but she and her women live alone. I would be happier knowing that she was protected."

"And I swear that she will be. Until you returned I had no idea that she lived so close. I will visit her."

I smiled, "She will surprise you, lord. I have never met a woman like her."

"And then, Sir Thomas, what will you do?"

"You are an honourable knight and we have fought in the same battle. I will not compromise you. Let us say I go to speak with Prince John and what else follows is in the hands of God."

He nodded, "Do not waste your life eh?"

"I will not. You have my word."

"And leave the carts with your aunt. I will fetch them when I go to speak with her."

When we reached my men, they were ready. The horses were tethered in a long line and the two carts were loaded. There were many people watching us leave. I waved the line forward and we headed past the gates to the town and west. This was familiar land but if things went ill this might be the very last time I would see it. I took in every blade of grass and every tree. I would cross the Oxbridge and take the greenway to Hartburn. If there were spies then I would confuse them. I knew the ways and tracks like the back of my hand. There was a trail that led to Wulfestun. It passed along a valley that had no farms for the ground was subject to flooding. It might take a little longer to reach our destination but I wanted to do so unseen. If we had travelled further north then the bailiff at the Bishop's Garth might have seen us and I wanted to remain hidden from him.

It was dark when we reached Wulfestun. My men joined the others and camped. My aunt had prepared food. William and I ate with her. She asked about the new lord of the manor. "Can you trust this Sir Richard?"

"I believe that I am a good judge of character. He was a Hospitaller."

She nodded, "My father gave Aqua Bella to the Hospitallers. Perhaps this was meant to be. We had better have your men bury the chests which can be buried."

"The weapons, mail, surcoats, shields and arrows we will take. We shall need them." She gave me a sideways look. "Do not worry I will not slay Prince John no matter how much he deserves it. My father's warhorses I will leave with you. I am not certain when I will get to ride them. I will need to take gold with me. We will have expenses and I have men to pay."

"If you need more then I have coin. Our father was generous to both Samuel and me."

"I thank you but you have been more than generous."

She noticed the signet ring on my finger, "I have not seen that since father died. I thought it had been buried with him."

"No, and I have this too." I took out the seal of Aqua Bella.

"Then you are meant to have them both. There were ten such signet rings. I wonder how many are left?"

"I will use it. Who knows, it may gain me an audience with the Prince. If he refuses…"

"If he refuses then you know where you stand. You return here. This land needs a knight to protect the border."

My plans were already made. When I returned from Derbyshire I would tell her of my plans to go to Stock Holm. That would be some time in the future. We would need a ship and, if all went as I planned, we would need to leave quickly. I was aware of my father's sister staring at me. I smiled.

"I know that look, Thomas. You look like my brother. You are plotting and planning. You are the last family I have. Do not throw your life away. You are the last of a line that goes back to the days of King Harold. Remember that."

Chapter 7

We left four days later. We took just two sumpters with supplies. Each of my men carried their own weapons. I estimated it would take us six days for I wished to avoid too much attention. We did not use the Roman Road which went south and through York. I knew that there would be many who would try to stop me. I was certain that the Bishop of Durham knew that I had returned. It would be in his interest to have me stopped. As I had committed no crime he would have to use others to do me harm. There were twenty of us. Each of us was an experienced warrior. If we were attacked then we would defend ourselves. I wish to avoid such confrontation until it was absolutely necessary.

The journey south was an opportunity for me to become reacquainted with my father's men and for the new men to get to know them. They had much in common. Within two days there were new friendships. David of Wales was happy to have other archers with whom he could talk. One of the chests had yielded five hundred arrows. We would need to make or buy more at some point but we had enough and that pleased my archers. They had divided them equally.

Edward son of Edgar had inherited many of the skills of his father and uncle. They had both been scouts under the legendary Aiden. Sir Richard had not known of his skills and he had just been used as a man at arms. I had him riding ahead with Will son of Robin Hawkeye. He too had skills in scouting. They became inseparable. The twins were also good scouts and they rode just behind them. At the rear, with the two sumpters, I had Phillip of Poitiers and Ridley the Giant. As unlikely as it was the huge Ridley and the much shorter Angevin got on well together. Phillip rarely shut up and Ridley was a gentle and almost silent man. I knew that our rear was in safe hands.

I rode with William for I was aware that I had neglected his training as a knight. I was glad now that I had given him the fine sword which I had taken from the dead lord of Aqua Bella. He now had a decent mail shirt. His had gone to Robert of la Flèche. Four of my men at arms were without a mail shirt but they had leather jerkins studded with metal. At least every man had a shield, helmet and surcoat. My banner remained furled. I would not advertise myself until I was closer to Bolsover.

We bought food in the towns we passed. I avoided visiting the towns with castles. Prince John had been ruthless about destroying strongholds of potential enemies. Any castles which remained would be held by staunch supporters of John Lackland. There would be many, such as I, who would have returned from the crusades only to find that those who had not heeded the call were now men of power. My great grandfather had fought for Prince Henry and his mother and now his son was throwing away that which had been gained. The further south we went the angrier I became.

I spied the castle in the distance. "Now, William, it is time to show the banner." I had not had the banner repaired. There were rents and cuts. The staff still bore the marks from the spears and swords of Ayyubid warriors who had tried to kill me. It looked tattered but that told a story. I wanted those who had stayed in England and lived off the blood which had been spilt to see it.

Bolsover Castle had a commanding position on a piece of high ground. Built towards the end of the civil war it had become Prince John's and he had made it a solid bastion. The road wound up to the gatehouse. I could see that it would take a mighty army to subdue it. I saw the Prince's banner. He was within the castle. I was stopped at the gatehouse. I had expected as much. My spurs and my banner marked me as a lord. I took off my helmet and William followed suit. I lowered my ventail and coif.

The sergeant at arms held up his hand, "I cannot allow you in with such a force of men lord. What is your business?"

"I am Sir Thomas of Stockton. I am recently returned to England from the Holy Land and I am here to speak with the Prince." The authority was in my voice.

The sergeant at arms looked nervously behind me. "I can admit you and your squire, lord, but not your men."

Turning I said, "David of Wales, make camp by the river. I will join you when my business is done."

"Aye lord and if you are too long then fear not. We will come to fetch you." He glared at the sergeant at arms. My men feared no one.

I smiled at the sergeant as I entered. I said, quietly, "And he means it! These warriors did not sit at home, they fought Turks and Scots."

He looked at them and nodded, "Aye lord."

Once in the inner bailey servants ran to take our horses. I took a silver penny from my purse, "Give them feed. They are good horses."

"Yes lord."

A chamberlain greeted us before we reached the Great Hall. "What is your business lord? It is unusual for a knight to come here unannounced." The criticism oozed from his mouth.

I smiled, "I am Sir Thomas of Stockton. I am recently returned from the crusades and I am here to petition the Prince. Is that so unusual with his brother held hostage in Austria? I rode with King Richard." He did not look impressed. I took off my glove and showed him the signet ring. "And I wear this!"

He nodded, "If you will wait, lord, I will pass your request to the Prince but he is busy."

I knew that we would be in for a long wait. I saw a servant, "Fetch us ale or wine; whichever is drinkable!" He hesitated and I just glared at him. He scurried off.

He brought us ale but it was good ale. I spied a bench and we sat upon it. We were not the only lords who were waiting but from the looks of the others, they were not warriors. I had heard that the Prince was in the habit of giving knighthoods to those who had money. Many wool merchants were ennobled. The door to the hall would open now and again to admit servants. Each time I heard laughter from within. The Prince did not seem to be conducting business. When I saw food being taken inside I knew that it would be some time before we would be admitted.

Surprisingly, a short time later, the door opened and a knight approached me. He was not like one of those who waited without. This was a knight. He held out his hand, "I am William Marshal. I knew your grandfather and father." I grasped his arm. He turned over my hand while it was in his. "Where did you get the ring? It is not yours."

"It was my grandfather's. It came into my possession when I returned from the crusades. Are you saying that I am not entitled to wear it?"

He smiled, "I did not say that. Do not be so touchy young hero of Arsuf."

"It seems to me that my family has everything else taken from them! Lands, titles, even bodies!"

He put his hand on my arm. He said quietly but with authority, "Peace my young hothead! I know you are angry and I know you are a fearless warrior but this is not Arsuf! Use your head. Your grandfather and father would have done so."

"And my father died protecting the King of England. What was his reward? I see little advantage in serving a king who forgets those who fought for him."

"Be careful, for you speak treason."

"I think, my lord, that there is treason which is much closer to home!"

He put his hand around my back and forcibly moved me into a corner. "I am trying to make you curb your tongue so that you do not lose your head. Now be silent and listen or I will have you and your squire carted off the donjon here! You will soon be forgotten."

I took a deep breath and nodded. I would bide my time and I would leave. This had been a mistake. I had thought that this knight would be on my side. If he was against me then I had little chance of persuading the Prince.

"You were a squire and then a knight. You had little time to learn the world of kings and princes. Your grandfather knew them well and that is why King Henry made him a Marshal. Your family was wronged! The Bishop of Durham had no right to do what he did but that is done and cannot be undone! You lost your castle. The Prince will not return it to you. If you are able to curb your tongue and flatter the Prince then he may give you a manor. That is a start. Your great grandfather began with a tiny manor without even a hall. You are younger than he was. You can do the same. Heed my words. I speak out of the respect I have for your family. If you love this country then you must accept that things may not be the way that you wish them to be."

I nodded, "And if I love my country and cannot accept the way things are, what then?"

He shook his head, "Then you find another country. You have to be a realist."

"In which case, you have given me good counsel and I am now secure in my mind what I must do. Tell me honestly, will I get to speak with the Prince or am I to cool my heels here until it is too late?"

He sighed and then smiled, "You do not compromise, do you? I will speak with the Prince but if you do speak with him then bend both your neck and your knee lest you lose your head!" He put his arm around me. "There are many of us who admire what you did at Arsuf. Your father's sacrifice should have been rewarded. Perhaps when the king returns it may turn out better for you."

He left me. The other lords in the chamber stared at me as though I had two heads. In that moment, I knew that King Richard would not reward my father's action. I doubted that he would even return to England. I would speak with the Prince and make my petition. When it was rejected then I would know where I stood. Prince

The Earl of Pembroke's words must have had an effect for we were admitted soon after. I made sure that William brought in the banner. The hall had twenty or so knights and they were seated along a long table. I saw the Prince in the centre. He was older than I was but he was a short, barrel-chested man. His seat was raised higher than the other knights. That was deliberate. He was a little man trying to appear bigger. I saw that William Marshal stood behind him. His hand was on the back of Prince John's chair.

"So, you are the knight who comes unannounced to disturb us."

It was not a good start. I saw the Earl's eyes as they begged me to curb my tongue. I nodded, "I apologise, Prince John, but I have recently returned from the Holy Land." I gestured to the banner. "This was the banner which marked the place where King Richard's loyal knights died to protect him."

The Prince said, "Little good it did my brother for he is now in a castle in Austria as a prisoner!" He laughed and the sycophantic knights around him joined in.

I took a deep breath. This would be harder than I thought. "I am here to petition for the return of my manor and for the punishment of Hugh de Puiset, Bishop of Durham, who desecrated the grave of one of my forebears."

The room fell silent. Prince John frowned. "Be careful young crusader! You tread a dangerous path. The Bishop of Durham was entitled to throw the bones of the unbeliever away for she was not Christian. And as for the manor! Your great grandfather is to blame for that! He did not ask permission to build the castle. He paid no taxes to the crown from the time of the death of the first King Henry to the coronation of my father. Some say that he never paid taxes! As a result, your family has forfeited the right to hold the land!"

"And what of Norton, lord? That was given to my family by your great grandfather. There is no castle there. Why can that not be returned to me?"

He smiled. It was the smile of a snake, "Because your family always had too much power. Call it a retrospective punishment."

I now understood. No matter what I asked I would be given nothing. I smiled and I saw the look of horror on the face of William Marshal, "So let me be clear, my lord, all that my family had has been taken from me and I can expect nothing from you."

"Very perceptive."

"And I will have to wait until the King of England returns to petition again?"

Prince John stood. It just accentuated how small he was. "That is treasonous talk!"

I spread my arms, "How is it treasonous to speak of the rightful King of England who, in the Holy Land, after the Battle of Arsuf, promised that my family would be rewarded?"

Before the prince could speak, William Marshal said, "That may be the case, Sir Thomas but while King Richard is incarcerated then Prince John is the Regent and all of us must accept his judgement. Do you agree with that?"

I smiled, "Of course, earl. I just wanted clarification so that I may plan what next to do."

The Prince, for the first time, looked worried, "And what will that be? Return to the Holy Land?"

"Perhaps, my lord but there is always La Flèche."

"La Flèche?"

I smiled, "Yes, my lord. It is my family's estate in Anjou. It was given to my family by Empress Matilda. It is in Anjou and not England. That cannot be taken away as a punishment by any save the Duke of Anjou." I smiled, "And that is King Richard. As you say he is a prisoner and therefore he cannot stop my claim."

William Marshal's eyes narrowed. He had not expected that.

I bowed, "I will take my leave and I thank you for listening to my petition."

I backed out. We headed directly for the stable. While the ostler saddled them, William furled the banner. The Earl of Pembroke appeared. "Well, that has set the Prince a problem! You are a fool!"

"But I am an honest fool and I still have my honour. Do you?"

"Be careful, Sir Thomas. I have never lost a combat and I would hate to have to slay you."

"I fear that one day it might come to that."

He shook his head and held on to my reins. His eyes and voice pleaded with me, "Be careful! The Prince surrounds himself with those who would do his bidding for what they could gain. You had best watch your back. Despite what you think I am fighting for England! We are on the same side." They were the same words Sir Richard had said.

I mounted Skuld, "Not from where I am standing!" I spurred her and we galloped out of the gate, scattering the guards who stood there. The die was cast. I was about to become an outlaw!

My men had made a good camp. They looked up as we galloped in. "Make the most of this. We leave in four hours' time at dark of night."

Surprisingly none seemed surprised. David of Wales said, "You received short shrift lord?"

"You could say that and I believe that men will come in the night to finish me off."

Jack son of Harold said, "Then we had best lay some traps and surprises for them."

William said, "You had better eat, lord."

I shook my head. They were all as mad as I was!

I confess that I felt better when I had eaten. I now knew what I would be doing. I sat with William, David of Wales and Jack, son or Harold. "We ride hard when we leave here. It took six days to get here. I would get back in four."

David of Wales asked, "Why the hurry?"

"I believe that Prince John will have men sent to kill us. I am an embarrassment. When his men do not return there will be a hue and cry to try to take us. We ride to Wulfestun. I need someone to go to Herterpol and secure a ship for us. We go to the Baltic."

William nodded as did David of Wales but Jack asked, "Why the Baltic, lord?"

"Firstly, because England will be unsafe. Every man's hand will be turned towards us and secondly, we have friends there. We can earn coin doing what we do best, fighting."

"A perilous cold place, lord."

David said, "I will take cold over heat any time. At least you can drink snow! You cannot drink the sun!"

"Then who will be best?"

"Edward son of Edgar, lord. He is clever. I would send him." Jack nodded emphatically.

"Good. Send him to me."

William asked, "And you still intend to end the life of the Bishop of Durham?"

"He will not be punished otherwise. I want to send a message to Prince John, I do not forgive and I never forget! If my message in there had him worried then think what the death of de Puiset will do."

Edward came, "You sent for me, lord?"

"I would have you and one other ride to Herterpol." I took out a pouch of coins. "Secure us a ship. If you have to buy one then do so but there should be enough here to ensure that we leave England."

"And what destination do I tell the captain?"

"You do not. Tell him we need the ship for no more than a month. Get the largest one that you can."

He took the purse and nodded, "And when do we leave?"

"Now."

He did not seem surprised, "I will take Garth son of Garth. An archer who is good with a dagger might be useful. When will you be there lord?"

"When I get there. Use the coin for lodgings. You have a small fortune there. Use it wisely."

He nodded and shouted, "Garth! We ride!"

I prepared myself for the fight that I knew was coming. My men returned, having set traps. We had a way out, to the north, but every other route was either barred or trapped. We would know when they were coming. We tethered the horses, already saddled, close to the escape route and then we lay down before a banked fire. My archers hid in the trees which surrounded the camp and the rest of us lay down, like bait!

As I lay down I said, "Keep talking and behave normally. Our men in the trees will warn of us of enemies."

A murmur of conversation sprang up. "How will we get to the bishop, lord?" William was resigned to my course of action and wished to know the details.

"Getting to him will be easier than getting out. We will go in disguise. When we have dealt with these knights and men at arms who come to kill us I would have you take two surcoats and cloaks from their bodies."

"You are certain that we can defeat them?"

"William, do you doubt these men that we lead? I am confident that they will give whoever comes to kill us a surprise. Keep your sword and dagger handy."

Mine were under my cloak. The murmuring gradually stopped as one would expect. Silence fell. An owl hooted. I heard the sounds of animals moving and pigeons as they roosted in the trees. They were the normal sounds one would expect. Then Skuld whinnied. An attacker would not worry. When it was followed by a whistle then I knew that they were coming. Our traps worked well. There was a shout as one of the men sent to kill us tripped on the cord strung between two trees. I heard the thrum of an arrow and then a scream. Realising that they had been seen the killers raced through the woods eager to earn the money their prince had offered and the reward for killing a nuisance.

William and I, along with my men art arms, were on our feet in an instant. I heard more cries as men tripped traps and others were slain by arrows sent from the dark of the woods. Even so, one of the knights I had seen seated close to

Prince John broke through and ran at me. He had a shield and a sword. He had good night vision for he came directly for me. I blocked his sword with my dagger. He held his shield to the side to block the swing of my sword. Instead, I rammed my knee between his legs. As his face came forward I punched him with the pommel of my sword and when his right hand fell plunged my dagger through the eye hole of his helmet. I saw William fighting a knight. He was losing. I stabbed my sword through his ribs so hard that the tip came out of the other side.

With all surprise gone and dead men littering the ground, I heard a voice shout, "Back to the castle! We need more men!"

I shouted, "William!"

"Aye, lord!" My squire went to seek the surcoats we would need for our deception.

"The rest of you, take what you will and then mount. They will pursue us!"

I took the helmets from the dead men. They were knights the same age as me. My experience in the Holy Land had been the difference. William quickly stripped two surcoats. I saw the men without mail taking the mail shirts from dead knights. I ran to Skuld, "Well done, my fine horse! You have saved us again!"

I heard horns from the castle. The survivors had sounded the alarm. We were half a mile from the castle. It would have to be enough of a start.

"Let us ride!"

I allowed William to lead. "David, keep the archers at the rear. If we can find somewhere to ambush them then so much the better."

"Aye, lord!"

As we rode north, towards the Roman Road, I realised that I was now a traitor and an outlaw. Prince John had sent those men. We had slain them. There was no stepping back from this road.

We did not stop until dawn. We were north of Rotherham, having skirted that walled town. We stopped in the shelter of the forest which stretched north for another fifty miles. We did not need the rest, the horses did. There was a house there. It was rude and crude and it was empty. We went to the water trough which was filled with unpleasant looking water. It would have to do. As the horses drank my archers spread out on either side of the road, hidden in the trees. Half of us rested in the middle of the road while the others saw to the horses. I heard the thunder of hooves.

"Ready!" This time we would need our shields and we stood in a loose line across the road. I wanted the enemy to see us. I saw that there were forty men. Two knights led a line of sergeants. They wore the livery of de Lisle, the castellan of Bolsover Castle. I guessed that one of the knights was de Lisle.

They had lances and they lowered them as they charged down the road at us. Few had fought since the civil war. Had they done so then they might have expected an ambush. Any who had fought the Turk always expected an ambush. There were just seven archers but they were all experts. Seven arrows found seven targets and then another seven followed. By the time they had realised it was an ambush, ten sergeants had been hit and four horses. The two knights bore charmed lives as did their squires. There were eight of us. I caught de Lisle's lance on my shield and I hacked my sword into the shoulder of his horse. The knight fell. His squire was butchered by Rafe and Ridley the Giant. The second knight had his lower leg taken. The squire threw down his shield and sword. He yelled, "Quarter! Quarter!"

The sergeants who had survived had fled. My men dragged the terrified squire from his saddle. The two horses we had captured were taken to join our others.

As de Lisle stood, somewhat groggily I used my sword to flip his helmet from him. I took his sword from his scabbard. "You are a lucky man today! You will live. I am not certain if your companion will. I will take your sword as a reminder to you that I could have taken your life. Tell your Prince John that we are now at war. I have men who can use the night and the dark. He will never be safe. When he sleeps advise him to have men sleeping by his doors. Until my estates and titles are returned to me then he is in danger. Do you understand?" I held my dagger to the bridge of his nose.

He said, "I will tell him but you are a dead man! Prince John will be the next King of England!"

I dragged the edge of my dagger down his nose and split it. "Then God help England! That is to remember me by." Turning to my men I said, "Mount! Let us ride!"

We now had at least a day start on the enemy. That would be time enough. With less than eighty miles to go, I was confident that we could make Wulfestun in two days. That would give us two days to get to Durham and then leave England. We headed up the road north. I knew that we could avoid any other enemies. With four spare horses, we could rest four horses every hour. We would make it.

Our horses were exhausted, one was even lame but we made Wulfestun after dark on the second day after we had fled Bolsover. We had camped on the high ground close to Loidis in a sheltered valley. If it had not had a stream and turf we might not have made it but the horses ate, drank and rested. We could sleep on the voyage to Sweden.

My father's sister's face showed her concern. She did not know what I had done. While her women saw to my men and William saw to the horses I sat with her before her fire. I told her all or almost all. "No matter what we did the result would have been the same. They will send men here. Too many people know that you are my relative and you live here. I would have you tell them where I have gone. You can say that I threatened you if that will make your life easier."

71

She shook her head, "I may not be a warrior but I will not be foresworn. Where are you going? The Holy Land again?"

"Outremer is finished. They may hang on to a few fortresses for a while but King Richard knew that he could not do what he said. That is the real reason he came home. He took the peace that was offered and he ran! We go to the Baltic and Sweden. I have been offered the chance to fight for pay for the Swedes against the barbarians and pagans of Estonia. We will take ship when we can."

"Have you coin enough?"

I nodded, "I have and all the men that I lead are worth the investment. They fought for what was right. I will not abandon them."

She nodded, "Sir Richard came for the carts. He is a kind man. He told me that you had asked him to watch over me. You are a sweet boy but I can look after myself."

"I would not be too sure about that. I listened to what William Marshal did not say. Prince John will do little to return King Richard to the crown. He will continue to gather power by ridding the land of all who oppose him. There will be another civil war. When that war comes then I will return. Until then I will be in Stock Holm at the home of Birger Persson. He is an important jarl in that country. We have faced death together."

She looked relieved. "And when do you leave?"

"We will be out of here by dawn. There are men pursuing us. It will take them time to get here but I would not make your home the scene of a battle."

She stood and embraced me. I felt the tears as she hugged me, "You are the only family I have and now you are going. This is not right. My grandfather and father made sacrifices so that this land would be whole and now to see it torn apart by a weasel-like John. When the king brought the boys to Stockton and they played he was the one who would pinch and nip others. He pretended that it was he who had been injured and his mother would berate us. Your father never liked him."

I laughed, "Well he has not changed overmuch."

I was tired but I did not get much sleep. I was busy planning how I would gain entry to Durham Castle and how I would kill the bishop. I fell asleep unsure of exactly how I would do it but when I awoke I had a crystal-clear idea. I would use Prince John as my unwitting accomplice. I took leave of Aunt Ruth. We had said all there was to say the night before. Besides both of us were close to tears. This could be the last time we spoke. I just nodded as I mounted Skuld and headed north. When we were two miles north we stopped. My men looked at me.

"I know how we will gain entry. William, the surcoats."

William had found four surcoats amongst the dead knights we had slain but two of them were bloody. I put one over my own.

"Robert of La Flèche, you wear the other. Rafe and Ridley, take off your surcoats. You will come in with us. My plan is simple. The four of us will say that we have a message about Sir Thomas of Stockton for the bishop. The rest of you will secrete yourselves in Durham. There is movement in and out of the castle and the cathedral. Cover your surcoats with your cloaks. You will be there to help our escape. When the deed is done we ride to Herterpol. Edward and Garth should have secured us a ship. If not…"

The men did not seem worried about the uncertain prospect.

"The archers will guard the horses and our baggage. Your arrows will be used to clear the gatehouse when we flee." They seemed satisfied. "We ride."

I had been to Durham on more than one occasion. The last time had been with Sir Wulfric when he went to admonish the bishop on my grandfather's behalf for failing to stop the Scots from attacking our lands. When we had ridden there that doughty knight had told me how my great grandfather had captured the castle from within. He knew of the secret ways in and out. We would not be needing those ways. I would enter by the front door and leave by the same. While we had been waiting to see Prince John I had discovered the names of some of his newer knights. I hoped that the bishop would not know them.

"Robert, you will be Sir Brian of Sheffield and I am Sir Thomas of Shenley. They are real knights and they serve Prince John. They had been on a crusade, albeit, briefly. We can pass for them. We will rely on speed to achieve our ends. Rafe and Ridley will cover our backs. I want the bishop dead. We may have to kill more but let us try not to."

"Aye, lord."

We stopped at the ridge just a mile from the castle. We could see it, through the trees on the other side of the river which looped around. It was a hard place to take and I wondered just how my great grandfather had done so. I nodded to my men. They knew what they were about. They had no need for a speech to inspire them. The four of us rode quickly towards the gate.

As we galloped towards the gatehouse there was a sudden flurry as the guard was called, "Who are you that you ride so quickly armed thus?"

I pointed behind me, "We have been sent by Prince John. I am Sir Thomas of Shenley and this is Sir Brian of Sheffield. We have news of the son of the Earl of Cleveland, Sir Thomas of Stockton!"

The captain of the guard said, "So it is true, the grandson of that devil is returned. Admit them!"

We galloped through the gatehouse and into the outer bailey. We walked our horses through the second gate after repeating our message and we found ourselves in the inner bailey. Our arrival had caused great consternation. Soldiers raced to us and I repeated my news a third time. They looked behind me as though an enemy was upon them.

"Watch our horses carefully. We have to ride to Stockton to warn Sir Richard after this."

"We can get you fresh horses!"

"No, these will do."

A priest hurried us through the castle to the bishop's chambers. The priest said as we hurried, "He is inside with two of his knights. He had heard that this devil was returned. Your news will be welcomed!"

There was a man at arms guarding the doorway. I said to Rafe and Ridley, "You two guard the door." I winked. "Let no one else enter until we leave."

The priest opened the door and entered, "My lord these men are from Prince John, they bring news of Sir Thomas of Stockton."

I saw that the two knights were mailed. I had only seen the bishop once but people had told me that I looked just like my grandfather. As soon as he looked up the bishop shouted, "You fool! That is Sir Thomas!"

Robert had quick hands. Even as the first knight's hand went to his sword Robert had run him through. I had my sword at the second knight's throat. "I do not wish to kill you but I will if I have to. Put your weapons on the floor and then turn around. Priest, do the same!"

I heard a scuffle outside the door and then the sound of something hitting the floor. The sentry had been dealt with. The priest obeyed my command immediately but the knight glared at me. I pushed my sword into his cheek and a tendril of blood dripped down his cheek. "I have nothing to lose. You will die if you do not obey!"

He reluctantly obeyed. I nodded to Robert. He spun his sword and smacked first the knight and then the priest on the back of the head. Both fell to the floor. Hugh de Puiset was defiant, "You do not frighten me! We have your lands! You will be caught and hanged!"

"What do you think we come here to do?"

He suddenly looked worried, "Why to rob me of course!"

I shook my head, "We are here to execute you. You desecrated my grandmother's grave and for that, you will die! I am the judge and I sentence you, Hugh de Puiset, to death."

"She was a Jew!"

"Confess your sins! You will die and I give you the chance to confess your wrongdoing."

I held my sword at his neck. "I confess that I did wrong. I was greedy and avaricious." He closed his eyes and began to mumble a prayer. I saw him soil himself. As soon as he stopped I swung the sword and took his head. It was over in a flash and I wished it had lasted longer. I sheathed my sword and we left. The four of us hurried out. The men were still there with our horses.

"That was quick."

"Bad news is best delivered quick. I told the bishop that Prince John said that Sir Thomas is heading here with an army! I would close your gates."

"Thank you, friend!"

Sword For Hire

We mounted and galloped out of the inner bailey. I saw some of my men at arms leading their horses up the hill towards the cathedral. Seeing me they turned and headed out. The captain of the guard looked at Jack son of Harold suspiciously, "Why the change of mind?"

Jack's sword was in his hand and the captain died before he could utter any more. Arrows flew and the other three guards fell dead.

"Ride!"

A couple of belated bolts flew from the walls but we were beyond their range and they clattered harmlessly onto the bridge over the Wear. We stopped at the top of the ridge and changed. "Now we head for Herterpol."

William pointed to the gates of the castle. "Lord, they are sending riders."

"Then we had better move."

I was confident that we would escape them. We had killed one of the senior knights and injured a second. They would head for Stockton. By the time they realised we had ridden due east, it would be too late. Everything now depended upon Edward son of Edgar. If he had failed then we would die.

Birger Brosa

Chapter 8

It was a wild ride to Herterpol. Just six miles separated my aunt's home from the port and the land between the two had few farms. Sir Richard had told me that while Stockton's fortunes had declined so those of Herterpol had grown. Ships did not have to navigate the tortuous Tees and now that there was a stone quay and the beginnings of a wall it would soon eclipse Stockton as a port. The Bishop of Durham had seen another way to have his vengeance on the Earl of Cleveland. My family had had little to do with the town. My great grandfather had rescued my great grandmother from it and destroyed one of the early halls. I hoped that their memories were short. It was late in the afternoon as we crested the rise just after Elwick. I saw masts in the harbour. Further out to sea I saw more ships. The seaways were becoming busier.

The wall did not extend all the way around the town. Soon it would and then those who wished to use it would be forced to use a gate and could be scrutinised. There were too many of us and we were too well-armed for the town watch to challenge. There was no gate yet. They had built the gatehouse and the four, portly men of the watch waved us through. Recognising a lord they knuckled their foreheads. We rode directly to the harbour and there I saw Edward and Garth. They were standing by a large ship. It was also an old ship. This one had had a hard life.

Edward looked relieved to see us. He beckoned us up the gangplank, "Lord, this is Henry the son of William of Kingston. His father used to sail your great grandfather's ship, *'Adela'*."

Henry, who had the weathered skin of a veteran sailor, nodded, "Aye lord. I am the youngest of the boys. It would be an honour to take you to Sweden. I have begun to sail those waters in the past couple of years. The iron ore they trade is of good quality. It is much sought after." He looked at the horses. "I fear my ship is not large enough for all the horses you have."

"How many can you take?"

"No more than fifteen."

I turned to Edward, "You know horses. We take Skuld and the best fourteen. Sell the others."

"Aye lord."

"David of Wales, get the gear on board and then help Henry here load the horses."

My men moved quickly. We all knew that there would be horsemen seeking us. It would take some time to get to Stockton and realise that we were not there. However, it would take time to load horses. I watched as Skuld was led up the gangplank. She was a seasoned traveller and she went easily. It would help to calm the rest. The loading might not take as long as I had thought for they would not need to use a sling. There was a ramp down into the hold. We needed to leave as quickly as we could. I did not know what awaited us in Sweden but I would need as many of my men alive and fit as I could manage.

I turned as an officious voice spoke, "I am John. the collector of taxes. Have you paid the port fees?"

I looked down at a little man. He was neat and had the look of a clerk. That was confirmed by his inky fingers. "Port fees?"

"We charge ships to land and we charge those who wish to use the port. Your captain has paid already for his ship. Now you must pay."

I saw Edward return. He had a small bag of coins from the sale of the horses. We could pay fees. If they went to Sir Richard then I would pay them.

"And to whom do the fees go? Who is the lord of this manor?"

The clerk smiled, "They go to no lord. They go to the Bishop of Durham."

The bishop had been a greedy little man. "Then in that case we do not pay the fees. I will pay nothing to Hugh de Puiset."

His mouth dropped open, "But he is the bishop!"

"I will not pay."

He looked around as though seeking support. There were none nearby. "I will fetch the town watch."

"You can fetch the bishop himself I will not pay." I leaned down so that my head was level with his, "And you cannot make me, can you?"

He suddenly took in my surcoat. He recoiled, "You are Sir Thomas of Stockton!"

I nodded and turned for the last of the horses was being loaded. "Captain, when can we sail?"

Henry looked over the side, "We either leave now or wait until the next tide, my lord."

"Then we leave now!" I stepped aboard. I saw John, collector of taxes pointing at us and exhorting the watch to do something. They were too far away for me to hear any words but the shaking of heads was enough. We had passed by them when we had entered and they had recognised us as men not to be crossed. We had just slipped our moorings and the tide and wind were taking us to the narrow entrance when I saw riders in the distance. They rode beneath the banner of the Palatinate. Had we delayed then we might have had to fight our way out. We had reached the mouth of the harbour when they reined in at the quay. I saw fists raised and waved.

Henry said, "I take it the bishop did not wish you to leave."

I said, "You should know, Henry, that I have slain the Bishop of Durham. You carry a killer on your ship."

He clutched his cross. His face showed his shock, "Lord, he was a bishop."

"He was an evil and a venal man. When you return tell them that I forced you to take us. They will believe it of us. I frightened the port official and he will confirm that I am a dangerous man. I swear that he deserved to die."

"Did you murder him, lord?"

"No, Henry, I executed him!"

I joined my men and we took off our mail. It would not do it any good to be subjected to salt water. I had a leather bag that was lined with sheepskin. After William had helped me take it off and we had used a sack of sand to clean and dry it, we folded it and placed it in the sheepskin-lined bag. William had a similar bag. We had bought them when we had landed at Cyprus on the way to Pisa. My men had to make do with hessian sacks. The bags were then placed in the hold. That took some time. When I looked up I saw that we were some way from the coast of England. Soon it would be a smudge and then it would be gone. When would I see it again?

I turned to descend into the hold. I saw that the horses were all secure. There was fodder for them. Each horse was tethered and supported by wooden walls. Henry had explained it stopped the cargo of iron shifting too much in bad weather. It made for good stalls. Henry had estimated the voyage to be between six and ten days in length. He said that it would depend upon the winds. I looked up at the pennant. The winds were from the south and west. God favoured us.

I headed to the canvas-covered shelter we would use while on deck and I slept. My men would eat but I needed sleep. I was exhausted and the execution of the bishop, although necessary, had wearied me. My spirits were also low for I had left England and the only family I had left. Sweden was new and was unknown. What if it proved to be like the Holy Land? My dreams were dark. I was grateful that, when I woke, I did not remember them. I opened my eyes to a grey day. The wind had veered a little and although still a westerly was now from the north-west and it was accompanied by flurries of rain. I wrapped my cloak about me and joined Henry. He was supervising the steersman.

"Lord."

"Henry. Tell me Henry what do you know of this Stock Holm?"

"I have used it before. This last year I have been there four times. In fact, I know it better than most other ports saving Stockton and Herterpol. They have iron mines close by and we carry that cargo. Usually, we travel there empty for there is little that they want from us."

"Stockton has iron too!"

"Aye lord, but since the Bishop took over the lands there is less of it mined. He taxes the miners. He charges too high a fee on the river. Herterpol will be the same. There are other ports further south which can be used. Hull has wool. The monks encourage ships to use that river and they do not charge high port fees. The iron mines can take their iron there. It takes a little longer but it is cheaper than using Herterpol or Stockton. He is… was strangling the valley."

I looked astern. My father would never have left England with his knights had he known the result. We had lost all. The people were now poorer and I felt as though I was abandoning them. I knew what my own crusade would be. I would fight for the Swedes but my purpose was to gain enough coin to be able to mount a fight against Prince John. I needed King Richard back on the throne!

After the mainly benign waters of the Mediterranean, the dark grey waters of this German Sea seemed almost malevolent. We were tossed and buffeted. Some of my men had not sailed before and they took some time to adjust to the motion. When we turned and navigated the passage called the Skagerrak even some of the more experienced sailors suffered. Once we entered it the Baltic was quieter and was calmer. It was also colder. I was glad that we had bought furs and thicker cloaks when we had left for England all those many months ago. William used the salve which Birger Persson had given him. When we had put the mail in its leather bag he had confessed that he was desperate to acquire more of the salve. England had been damper and colder than was good for his wound. It helped him to sleep.

I know not what I was expecting of Sweden but the archipelago was not in my mind. It was a mass of inlets, rocks and shoals. Captain Henry had to use all of his skill to navigate the channel and reach the harbour. It was a smaller place than I expected. There was a wooden hall and a wall. This had been a small settlement and now it was growing. Perhaps that was the result of the iron. I could see building work. They were making a stone castle and other buildings were being erected. I now understood why Jarl Birger had had such old-fashioned armour. This land was, compared with England, somewhat primitive. There was little point in bemoaning my choices. If I had not come here then I would have had to return to the Holy Land and that was not a choice I was willing to make. I had sworn to the Turk that I would never return and a knight did not break an oath; even to a non-believer. We donned our mail before we docked. We were warriors and I wanted The Jarl Birger Brosa to know that.

I was lucky that we had found Henry to bring us. He spoke some of the language and he was able to tell the officials that I was here at the request of The Jarl Birger Brosa. His name was known and we were able to offload our horses and our baggage. We had paid for our passage before we had left England but I pressed another bag of coins into Henry's hand.

"Lord, you have paid me."

"This is so that you will continue to act for me and let me know how things are in England. I know not where we will be living but I will find someone here with whom you can speak and leave messages. You will be my link to England. You will tell me how my land and my valley fares."

"I will, lord. And I will pray for your soul too." He left me to negotiate for a cargo to take from the port.

David of Wales came over to me, "Well lord, what now?"

"The horses will be of no use to us until they have their land legs and we need more horses. Let us see if we can find some accommodation." I turned to my men. "Wait here while I go with William to see if we can find a bed for the night."

As we headed towards the hall William said, "I had thought this would be a bigger place from what Jarl Birger Persson told us."

"You are right. However, it is too late to do anything about this decision now. Henry will be sailing back and we have few other choices. We will have to make the best of it."

The walls of the settlement, it was not large enough to call a town, were made of wood but I could see, beyond the wooden enclosure, masons toiling to make a stone keep. As we neared the gate a handful of Swedish warriors, wearing blue surcoats with a gryphon device, walked towards us. That was the first time I met the legend that was The Jarl Birger Brosa. He was much older than I was and unlike me, this knight held power; real power. Married to the daughter of the King of Norway he controlled the destinies of many Swedes. He was second only to the king and he ruled this part of Sweden like a king. Despite the fact that he was older he had bright alert eyes and an enquiring mind. He was full of enthusiasm.

I saw him and his men pointing to our surcoats. They were very similar to the ones I saw the jarl wearing. To my relief he spoke my language, "I am guessing that you must be my cousin's friend, Sir Thomas from England. I recognise your device."

His manner and tone invited a smile and conversation, "And you must be The Jarl Birger Brosa. I am relieved that you speak our language."

He nodded, "My wife and I visited Rome and the Pope. We found it easier to speak their language. Tell me what brings you here? My cousin said that you were returning to your manor in England."

I decided that honesty was the best policy. "My lands and titles were taken from me while on crusade. There was nothing left for me in England. Birger Persson said that a warrior could earn money with his sword in these lands." I looked at the jarl, "Was he correct?"

Laughing he put his arm around my shoulder, "You are an honest man. Yes, he is right. This will be a formidable citadel one day. I am recruiting men to bring Christianity to the pagans of Estonia. It will cost less to hire men such as yourself who are armed and trained than training men myself. I see that you all have fine mail and modern helmets. My cousin told me that the men you brought were good warriors who knew how to fight. That is what we need here."

We had entered his gates and I saw that his halls were not the same as ours. They were more like upturned boats. They had just one floor. Many of our halls, even the ones built by poor knights, had two storeys. The keep, I could see, would be more like the ones I was familiar with. It was square with steps leading to a door four paces up the wall.

"And of course, there will be the opportunity for you to take treasure and slaves. Any who convert will live and be freed but the others will be sold as slaves. Bishop Albert and Pope Celestine are adamant that the Baltic will be Christian. And I too would have the Baltic at peace."

His wife came to greet us as we entered the hall. Lady Brigida Haraldsdotter was a beautiful woman. She was also very gracious and William and I were greeted like honoured guests.

"You will both stay in our hall."

I bowed, "Thank you, my lady but I have my men and horses to see to."

The jarl said, "Sverre, see to Sir Thomas' men and their horses. You can use the warehouse we use to store the iron. I am guessing that it will be loaded onto the ship which has brought Sir Thomas. When you have done that send a rider to my cousin and tell him that his friend is here."

"Aye jarl."

He led me into the hall. It was warm and comfortable. "We will discuss terms over food this night."

The hall had but one floor. There were no stairs. It looked to me as though there were chambers for sleeping off the main hall. Lady Brigida Haraldsdotter clapped her hands and servants appeared. She rattled something off in Swedish and they disappeared. She smiled at me, "Come, I will show you your chamber. My servants have gone to fetch your bags." She examined my face as we walked to the chamber. "I can see you have been in the sun. Here, when it is winter, we are lucky to see the sun at all. I liked Rome. It was hot although I did not like their food. I suppose you cannot have everything." She moved aside the curtain. There were two mattresses. They looked to be filled with some sort of feathers. There was a table upon which there was a pot of water and a bowl. "You will want to clean up after your journey. I will send a servant to tell you when it is time to eat."

When we were alone William said, "That was easier than I had expected, lord."

"It was but I trusted Birger Persson. This jarl seems an honest man. Help me off with my mail. I do not think we will need it while we are here. None of the men we saw was wearing mail."

81

Sword For Hire

The curtain opened while William had my mail halfway off. The servants placed our bags on the floor and scurried out. We washed and then combed our hair and beards. We had fine clothes we had brought from the Holy Land and we wore those. We organized our clothes. I did not know how long we would be here but warriors are organized. They like everything in its place.

The servant who had brought our bags summoned us to the hall. The table had been laid and I was seated to the right of the jarl. William was on my right. I noticed a space next to the jarl's wife. Jarl Brosa smiled, "My cousin will be here. He does not live far. I know that he is anxious to see you." There were no other guests. It was an intimate gathering.

The food was interesting. There appeared to be more fish than we might eat in a month at home and a lump of meat I was told was reindeer. It tasted like venison. The jarl and his wife were excellent hosts and they told us of the wars that were rife in the region.

"The Danes and the Norwegians have civil wars and wars with each other. We try to be a haven of peace and do not become involved. However, our greatest danger is the barbarians who live close by. There are Estonians and Karelians who continue to raid us. The Rus and the Slavs also plague us. The crusade we will undertake is for our own safety as much as anything else. They raid for slaves and they raid for our animals. The heathens are lazy and godless. They do not like to work themselves. It is easier to plunder and to take. That is why we will build stone walls and a keep. This will be the first but soon Sweden will be ringed by walls of stone defended by men of steel."

Lady Brigida shook her head, "They are an evil people. Christian priests are abused. Some are burned alive. It has to stop. Tell me, Sir Thomas, the men you brought are they good fighters?"

I nodded, "They are the best. I believe that man for man they are the equal of any knight and superior to many. We are small in number but we will not let your husband down."

He nodded, "And I am intrigued that your surcoats have a very similar design to mine. I would have thought that you sought to flatter us had not my cousin told me that your family have used this for three generations."

"My grandfather went on the Second Crusade. He chose the design in Constantinople, the place you call Miklagård. It has served us well."

Just then the door burst open and Birger and Petr stood there. He did not stand on ceremony but ran the length of the hall to embrace me in a bear hug. "I hoped you would come but I did not expect it to be so soon! This is good news."

Birger Brosa shook his head, "My cousin has always been the impetuous one. Sit, cousin! Give your friend the chance to tell you why he is here."

Birger made up for lost time by devouring fish, reindeer and bread as I told him of the events which had followed our landing. I realised that I would have to be brutally honest with my hosts and my friend. I stopped abruptly when I reached the point in the tale where we reached Hull. "There is something which you need to know. It may change your opinion of me but I cannot serve you while there is a secret between us."

I was aware that silence had descended. The four of them looked at me. William looked crestfallen. I think he had hoped I would remain silent. I could not. If the jarl heard what I had done from another then it would be worse than if he heard it from my own lips.

"My grandmother was a Jew. She was not Christian but she was a good woman. When she died she was buried in the same tomb as my grandfather in the church at my castle; my former castle. My father had her effigy carved upon a stone slab. While my father and I were in the Holy Land, Prince John and the Bishop of Durham plotted and the castle was given to the Palatinate of Durham. I could have lived with the loss of my castle but the bishop then had my grandmother's bones thrown into the river and her slab destroyed."

I saw the jarl's wife clutch her cross, "Monstrous! That is not the act of a Christian! And he calls himself a bishop!"

I shook my head, "He is more of a politician than a man of God. I went to the Prince for justice. I was treated badly and he sent men to kill me."

The four of them shook their heads in disbelief. The Jarl Birger Brosa said, "A regent does not do that. There has to be justice. If there is not then there is anarchy!"

"That was when I decided to take matters into my own hand." There was no long-winded way of telling them what I had done. "I rode to the bishop's castle and executed him. I gave him the chance to beg forgiveness of God before I did so but I took his life." There was silence in the hall. The servants had not understood a word, of course, but the four Swedes looked at each other. "I understand this may change how you view me and my men. If you wish us to leave then we will do so but I will not fight under false colours. I am an outlaw in my own land and I killed a churchman."

"I admire your honesty, Sir Thomas. We will do nothing that is hasty. Bishop Albert is visiting here next week. He will give us advice. Until then you are our guest."

I was amazed. My confession did not change the way they spoke to me. Sweetmeats were brought and honeyed wine. It was my confession apart, a very pleasant evening. The jarl and his wife took their leave of us and I was left to speak to my old friend.

"Life is never dull with you around, Thomas. I am glad you have come. I wished you had not slain a churchman but then you could not have allowed him to live."

"Would you have killed him?"

"Probably but in a less public way. You have told the world that you did it. You were right to tell my cousin. He is ever honest and he likes honesty in others. When the bishop has visited I will take you to my home and we will hunt and fish."

"If the bishop allows me to stay."

"It is my land and you and your men shall stay with me no matter what his judgement."

Chapter 9

I spent two days riding the jarl's lands. I discovered that my men were being treated well. They were enjoying the life. They had food, good beer and they got on well with the jarl's men. All appeared to be well until Jarl Birger Persson's rider brought dire news. He arrived in the late afternoon. His horse was lathered and his surcoat was besmirched with blood. He threw himself from his horse and said, "Jarl Birger, our home has been sacked and burned. The Karelians came in the night. They have taken many of our people as slaves and slain many of our men. The survivors are heading here now."

They say you judge a man by how he reacts to adversity. Jarl Birger showed me that day that he had steel for a spine. He said, "Then we will seek help from my cousin and we will teach these Karelians a lesson. Eystein, find a fresh horse and have some food."

"Aye jarl."

Turning to me he said, "Would you and your men fight at my side?"

"Of course, need you ask? I will get them."

"And I will find my cousin. This is what we both feared. We have waited too long to deal with these barbarians."

I sent William for our mail and I ran to the hall our men were using. "Arm yourselves. We go to war. Saddle all the horses we have. Some of you will have to march."

None seemed surprised and they greeted the news that we were going to fight in a strange land with stoicism and practicality. David of Wales asked, "Are we to fight knights lord or folk like the Turks?"

"Neither. They are barbarians who have sacked a town and taken the people as slaves."

Jack son of Harold said, "Like Scots then! I was ready for a fight."

By the time I reached The Jarl Birger Brosa's hall the whole of the town was aroused and men were racing hither and thither. William helped me on with my mail. We had just stepped out into the light when Birger Brosa appeared. He was mailed with a surcoat and a helmet. His squire had his horse. He nodded towards me. "It seems you will be fighting alongside us, Sir Thomas! I look forward to seeing how Englishmen fight!"

Skuld was brought over and I mounted. William handed me my shield and my spear. I saw that Ridley the Giant and three others were prepared to march. As most of Jarl Birger's men were also on foot it would not be a problem. My men formed up behind me in a column of twos. Birger Persson and Petr were next to The Jarl Birger Brosa. He turned to me, "Do not take offence, Englishman, but you do not know our country. I would have your men at the rear. The Karelians are fond of ambush and this raid may be a trap for us."

I nodded, "We will do whatever you ask of us, jarl. I have eight archers who never miss."

"Then they may be useful. The Karelians are good archers too."

We headed northeast. I had not travelled the land yet. We had had rain recently and I saw that they did not use stone for their roads. The result was that the track we followed soon became a muddy morass. Nor did it travel in a straight line. It twisted and turned around rocks, inlets, rivers and ponds. There appeared to be little farmland along the path we trod. It was late summer but, when we had been speaking with our hosts, we were informed that winter set in early. Rather than deterring fighting, it encouraged it as the frozen ground was easier to travel than wet.

William said, "There are not many men, lord."

He was right. There were less than forty Swedes ahead of us. This was not a large army. I hoped that they knew what they were doing. Only the two jarls and their squires wore mail. Although most of the others had a helmet and shield the majority did not even have a leather jerkin. They reminded me, however, of some of the men who had served my grandfather. They had been descended from Vikings!

As we marched I looked at the sky. Night was not far away. I did not know how far away was this village of Sigtuna. Although I was at the rear I could see the two jarls, their squires and the warrior, Eystein, on their horses. They were the only mounted Swedes. Even the standard-bearer went afoot. I saw a hand raised and they stopped. Beyond them, I could see the remnants of Jarl Birger Persson's men. These were the ones who had escaped the Karelians and the raid. There appeared to be less than twenty and I saw bandages and litters. To the side stood a forlorn huddle of women and children. There were not many.

Behind me, I heard Will son of Robin say, "This looks all too familiar, lord. When the Scots raided and came south of the border this is what we saw. Then your father and grandfather would take us north to wreak revenge."

"One day, Will, we will return home and do so again. This is not our destination. This is just part of our journey."

We moved on and marched into the twilight. We stopped at the burning remains of Sigtuna. It looked to have been a fine settlement. There was a ditch and I could see where the wall had been. It looked to have had a quay. Ships could sail here. The hall was now just a pile of burning embers. My friend had lost his home. I heard him shout, "We will camp here tonight! We bury our dead first."

It was a distressing operation. Many of the older folk had been burned alive in their huts. I saw the body of a child, no more than seven summers old. Her skull had been caved in. There were many other careless deaths. My men were used to seeing warriors dead and maimed but not the old and the young. It hardened the hearts of my men. We placed a good guard around the camp. No one was in the mood for food. We rigged up shelters and made sure that the horses had grazing and water.

I sat with the other knights. "What do we do on the morrow?"

The Jarl Birger Brosa pointed across the water. "They came by boat. They use an island as a base from which to raid. If this was winter we would march over the ice and we would be slaughtering them already. But it is not yet winter and they chose this time to raid because there is no ice. We will have to march around the headland and cross the shallows to reach them. It will take all day."

I looked over to my friend. He was deep in thought. "You can rebuild."

He nodded, "Aye and like my cousin I will build in stone. When I came back from the crusade I had such ideas. I was putting them off until I could hire a good mason. It has cost my people their lives. When we have punished these animals then we build in stone."

The Jarl Birger Brosa shook his head, "But not here, cousin. I would have another castle but I would have it on the island these animals use. Let us deny them a base and use it ourselves."

"But this is the home of my people. My family farmed here."

"Look around. It is a charnel house. Start again!"

It was as though he was talking to me. It was what I would have to do. I would never be given Stockton again. There was little point in yearning for what I could never have. The castle was gone. I would have to begin again.

The Jarl Birger Brosa continued, "Besides you have told me that the channel was becoming silted. The island will be not only more secure, but it will also be better for your fishermen."

My friend nodded, "You are right and I have been away at the wars for too long anyway. Sir Thomas, will you help me? You English know your castles."

"If the bishop allows me to stay then I will."

It rained in the night but with the rain came sleet and that promised snow. The men I had brought from the Holy Land would suffer more than the others. The women and children, along with the wounded men were sent back to Stock Holm. They took with them all that they could carry. They would build a new home. Others would come to Sigtuna and it would be rebuilt but it would always be a poor and mean place. It would be haunted by the memory of the dead.

Rather than riding our horses, we led them. We were going at the pace of the men on foot in any case. I hung my spurs and helmet, along with my shield, from my saddle. With my coif hanging loose I kept my head dry with the hood of my cloak. The trail we followed was a circuitous one but through the grey murk, we could see, ahead of us, the darker shadow of the island. Petr dropped back to speak with us as we went.

"My brother has sent me to give you more information about this place we seek. We will need to attack at low tide. It will be in the dark of night and that suits us. You and your men know how to use the night." It was not a question. I nodded. "He wonders if you and your men could cross first and slay their sentries. We would attack their main band. All that we would require you to do is kill those who watch for us."

I smiled, "Petr, we will do whatever is needed. We are warriors for hire. We need to prove ourselves. I know that. Tell your brother he need not worry about us."

He seemed relieved and he mounted his horse and headed back to the head of the column.

I said, "David, Will son of Robin."

My two archers led their horses next to me, "Lord?"

"We are going to have to cross the water and slay their sentries. Bows or knives?"

Will looked up at the sky. "Our strings will not be taut enough in this rain and we have not scouted their positions. Better that we sneak ashore and slit their throats. We can take our bows and then defend the Swedes when they attack."

I smiled, "You were listening."

They nodded, "Of course, lord."

The sleet turned to snow in the afternoon. We were all soaked through. I heard Will say to David of Wales. "It will get us used to the wet then, eh David?" They saw positives in everything.

By the time we reached the shoreline, it was dark. The island could be seen now as a large dark shadow ahead of us. We halted at the waterline. The sound of the sea rolling over the stones meant that we could speak without being heard. I took off my surcoat and then waved William over and I held my arms out so that he could pull my mail shirt from me. Petr came over. The two jarls were deep in conversation.

"Sir Thomas, what are you doing?"

"A man does not order his men to do something he would not. I will lead." I took off my chausses too. I replaced my surcoat.

The two jarls came over, "You need not do this, Sir Thomas."

"I know but I shall. When we spoke in your hall of the coin you would give us it was for my whole company. I am part of that company. I will lead." They both nodded. Birger Persson understood more than his cousin, I could see that.

"William, you take charge of the men at arms. Bring them over when you are ordered." Glancing down I saw that the tide had already gone out a little. "How deep is it?"

Birger Persson shrugged, "To be truthful I am not certain. At low tide, a knight on a horse can walk across and his spurs will be dry."

"The sooner we get across the better." I fastened my baldric over my shoulders so that my scabbard hung down my back. I carried my sword. I raised my arm and waved my archers forward. The water was icy. The sleet had stopped but the water felt as cold as snow. I held my sword above me so that it would not be immersed in the sea. My men followed me. The water was just up to my ankles but, as I headed towards the island, it began to rise. I had no idea where the deepest point was. If my mouth dropped beneath the waves then we would stop until the tide receded some more. There was an awful shock of cold as the water hit my lower body. It was painfully cold but then the water level dropped. We had reached the deepest part. I could see the water breaking on the shore of the island. The masts of Karelian ships could be seen on the far side of the island. They were like trees without branches. When the water just covered my ankles, I stopped. I sheathed my sword and drew my dagger. I looked around. My men were close behind me. We moved very slowly towards the shore. It shelved and the last thing we needed was for one of us to slip. A sudden splash would alert the Karelians.

As I stepped onto the sandy rocks I winced as a sharp rock cut my foot. I should have worn boots. I ignored the pain and stared into the dark. My archers spread out behind me. They had carried their bows and now they began to string them. Their arrows had been carried in a quiver on their backs. The tips might be wet but the feathers would be dry. My patience was rewarded. Two men, just fifty paces from me, were talking. I had no idea what they were saying. From what I had been told they spoke a language that even the Swedes could not understand.

I tapped David on the shoulder and pointed. We dropped onto all fours and crawled towards the two men who were talking. We did not have to look up, their voices drew us to them. I found that I could smell them. It was the smell of rancid fat and seal oil. We were three paces from them. The fact that we could smell them meant that the slight breeze would not allow them to smell us. I looked at David. He nodded. We rose as one and stepped forward. I grabbed a handful of hair and pulled the Karelian's head forward. Ripping my dagger in a sideways motion I tore open his throat. Blood flooded onto my surcoat. I lowered his body to the ground. David's sentry lay in a widening pool of blood.

I turned and waved my men forward and they spread out to find the other sentries. David and I moved towards the crackling fire we could see in the middle of the island. I reached over my back and drew my sword. My men could take care of the other sentries. David and I kept moving forward. He had an arrow ready. We stopped when we saw and heard the people by the fire. The men were drinking. By the light of the fire, I saw that the captives were tethered together. If one tried to escape they would have to take all of the others with them. It was an effective way to keep them under control.

Karelian numbers were hard to estimate for it was dark and they were moving around but there seemed to be more of them than the force we had brought. However, as I looked at them I saw that none had mail and most had either a bow or a short sword. Our job was done. We had to wait now for the Swedes to attack. As I looked to my left and right I saw the faces of my men. They had all survived.

Suddenly there was a shout. It came from behind me. One of the dead sentries had been spotted. Then I heard Jarl Birger Brosa as he shouted something in Swedish. I heard hooves. The Karelians grabbed their weapons and ran towards the beach. We were in the way!

I shouted, "Archers, one arrow and then take cover!"

There was a chorus of 'Aye, lord'. Then I heard the crack of bow strings and Karelians fell. The others stopped and that allowed my archers the chance to flee. I did not move. If I stayed still then they had less chance of seeing me and, behind me, I heard the sound of our men as they charged to get to grips with their enemies. A Karelian ran straight at me. He had seen me. Wielding an axe and screaming he charged me. I was taller than he was. He swung his axe at me but I had anticipated it. I swung my whole body in a circle. The axe head tore my surcoat but did no damage to me. My sword bit deep into his side and jarred against his spine. As I withdrew the blade two more ran at me. Both fell with arrows in their chests.

I waited for the next wave to attack me but none materialized. The Jarl Birger Brosa galloped past swinging his sword. His squire, Jarl Birger, Persson, Petr and William followed. The five of them swept through the advancing Karelians. Moments later my men at arms and the Swedes arrived. The slaughter was about to begin. I shouted, "My warriors, Stockton, stay with me!"

I was acutely aware that we had not fought with the Swedes before. I wanted none killed or hurt by mistake. William was charging ahead and had not heard me but the rest raced to my side. My men at arms flanked me and my archers stood behind. Those who had yet to string their bows were now doing so. As the Swedes ran towards the enemy I raised my sword, "On!"

We moved steadily towards the whirling blades and screaming men. Later, when it was all over, I wondered what had put the thought in my head for I saw that there were more Karelians than I had first realised. It was a large warband. The Swedish foot had been eager for vengeance and hurled themselves into the barbarians. Even worse I saw that the five horsemen were now surrounded and fighting off barbarians who were hacking and slashing at man and beast. If we had had shields then I might have ordered a wedge. As it was we had neither mail nor shield.

"David, as we move clear the men from around the jarls."

"Aye lord."

"The rest of us will carve a path to them." Our delay in organising a line had worked in our favour. The Karelians had swarmed around the rear of the Swedish warriors. I saw arrows flying overhead and men screamed as the deadly arrows plunged down into bodies without armour. The first that they knew of our approach was when men began to die. They had no armour and I rammed my sword through the back of one warrior as I stabbed down into the neck of a second. With Ridley on one side and Jack on the other, we had soon cleared a path before us. The next men we struck were fighting Swedes. Attacked from two sides they were soon despatched. I saw that only three horsemen could be seen. Language was now a problem. The Swedes were neither as disciplined nor as organised as we were and they were in the way.

The warrior called Sverre must have realised that they were not helping for he roared something and the Swedes parted. I raised my sword and shouted, "For God!"

My men roared. Arrows sailed over our heads. David and his archers were just two paces behind us and using the space we had cleared. Their arrows were aimed at men less than thirty paces away. They could not miss. I saw that William was still mounted. A Karelian jumped onto the back of his horse and raised a wicked-looking dagger. He fell with two arrows in his back. William's predicament spurred us on and we ran. The enemy knew we were coming and they turned to face us. A spear was thrown at me from less than ten paces. Even as it clanged from the side of my helmet I had rammed my sword deep into the guts of the would-be killer. I had always had a strong left hand and I used sword and dagger to strike, stab and slash at those before me. Their numbers did not help them against my men. The Karelians were raiders. The mail and helmets of my men made them almost impervious to their weapons. They struck and fled. My men were warriors who had stood in shield walls and faced disciplined Turks or organised Scots. They killed with cold efficiency.

A chieftain ran towards The Jarl Birger Brosa. He had a helmet and a shield. There were two others similarly armed flanking him. I saw him swing his sword at the jarl's horse. David's archers killed one of the men with him. The chieftain hacked into the jarl's horse which fell, taking the jarl with it. As the second warrior raised his sword I watched as William pulled back on his reins so that his horse reared. The Karelian's skull was crushed like an egg. The chieftain, who had been on the verge of ending the jarl's life was forced to stop by the rearing horse. I just ran at the chieftain. He turned and saw me. As I swung my sword he raised his shield. I stopped my sword before it struck and I grabbed the edge of his shield with my sword hand and pulled it towards me. He had not expected that. I saw his bare throat and I rammed my dagger deep into it. He just collapsed at my feet.

Jarl Birger Persson shouted something. There was a cheer from the Swedes and then the remaining Karelians began to flee. He and William galloped after them. The Swedes followed. I shouted, "Hold!"

I sheathed my weapons and went to Birger Brosa. He was not moving. "Ridley!" My giant came. I handed him the jarl's spear. "Try to lift the horse a little and I will pull out the jarl."

"Aye lord." He took the dead chieftain's helmet to use as a lever. I put my hands under the jarl's armpits. He appeared to be breathing. Ridley nodded, "Ready lord." He pushed down. The dead horse moved a little and I pulled. The jarl popped out. He gave a moan as he did so. We had a priest with us but he was back on the mainland. I took the jarl's helmet from his head and remove his coif. I saw blood. I knew enough, from the Hospitallers I had met in the Holy Land, to know that you laid someone with a head injury on their side and tried to avoid moving them. I wondered if I had done more harm than good by moving his horse. Then I saw that his leg was hurt too. I had done the right thing.

I stood, "David, release the captives. Jack finish off the enemy wounded and bring our own here." The Swedes had followed the Karelians who had fled to their ships. I had a handful of men left. I did not know if there were more enemies left on this rock! To my relief, I saw The Jarl Birger Brosa's eyes open. He saw me and smiled. Then he closed them again. "Alf, fetch water."

I heard a cheer from the far end of the island and knew that we had won. The sky was beginning to become lighter. Alf brought a water skin. I dribbled some into the jarl's mouth and then used some to wash his scalp. Here there was plenty of water. Had this been the Holy Land then we would not have wasted precious water in such a fashion.

"Have we won?" The jarl croaked.

"Aye Jarl Birger. You rest. When I can send for a priest to heal you I will do so."

The captives, having been freed, stayed close to David and his archers. There was an occasional cry from the battlefield as wounded and dying Karelians were given a warrior's death. The wounded Swedes were brought to where we waited for relief. I looked up as Birger and William rode up. I saw Petr, bloodied but alive, walking behind. Birger looked down at his cousin. "Is he alive?"

"He is but we need the healers."

"The tide is in. We are trapped."

I stood and laughed, "I can see at least three ships from where I stand. Fetch them!"

Birger hung his head, "I should have known that." He turned and shouted something. Eight men ran back towards the ships whose masts could be seen in the distance. They stood out against the lightening sky.

Daylight brought us the priests and food. It also revealed the extent of the slaughter. There had been far more Karelians on the island than the two jarls had expected. The Swedes had lost heavily. There were just twelve men without wounds. The reckless charge into the night had cost them dear. Their jarl had almost been killed and there was a sombre mood in the camp as the wounded were attended to. We found Birger's squire, Lars. He and his horse had been butchered. Petr's horse had also fallen. We would not be able to leave until low tide.

I pointed to the ships, "Why not use those to take the captives and wounded back to Stock Holm? We can march but I feel a chill in the air. That sleet we have felt makes me think that there may be snow on the way."

"You are right. I fear I have asked you to come here and fight in a battle we cannot win."

"You are wrong. You can win but your men need to fight as our armies did in the Holy Land. I know he is your cousin but a reckless charge in the dark against an unknown enemy is a dangerous thing to do. He is brave but his men have paid a fearful price."

He was silent. My words had struck home. We reached The Jarl Birger Brosa. He had a bandage around his head. "Sir Thomas suggests that we send the wounded and the captives back to Stock Holm in the Karelian ships. Snow is in those skies."

The jarl nodded. He put an arm out for the priest to help him to his feet.

"Do we have slaves and captives?"

"No, cousin. The few who tried to surrender were slain by our men. They were in hot blood. The rest jumped into the sea." Birger Persson pointed to the mainland. "The ones who survived fled west. We can hunt them down at our leisure. It seems they had raided others and gathered them here. It is the end of the raiding season. Perhaps the attack on my home was the last one."

I pointed east. "And that is why you need a castle here. It would control the seas. I am certain that there will be more ships coming in the next day or two. They could not have transported all their men, animals and captives in those three ships. If you had a castle here that could not happen."

Birger Persson shook his head, "I agree it is a good site but it is cut off from the land. If raiders came and it was high tide, what then?"

"When we walked across last night there was just one place where the water was deep. Raise the causeway and leave just the one channel. There you build a bridge. You and your men could leave the island whenever you chose. The island would be protected." I knelt and tapped the ground. "This is good ground. Build in stone and the enemy will be curbed."

"I am guessing that is how you control your enemies at home?"

"Yes, Birger Brosa. We line the borders with stone castles and have riders within them. They can patrol far and wide. A few men on horses could deal with these barbarians."

"We have much to learn. When you return to the Stock Holm we will talk further." He looked to Sverre, "Have the ships loaded."

By the time the ships had been loaded, it was low tide again and we crossed back to the mainland. The water was still icy but it was easier in the dark. The passage was only a hundred paces. In the night, it had seemed further. The ships sailed as I fed and watered Skuld. Birger Persson had just four men to walk back with us. I had lost none. There were wounds but they were cuts and knocks. They would not even merit a story when my men sat and drank. We would not reach Stock Holm quickly. It would take at least two days. The skies were laden with the first of the winter snows. This was a baptism of ice we would have to endure.

We did not ride our horses. Instead, we used them to carry our weapons and the food that we had with us. The Karelians had great stores of food that they had ransacked. We would not starve. Nine men did not have horses and we went at their pace.

As we walked Birger Persson and his brother plied me with questions about castles. "We saw the castles in the Holy Land. They were enormous. You are not suggesting we build one as big on that island, are you?"

"No, my friend. You need a wall with a gatehouse and two towers. On the island that would be where the causeway lies. You need a hall within for your men. If you build one with stables on the ground floor then that will be easier to defend. At its simplest level that would do. However, if a determined enemy landed on the island you would need towers filled with archers."

Petr said, "That sounds like a lot of work."

"It would take a year at least to build and you cannot start yet for you have no stone and I am guessing that the ground will be frozen until spring."

Birger Persson was in a thoughtful mood, "We need to build homes for my people at Stock Holm. My cousin has plenty of food but shelter is scarce. When we have built the shelters for them we will see if we can get more horses. We will have to trade for them. There are not as many here as in England."

"Then why not send to England? The ship on which we travelled will be returning for more iron ore. The captain does not like to travel empty. It would be in his interest to fetch horses."

"A good idea but we do not know where to get horses."

I smiled, "We do."

William looked at me, "Beverley!"

I nodded, "There is a horse farm there and they have good horses. The port of Hull is small and we could land there and make the purchase unseen."

"That would be a risk. If you were seen, Sir Thomas, then it would mean your life."

"If Bishop Albert judges against me then I might not have a choice. We would go in disguise. We have three surcoats we took from dead knights in England."

"Then I would come with you and share the risk."

The snow began to fall. I looked up, "Besides there will be little else for us to do. When the snow falls I fear there will be no fighting."

"There you are wrong, Sir Thomas. When the seas freeze we use them as roads. But you are right. The ground will not be frozen for at least a month. There will be time to sail to England and buy the horses."

We had it all worked out by the time we reached Stock Holm. The jarl's wife had set men to work building the houses. There was a great deal of activity. As we neared the hall I saw the jarl, still bandaged emerge. He was not alone. Birger Persson said, "And that is Bishop Albert. You will soon know your fate, my friend."

Bishop Albert

Chapter 10

When I had been growing up my grandfather had a warrior priest called Brother Peter. I had barely known him but as soon as I saw Bishop Albert I was reminded of the Knight Hospitaller who had served my grandfather. He was a big and powerful man. He had fanatical eyes and a voice to match. He glowered and glared at me as I approached.

"So, this is the killer of priests! This is the enemy of God!"

It did not bode well. I bowed my head and said, contritely, "I am ready to hear and accept your judgement, Bishop Albert."

He nodded and appeared somewhat mollified. "It is not good to talk out here. Let us go into the jarl's church." He gave me a wicked grin, "Unless that would offend you, priest killer?"

"No, bishop, I am happy to enter the church for I do not think there will be any desecrated graves within its walls."

He gave me a sideways look. "I heard you were an interesting man. The Bishop of Uppsala, Henry, was Englishman. He is a saint. I fear that you are not made of the same material."

We had entered the church which was lit by just two candles.

"I do not think that anyone will canonize Hugh de Puiset!"

I heard Bishop Albert sigh, "Sit and tell me your tale."

I did so and I omitted nothing.

When I had finished there was silence. "You fought in the crusades with Jarl Birger Persson?"

"I did."

"He told me that you were knighted when you defended your father and your squire while saving King Richard from certain death." I nodded, "And that you and your squire saved the life of The Jarl Birger Brosa in the recent battle with the Karelians."

"We helped."

"That offers me hope. You are an enigma but I believe that you have been sent here for a purpose. You are here to make us better warriors and convert the pagans. You shall have absolution from your sins when we have converted the heathens of Estonia. I will give you absolution when you have done enough to outweigh the killing of a priest."

I hesitated. I would be committing myself to a battle we might not win. Would I ever get home? I had no choice. Some power other than that of mortal man was controlling my destiny, "Thank you, Bishop Albert."

When we entered the hall, it was as though this was Bishop Albert's home and not the jarl's. He was an ebullient man who was full of life. His passion was the conversion of the barbarians and he was not afraid to use force to do so. As we ate that night in a hall that was filled with priests, clerics and other knights who followed the banner of Bishop Albert, I was questioned about the way we fought and my ideas.

Bishop Albert seemed enthusiastic. "We have horses but they are smaller than yours and only ridden by our jarls. I think we need an order of knights such as the Templars or the Teutonic knights. I have the name already, the Livonian Sword Brothers." He turned to Birger Persson. "When you were in the Holy Land did you discover how we might create such an order?"

Birger looked at me, "The problem I see with such orders is that although they work for the Church, they do not appear to answer to them. You would need a master who would ensure that what they did was for God and not for themselves."

Lady Brigida was a little innocent where war was concerned. It had barely touched her home for Stock Holm was well protected. "Surely the Holy Orders are priests who are also knights."

I shook my head, "Most are, my lady, but there are enough who are not, to give rise to the belief that there are self-serving men in positions of power within the orders. They are rich and they are powerful. Kings jump to their commands. When the Hospitallers chose to charge at Arsuf it was against the King of England's command."

I saw Bishop Albert did not approve of my criticism for he frowned and flashed me an irritated look. "I see. Then I will have to choose carefully. But the principle is a good one?"

Birger nodded, "They serve for a minimum of one year. That is often enough. They have knights and they have sergeants. Both are mounted and well-armed. They are highly trained and very disciplined. Some would call them fanatical."

I nodded, "My grandfather was at the siege of Ascalon. The Master of the Templars led many knights to their death when they charged a breach in the walls. Had they waited then they would still have won and over sixty knights would be alive. Their lives would not have been wasted."

Bishop Albert drank some of the honeyed wine they seemed to like in this part of the world. "Then horses are what we need. However, you cannot possibly bring back enough for our needs, Sir Thomas. I would have you acquire a mare and a stallion so that we may breed."

"You mean a war horse?"

He nodded, "As far as I am aware it is the blood of the stallion which will make strong offspring."

"They are almost impossible to buy but…"

Birger looked at me and laughed, "I know that tone. Sir Thomas has a plan."

"I know where there is a warhorse and two good breeding mares. They belong to me."

"You forfeited your land!"

"I did but there are still some honourable knights. My father's war horses are still there. I had thought to let them see out their lives grazing but this would be better."

"Are they close to this place, Hull?"

I smiled happily, "Oh no, they are sixty miles and a river away. It will not be easy but I fear that my penance will be a more difficult one than that my grandfather's." I swallowed the goblet of wine, "But now we wait for the arrival of Henry and his ship."

Henry came six days later. The snow had not stopped in that time and both the jarls and Bishop Albert feared that the Baltic might freeze early. When we saw the old ship tacking towards Stock Holm, The Jarl Birger Brosa, much recovered from his wounds, said, "You have a month, at most, to complete your task. Once the seas around the coast freeze then we are cut off."

Bishop Albert had spent four of the six days gathering coin from his flock to pay for the horses. He would not need to pay me. I would however make a profit when the mares began to have foals and colts. The Jarl Birger Brosa had contributed half for he wished to have as many mounted men as we did. Henry had brought a letter for me. I saw him privately, "Where did you get the letter?"

"A one-eyed man who knew my name said would I deliver it to any from the family of the Warlord. He said he would be waiting for my return in case there was an answer."

"You did not know him?" He shook his head. "He was alone?"

"He was." I wondered who had sent him for I knew no one-eyed men. "You are declared outlaw, lord. Any man who sees you may kill you. Prince John and the Archbishop of York signed the decree."

I nodded.

"But there is good news too, lord. King Richard is now freed from imprisonment. He is at his castle in Chinon."

I felt my spirits soar, "And he returns to England?"

He shook his head, "I spoke with other captains. He campaigns in Normandy against the French and rebels. His nephew, Arthur, seeks Normandy. Prince John still rules England."

Just as swiftly as they had been raised my hopes were dashed. King Richard sought glory and his people would suffer.

"You have a commission. Where do you take your ore?"

"Herterpol, lord."

"Then I would have you let me slip ashore there with two men. The jarl wishes you to sail to Hull so that he and William might go to Beverley to buy horses."

"Hull will not be a problem. I have sued the port before but Herterpol! That is dangerous lord! You risk your life."

"I think not but I would need you to pick me up from the beach which is south of Herterpol on the way back. Would it be possible to take three horses from the sea, using slings?"

"It is not easy but it could be done."

"Then that is what we will try to do. I will work out the details. You had better speak with Bishop Albert and the jarls. They are the ones who wish to buy the horses. They want as many as you can bring. It means you will have cargo both ways. This will mean coin for you."

"Coin is nothing, lord. I would have you safe!" He meant what he said. My grandfather's people were loyal.

The letter was in my aunt's hand. I did not know how Henry had managed to get the letter but Ruth was a resourceful woman. I opened it. I saw that there was no name upon it. When I turned it over I saw that the outside was blank too. She had been careful.

You know who you are and what you have done!

Sometimes men have too much honour. However, if my father had not had such high ideas of honour then my brother and I might not have been born. I beg you to stay away from England. Until we have a king again this is a dangerous place for you. Fear not for me. I have a protector and from the most unlikely of places. You know him but I will not name him. I know not exactly where you are. That is for the best. I cannot betray you if I do not know. I have an idea how I can get this letter to you but it may take some time. I pray that you read it before my time on this earth is over.

Know that I love you as though you were mine own. Whatever you need from me is yours. You are a true knight and an honourable knight. That gives me comfort in a land riven with treachery, deceit, and dishonour.

Xxx

That was it. There was no signature and no seal. She had used no names. If this had fallen into the wrong hands it would have availed them little. I folded it up and tucked it inside by surcoat. I would reread it later on and work out the messages between the lines.

While Henry negotiated I chose my men. William would go to Hull with Jarl Birger Persson. I would take Will son of Robin and Edward son of Edgar with me. Both were quick thinking and we would need that. I had yet to work out how to get out of the port of Herterpol and then across to Wulfestun. It was Edward who gave me the solution. He pointed to Bishop Albert. "It is simple, lord. We dress as priests. We have all picked up a few words of Swedish. We pretend that we are Swedish monks and that we go to Durham. We put on a false accent. The people of Herterpol see few foreigners. That church official will bend over backwards to accommodate us."

Will nodded, "He is right, lord. The robes would hide our swords and the hoods our heads. We get Henry to make the introductions."

I shook my head, "No, for that would put him in danger. We get Jarl Birger Persson to speak for us."

It was a better plan than any I had. Bishop Albert agreed, reluctantly, to get us robes. He did not like the deceit but the greater prize of the conversion of pagans swung him in our favour. We left as soon as the ship was loaded. We had been given a month but Henry hoped we could manage it back sooner. Birger Brosa suggested that we wear sealskin boots. They were common in Sweden and would make the walk to Wulfestun easier.

"How did you avoid trouble when you returned to Herterpol?"

"I told them the truth. I said that you forced me to take you abroad. My men backed me up. All of them have family in Stockton. I just said that I was forced to take you to the land of the Danes." That was good. Even if they knew we had come to Sweden it would not help them. So long as I was with the leading lord of the land then I was safe.

We spent time, as we sailed west, finalizing the details. It would take up to four days to sail from Herterpol to Hull and to buy the horses. That gave us plenty of time to get to Wulfestun, unseen and undetected, and then to fetch the horses to the sand dunes. At the end of autumn, it would be bleak beyond words. We would have to lift the horses from the sea. That would not be easy. Henry had block and tackle. He showed me how the slings would work. "Of course, lord, you would be in the water and you would have to fit the slings. The sea can kill a man at this time of year."

I nodded, "If you use the mouth of the Tees then you should be able to get closer. There is a deep channel there."

"I know, lord, they call it Snook Point. It is close to the Greatham Fleet. I have my father's charts. If you are willing to take the risk then I will be there. We will need a signal."

"We will have to risk a fire. It will be cold anyway and I hope that there are no prying eyes. We will be there three nights after we are dropped. We will wait until you reach us."

Sword For Hire

Neither William nor the jarl was happy but they agreed that there was no other way to get war horses. A rouncy would cost a horseman eight pounds but a war horse, if one could be bought, would cost ten times that amount.

Churchmen were normally clean-shaven. The three of us had to lose our beards. Although my men were not happy I knew that it was necessary. It would change my face so that I might not be remembered. They would grow again. I felt naked without mine and my face felt cold. Our cheeks were red raw but they would settle as we headed west.

We reached Herterpol in the middle of the afternoon. Henry had told us that, since our escape, they kept a stronger watch upon the walls. The lateness of the hour suited us. The market had finished long ago. There were three ships about to leave the port and, with the turning tide, they would expect Henry to turn his ship around quickly. He had his fees ready.

We had barely tied up when the officious little man appeared. I stayed in the background. Will son of Robin would do the talking and Jarl Birger Persson. The official came to Henry first, "You have a profitable business, captain. Perhaps I should charge you more."

"I thought that Bishop Albert set the fees, What difference can my profit make?"

Jarl Birger stepped ashore. "There is a landing fee?" I saw a frown crease the jarl's face. The official had the kind of face and manor that made you want to strike it. "I am not landing but these three penitents are." We stepped forward. I was at the rear and I kept my head down.

"Then they will still have to pay a fee."

"They have been sent by Henry, the English Bishop of Uppsala. They have messages for the Bishop of Durham."

I heard the intake of breath from the official. I guessed that landing fees were a way of lining his purse. He would not want the Dean or Canon to know that he had charged priests. "In that case, you may land, brothers." He turned to us, "Do you wish horses?"

We had rehearsed this part on the ship. Birger asked us in Swedish and Will answered him in the same language. The jarl said, "No, the priests say they will walk. It is good for their souls."

The official mumbled, "And hard on their feet." He added a little louder, emphasising each word as though we were imbeciles, "Go with God!"

Will made the sign of the cross and mumbled something in Swedish. He was enjoying this too much. I nudged him in the back and we began to walk slowly, as penitent priests, towards the gate. We did not look back. The sentries had seen us land and noted our robes. We were not a threat. They opened the gate and we stepped through.

We walked slowly. I had watched priests before and none moved quickly. When we were out of sight then we would hurry. We took the road west and north. It led through Elwick. We would get nowhere near that place. As soon as we reached the ridge we would head south. When we were out of sight, where the ground dipped on the other side of the ridge, we took the smaller trail south and west which led to the tiny farm of Dalton. We could then take the track east. We intended to scout out the beach. It would add a few miles to our journey but it was important to see what problems we might find. We passed between Seaton Carrowe and the Grange at Seaton. It was almost dark when we did so. People might wonder what three priests were doing there for there was no church but by the time someone investigated we would be long gone.

We saw fishing boats drawn up on the beach as we climbed the dunes. It did not take us long to reach the river and Snook Point. There was no one around. The wind blew the sand too much for there to be tracks but there appeared to be no footpaths. The landing sight appeared to be safe. We headed due west. Edward was, like his father, a natural scout and he took us on the path which would be hard to see and yet which kept us hidden. The grass was sharp and I was glad that we had opted for the seal skin boots. I was the one least familiar with the paths and tracks across the marshland. I was glad when we saw the tower of the church in Billingham to the south of us. It meant the ground would soon become firmer.

It took some hours to reach the estate. The doors to the hall were barred. I did not want to wake anyone and so we slept in the stables. It was warm and we were tired. I was awoken by Gonfanon licking my face. My two companions were nowhere to be seen. It was daylight, which meant I had slept longer than I had intended. I stood and used Gonfanon's water to wash the sleep from my face. Edward ran in and raised his hand. Will followed with his fingers to his lips. I drew my sword.

Creeping to the door I heard the sound of horse's hooves coming through the fallen leaves. It was just one rider. This was not the time of day for visitors. I was hidden by the side of the building and I had a good view as the horse turned the corner. It was Sir Richard. What was he doing visiting my father's sister? One of the farm workers took his horse and I saw him disappear inside.

"That does not bode well, lord."

I looked at Will and shook my head, "No, it does not. It means we may not be able to take these horses."

Edward said, "You should speak with him, lord."

"What?"

Edward shrugged, "He is a fair man lord. When I said I wished to leave his service he gave me a good sword and a gold coin. He told me to watch over you." I stared at him. "Lord, I am a good judge of horseflesh. I can speak with dogs. I also like to think that I know a good man from a villain. Sir Richard is a good man."

"Would you bet your life on it?"

He said quietly, "It was how I judged you lord and I am right about you."

"Very well but you two remain here. If this is a trap and I am taken then you two must get to the ship and tell the others."

I strode towards the door of the hall. I opened it and I heard voices from inside the room. I listened. I heard my aunt's voice, "It was the same ship?"

"Yes, lady, but the captain did not stay. My man watched from the shadows. He hoped to catch the captain when he stepped ashore. Three priests disembarked but no other. He unloaded and then sailed south. If there had been a letter then he would have tried to give it to my man."

My aunt said, "Then perhaps he is dead or he has left the land of the Swedes. Thank you for your efforts, Sir Richard. You are a kind man to help a widow like this."

I opened the door, "No, I am still alive."

She threw her arms around me, "You are a fool to return here! Why?"

I looked pointedly at Sir Richard. He smiled, "I told you once, Sir Thomas, I am not your enemy. You are, however, a hunted man. If any discover that you are in this land then it will mean not only your death but your aunt, her people and, me. I have lived long enough but the ladies here…"

"I promise you that we are here but briefly. We are here for the three warhorses."

"Sit and tell me all."

"Before I do I shall summon my companions." I went to the door and whistled. Edward and Will appeared.

Sir Richard said, "Three priests. You are not as foolish as I thought. Tell your tale."

"Is there food? We slept in the stable o'er night."

Ruth shook her head, "I am forgetting my manners."

I waited with my story until the food and ale had arrived. I told them everything including my penance. They both seemed relieved. My aunt put her hand on mine. "Then you will not be spending eternity in hell. I am pleased."

Sir Richard stood, "I had better get back. Prince John has a spy in my hall. He knows too much about my finances and my comings and goings. I have yet to discover his identity. You take care, Sir Thomas."

I clasped his arm, "Thank you, Sir Richard, and I am sorry for having doubted the word of a Hospitaller."

I enjoyed the time I spent with my aunt. She told me how Sir Richard had been a rock and helped her whenever he could. She had begun to use the church in Stockton once more and I was relieved. I had worried that she might be in danger. Now I knew who her protector was.

We left the following afternoon just as dusk descended. Our parting was less poignant for we were both relieved to spy hope in the life of the other. We had food and ale. We used bridles and reins but no saddles. We rode bareback. The horses would have plenty of time to recover. If anyone saw us then we would be in trouble for three priests riding horses was a sight most men would not forget. God was on our side. We reached Snook's Point unseen. We lit the fire, for there was plenty of driftwood, and we waited but no ship arrived.

We had the fire doused well before dawn. We gave half of the water to the horses. There were dells amongst the sand dunes where the grazing was not too salty and the horses ate. We eked out our food. One of us always kept watch to the north and Seaton Carrowe. We saw nothing.

As darkness fell we built the fire with the driftwood we had collected. We waited. It was Gonfanon that gave the alarm. He whinnied. Edward was watching the river and Will the beach to the north. When Gonfanon whinnied I climbed to join Will. At first, I saw nothing and then I saw shadows moving. They were more than a mile away but it was a clear sky and we saw the moving shadows. It had to be men. What should we do? We could mount and flee. The men were afoot but then there would be a hue and cry to find us.

"Lord, a sail!"

I whipped my head around and saw a sail fluttering in the river as a ship turned. It had to be our ship. "Quick, into the water!"

I grabbed Gonfanon's reins and led him through the dunes to the river. The ship was a dark shadow. None had shouted yet and it could be any ship but I had to believe that it was Henry. I slipped onto Gonfanon's back and he walked into the water. Henry had brought the ship as close as he dared. We only had thirty paces to swim. The river water was icy. I lay along Gonfanon's back and kicked to make his task easier. I saw that we were being pushed out to sea by the current. Gonfanon was strong and I heard Will shout. "A little further this way, lord!" He was with his mare and they were already beginning to haul her up.

I looked and saw the sling waiting for him. I turned his head and smacked his rump. Even as I did so I heard shouts from the sand dunes. Our pursuers were closing. I grabbed the slings and pulled them under his middle. I was doused by the sea but Gonfanon was more patient than I had expected. I fastened them securely and shouted, "Haul away."

As he was pulled up I saw that Henry had lowered his sails so that the ship was drifting at the same pace as the horses. I swam to help Edward. His mare, Rona, was too far away from the ship. I swam to her rear and pushed her. It took some time and by the time we had her near to the ship the first mare was halfway up. Suddenly an arrow thudded into the hull. Will swam to help us with the last mare. She was terrified. It would be a tragedy if she panicked and drowned. Edward began to sing to her. Amazingly it quietened her. When the sling was lowered the three of us had her fastened in very quickly. As she was hauled up more arrows hit the sea and the hull. They were sending them blindly. A blind arrow could still kill.

Three ropes snaked down and Will shouted, "Hurry lord, we need to move. We are drifting too close to shore. Henry fears we may be grounded."

I grabbed one of the ropes and began to climb up the side. The habit was sodden and was dragging me down. My arms ached and my legs were so cold that I could not feel them.

I heard Will shout, "Pull! Heave on the ropes!"

We began to move quickly. It was as though we were flying. As we flopped onto the deck I began to shiver and my teeth chattered. One of the sailors laughed, "Well these are the three biggest fish I have ever caught and no mistake!"

Chapter 11

The horses recovered well, once we reached Sweden. Rona, who had been the most distressed, took the longest. Bishop Albert had not been idle while we had been away. He had ordered men, including my own, to build new stables. The horses would be comfortable. The two jarls now had twelve more horses for their men. It would take time to breed warhorses but Jarl Birger Persson had bought palfreys from which Bishop Albert could breed. They had also managed to throw up a small hall for me and my men. That had been the doing of Lady Brigida Haraldsdotter. For some reason, she had taken to me. Jarl Birger thought it was because her own son, Philippus, was in the service of King Sverre. I reminded her of him.

The hall was similar to that of the jarl. Hull shaped and covered with turf it was warm. My men quickly settled into it. They all found their own space in the hall. William rigged up a curtain so that he and I would have some privacy. I was not concerned but my men thought it inappropriate that their lord should be on public display.

If I thought that winter meant peace I was wrong. We spent a month preparing for a campaign against the Karelians who lived in the north of the jarl's land. Maps mean nothing in this land of inlets, islands and, in the winter, perpetual ice and snow. The Swedes talked in terms of distance and directions, not places. They lived four days travel to the north. When I was told this I wondered, for the days were drawing much shorter and by the time we left the length of a day could be the blink of an eye. My friend told me that they marched while it was dark. The dark nights of Sweden did not stop Jarl Birger and his men. They constructed sleighs which horses would pull. These would prove to be faster than carts and wagons. We could take supplies on campaign. My men and I had cloaks and some thick furs but Jarl Birger Persson provided even more. I discovered, on the campaign, that most of them had come from defeated enemies. Where we had only taken weapons and mails, here in the land of the midnight sun, furs were as necessary as mail.

My men and I were tasked, while all this was going on, with the training of the Swedes. The men of the jarls were brave enough but they tended to fight as individuals. We had to teach them to fight as one. That included the archers.

Bishop Albert was ever-present. he wanted to know what we did so that it could be replicated elsewhere. We were the first part of a larger crusade. Once we began our campaign his work would begin. He would seek help, both financial and military, from the kings of Norway, Sweden and Denmark. This was despite the fact that they were normally at war with one another. He saw the crusade as a way of uniting Christian kings. He had not been in the Holy Land. If he had then he might have had a different view.

He brought two priests who would accompany us. Both had swords and wore mail. "This is Brother Magnus and this is Brother Harald. They are both healers and they are warriors. They will carry my banner against the heathens!" I saw that Brother Magnus was little older than William but Brother Harald had grey hairs. They were the start of what would become the Livonian Order of the Brothers of the Swords. Their shields bore a yellow cross on a blue background as did the surcoats they wore. If they proved to be as good as the Hospitallers I would be happy. If they were as fanatical as the Templars then they would be a liability.

Before we left he held a service in the church where he had heard my confession. Lady Brigida had made a banner. It was of the Virgin Mary, and in her arms, she held a yellow cross. The background was blue and from the distance, it was not dissimilar to The Jarl Birger Brosa's banner. Lady Brigida and her ladies had made it. The ceremony blessed it and holy water which had been brought from Rome by the jarl was used to anoint it. The two priests were excited to be carrying such a holy item.

The intention was to begin the campaign when the days began to lengthen a little. We would travel north when the Estonians were huddled in their homes. They had their herds of animals, mail reindeer, close by them. The Jarl intended to strike at the five settlements which lay close to his borders. In the summer, the swamps and rivers gave them natural barriers. When the land was frozen there was no obstacle.

The Swedes did not celebrate Christmas in the same way as we did. My men were amused by their customs and the foods they ate. For those who had been in the Holy Land, it was refreshing. For those from the valley, it took some adjustment. We had all begun to pick up the language. It was necessary and the Christmas celebrations, with the inevitable drinking, accelerated the process. The result was that when we left Stock Holm we all understood the commands and there would be no confusion. The Jarl Birger Brosa was an organized man and he had drilled us all to his signals and commands. None had to march for we used the horses to pull the sleighs.

This time I did not ride at the rear but at the fore with the two jarls. Four young knights had joined us and with the two warrior priests, we had nine knights and seven squires. As we were all mailed we were a potent force. The Swedes had yet to equip their men at arms in the same manner as mine and the ten men at arms of mine, all mailed, would form up with us. We had thirty other men at arms from the two jarls and the four knights. In addition, there were ten more archers and twenty men of the levy. Little better than the men we would be fighting they would be handy when it came to guarding the sleighs and horses. I had impressed upon the two jarls the folly of using them for fighting. Bishop Albert and the jarl's wife saw us off. Lady Brigida smiled and waved. Bishop Albert sang a holy paean in our honour. We left in the dark and headed across ice-covered roads flanked by snow-filled forests. After the Holy Land, it was a huge contrast.

We would be heading through the land ravaged by the Karelians. It took two days to reach Sigtuna. Jarl Persson and his men were distressed by the skeletons of the buildings. This had been their home. Others might come to live here but it would not be for some time. I spoke with Birger to take his mind off the sights which surrounded us.

"Do these Estonians have a king?"

"No, they live and fight much as the Vikings and the Rus used to. They have warbands and fight in clans. They are nomadic and move in the season of the grass from grazing to grazing. When they are not raiding us then they fight amongst themselves."

"Then there is no one to whom you can appeal for peace? There is no one who can bend a knee to your king?"

He looked at me, "It is why I was sent to the Holy Land. When the crusaders first went they conquered and subjugated the people there and made them Christian."

"Except that they did not. You, of all people, know that."

"True, my cynical young friend, but the difference is that there we were fighting Islam. Here we are fighting people who had the same beliefs my forebears did. They have been led astray and we will put them on the right path."

"And conquer them!"

"For their own good. We will give them protection. We will give them order."

I was not certain that they would see it that way. I was here to do penance but if I was The Jarl Birger Brosa I would have done what we had in England. I would put a line of castles to protect our border and just stop the barbarians from raiding. I could see that I would have much to learn. I hoped it would make me a better warrior. My destiny was not here in Sweden but on the borders of England. I now knew that my time in the Holy Land and here in Sweden was to prepare me for something greater. This was not my war. I was a tool. I was the sword that would clear the land of barbarians.

The Swedes had good scouts. They were from the levy but they knew the land. On the fifth day, they returned to tell us that they had found a large warband of Estonians. They had seen Swedish slaves complete with thrall's yoke.

"Jarl, there are over a hundred warriors. They have skulls mounted outside their huts."

The Swedes saw that as evidence of their paganism. I was more concerned about their defences. I asked, "They do not have walls?"

Birger Persson shook his head, "They are nomadic. They move around. That is why this is the best time of year to catch them. They stay in one place while the snow covers the ground."

"Do they have horses?"

"They have reindeer and sometimes ride those but they do not ride to war as we do. They are primitively armed but do not underestimate them. They have thick hide armour. Arrows cannot pierce it save at close range. It resists swords and spears too."

I was not certain that it would resist the arrows my archers used but I said nothing.

The Jarl Birger Brosa said, "We strike quickly before they know we are here. We will charge in and use the speed of our horses to reach them quickly."

I shook my head, "The ground is slippery and slick. Horses risk damage. Better we take the horses around to the far side and attack with the men on foot and the horses."

"And the knights just watch and wait?"

"No jarl. We attack from the far side. Hit them simultaneously. They will be confused and in the confusion then order will win. If their hide armour resists cuts then we use the weight of our horses and mail to do the damage."

Jarl Birger Persson nodded, "He is right. We need them all captured or killed. If some escape then they will tell the other clans. If they band together then we will lose." He pointed to the two warrior priests, "The two brothers can lead the men on foot with the cross."

The priests seemed happy to be placed in such danger.

We took a wide sweep around the village. I could not see it but I did spy tendrils of smoke, and as we moved around I could smell both the animals and the wood smoke. It was a well-hidden settlement.

Once we were in position, in the cover of some spindly pine trees, I readied my spear. I preferred a spear to a lance. I noticed that the others had copied me. I saw the huts some two hundred paces from us. The light was fading and we were approaching from the east. We would be harder to see. The nine knights were in the front rank with William. He did not have to carry my banner. We had six already. I wanted him next to me and able to defend himself. He had improved since the battle of Arsuf.

The Jarl Birger Brosa turned to his squire who held a cow's horn. "Give the signal!"

Two blasts were sounded on the horn and we moved forward. We had four lines. We were compact and we did not gallop. We did not wish to risk a slip. As soon as the horn sounded I saw Estonians race towards the sound. I guessed they had never seen so many horses at one time. How would they react? I saw that someone was organizing them to make a rudimentary shield wall. As we closed I saw that it was an illusion. The shields just touched each other. They did not overlap. I saw The Jarl Birger Brosa spur his horse to go a little faster. We had to copy him but I hoped it was not a mistake. I brought up my shield and it was just in time. Arrows flew towards us. One of the young knights was either too slow to bring his shield up or too arrogant to believe that a primitive weapon such as a horn bow could hurt him. He was proved wrong and the arrow hit him in the shoulder and he fled to the snowy ground.

When the Estonians cheered it showed that they thought they could beat us. At thirty paces, I lowered my spear and held it slightly behind my body. When I had been a young squire my father had made me drill for hours at a time until I could hit the tiny ring in the tilt yard with my spear. I had not forgotten the skill. I picked out a huge Estonian. He had a leather cap and a round shield with a wolf's head crudely painted upon it. He had a spear with a bone head. I was under no illusions. A bone head could penetrate mail just as easily as a steel head. Our line would meet their line man to man. The warriors on the side of their line would slightly overlap ours but my men at arms would deal with them. It meant that I had one man to deal with. Others were racing to join their first line of defence but, for the moment, it was one rank deep. I stood in my saddle and pulled back my arm. I rammed it forward. Skuld flicked her head to one side to avoid the boneheaded spear and it gouged a line across the cantle of my saddle. My spear smashed into his face and out of the back of his skull. Those racing to join him were spattered in blood, bone and brains.

The ones behind held their shields too low. I pulled back and powered my spear into the throat of the next warrior. His sword did not even get close to Skuld. The warrior next to him was thrown to the ground by Skuld. I pulled back my arm and sought another target. I could see, ahead of me, the priests leading the men on foot to engage the enemy there. The confusion meant that there were many Estonians torn between which enemy was the more dangerous. That suited us.

My efficient and deadly strikes meant that I was ahead of the rest. I could wheel Skuld and choose my targets without fear of hitting another horse. One warrior who ran towards me was quick on his feet. He jerked to my left when Skuld approached him. Using my knees and jerking on the reins I struck him in the shoulder. The hide armour was tough but it only covered his upper arm. My spear pinned his shield arm to his body. I pushed and, as he fell, he pulled the spear from my hands. I drew my sword and wheeled Skuld to the right. A horseman with a good horse and a sharp sword can do serious damage to men on foot who are without order. I leaned out to the side as I swept my sword at neck height. These warriors were shorter than the ones I had fought before. The first two were facing me. They misjudged my speed and my blade. Both paid with their lives.

Sword For Hire

As I looked up I saw that the two priests were being beleaguered and likely to be overwhelmed. I yelled, "William!" I needed at least one other horseman by my side. That way we could hack and cut our way through the Estonians and relieve the pressure on the priests. The Jarl Birger Brosa and the other Swedes had forgotten that the men on foot would not be having such an easy time of it.

I glanced behind and saw Edward and William hurrying towards me. The ground was no longer frozen. The Estonians had been tramping over the ground. If anything, it was muddy. I raised my sword and shouted, "England!"

The Estonians would not know my shout but my men at arms would and I hoped that they would hurry to my side. It made some of the Estonians turn and that allowed our hidden archers to send arrows into flesh rather than catching on the hide armour. Four of the Estonians turned to face us. I was still ahead and to buy me time and also to terrify them, when I neared them I pulled back Skuld's reins and stood in the stirrups. She was a frightening sight for a warrior unused to fighting horsemen. Skuld's hooves smashed the skulls of two of them and, as he landed, I brought my sword across the neck of a third. Edward still had his spear and the fourth was pinioned by Edward's weapon.

"We are coming, lord!" I heard Henry Youngblood's voice and the three of us took heart and charged the Estonians. They were caught between our blades and horses on one side and the priests with the banner blessed by Bishop Albert and backed by our foot on the other. We ground them into the ground. The white snow flowed red.

As the last of those before us fell I saw that we had not had it all our own way. There were many dead pagans but twelve of the Swedes were also dead. Others had suffered wounds. I heard a cheer behind me and the Swedes chanted, 'The Jarl Birger Brosa, The Jarl Birger Brosa, The Jarl Birger Brosa' over and over. He had his first victory.

Edward nudged his horse next to mine and stroked its mane. He said, quietly, "That was your victory, lord. If you had not brought us to the aid of the priests then the battle would not have been won."

I shook my head, "We are swords for hire, Edward. We take the coin that we will be paid. If we lose it will be our fault and if we win then the glory will go to someone else. This is a means to an end. When we have enough treasure, men and weapons, then we return home and take back that which is ours!"

There were many captives whom the Estonians had enslaved. Most were women and there was great bitterness when they were released. Some children and some of the old had been mistreated and had died. If the priests had not been there then I think there would have been a great slaughter. I did not understand enough of the words to follow the argument but I could tell, from the actions and gestures, what was going on.

Jarl Birger Persson joined me, "This is more satisfying than fighting the Turk, Thomas. These are our people we have rescued. Some of these were taken five years ago."

"And what of the Estonians?"

He pointed to The Jarl Birger Brosa who was speaking with them, "He is giving them a choice. Become Christians and stay in his lands or head north."

"They will die."

He shook his head, "They are tougher than you might think. They will survive but the Karelians or the men of Novgorod will enslave them. They will convert. The ones who are attractive to our men will become brides and the rest will be employed in our halls."

I saw the drooped shoulders of the Estonians. Birger was right. Christianity was a better option. They would pay lip service and still worship the old gods but they knew how to appease the priests. They were not like the Mamluks who had been Christian and when they converted to Islam became even more ferocious and fanatical than the Seljuk Turks themselves.

I dismounted and handed my reins to Edward. Until I managed to get another squire Edward would help William. Petr took Birger's horse. Birger pointed to one of the large huts. "And in there is your treasure. The jarl is pleased with how you fought. It did not escape his notice that it was you and your men who saved the priests."

"There is gold in there?"

He laughed, "The Estonians have little gold. There will be coins but their real treasure is in their hides and furs, their skins and their seal oil. It will be sold back in Stock Holm or traded. You are well on the way to becoming rich."

The days were short. When dawn did arrive, the jarl decided that we would use it to rest. There were two more camps he wished to eradicate. Thirty or so of the villagers had headed north across the frozen river. To make sure they did not return he had his men break open the ice with war hammers.

There were enough huts for us to be given one to ourselves. It was surprisingly cosy. I had thought that we would need to be covered in furs but we did not. There was reindeer meat for us to eat and some fermented milk. I was not keen on the milk. Henry Youngblood was picking his teeth with a piece of bone, "I can see why they need us, lord. They are keen and they are fierce but they are not yet warriors."

The others who had been on the crusades nodded their agreement. Edward said, "Then you have never seen the Scots fight. They are almost the same except they have even less armour. I have seen them fight naked."

"Do not forget that they are hard to kill."

"As are the Estonians. Our arrows bounced off the hide when the range was too great. Will and I examined one we took from a dead warrior. It is not just hide. It is hide covered with seal skin. It reminded me of the layers the Turks wear. You have to aim for flesh."

Will nodded his agreement, "And their archers have good bows. They are shorter than ours but equally powerful. It is how that young knight was wounded."

I stretched, "We have two more villages like this. Edward, divide us into two watches. William will command one and I the other. William, wake me at noon, or whatever passes for noon in these parts."

I rolled in my fur and was asleep almost instantly. After William had woken me and I had made water I went to speak with the other sentries. Jarl Birger had made sure that we had half of the men watching at any one time. He was up. "I have sent back the captives and the converted Estonians with Brother Magnus and Knut, the knight who was wounded today. There are enough men with light wounds to guard them." He waved a hand, "I used the Estonian sleighs and the reindeer they use to pull them. We will travel faster."

"Are the next two villages far?"

"They are closer to our home. This was as far as I wished to come. We will be heading home when we take them. We wish to approach them from the side they feel safe. They should be smaller than this one. The chief here led the most successful of the clans who invaded our lands."

"Then this is not where they normally live?"

"No, their land is across the ice. They came here some years ago and they crossed the ice to do so. At first, they just moved their herds around and we tolerated them. Then, some four or five years ago they began to raid the outlying farms. It was not a major attack and we were too busy doing other things; we went to Rome, we improved our home. We ignored it and that was a mistake. In the past two years, their attacks have increased. They have made the land to the north of us a wasteland. Even now Bishop Albert is seeking the support of King Sverker to invade Estonia and end these raids once and for all. It is not just us who are suffering."

"That would not be in the winter."

"No, it would not. We would use ships to transport an army." He leaned to me. "My daughter, Ingegerd, is at court now. The king's wife is not well and he has shown an interest in my daughter. She is not averse to a marriage with the King of Sweden. Her mother, after all, is the daughter of the King of Norway. If she marries him then we will have more influence."

I saw politics here rather than anything else. I saw now why Birger Brosa had been so keen for me to train his men. He was becoming the most powerful man in Sweden. If his daughter married the king then, with his connections to Norway, he could rule the region. He reminded me of some of the Dukes and Counts of Normandy and Anjou.

He smiled at me, "Your coming was quite propitious. I saw, last night, that you and your men are superior to mine in every way. It is not just your armour; we can make and buy mail and helmets such as yours, it is the way you fight. We fight as though it is like the hunt. You fight ruthlessly. I need you to teach me to be as good as you."

"You need to become better riders. Did you notice how I rode Skuld with my knees?"

"Skuld? She is one of the Norns."

"I know. She is bred from a line that began with a horse thus named. A Norwegian named her. The line seems to have the ability to sniff out danger before it is seen. That is why the name is used in every generation. It would be bad luck to change it."

"And that is something else, "The gryphon on the blue background and your chance meeting with Birger Persson, it is almost as though you were meant to come here."

I laughed, "Realistically I had nowhere else to go, being an outlaw."

"And will you go back?"

"When I have earned my penance and made enough coin, I will go back. I will return when there is a king of my country who deserves my support."

"Then you will go back a rich man. Your share has been sent back to Stock Holm. By the time we are done here, you will have a chest of gold!"

We left in the middle of the night. The jarl wished to attack at dawn. We had fewer men but then again there would be fewer men in the village we were going to destroy. This time he reversed the plan. He had the men on foot and the archers work their way around the village and we would attack. He had seen the benefit of horses with mailed men charging an enemy.

We only had twenty miles to cover but the icy path had banks of snow on both sides. It was barely wide enough for three men abreast. Jarl Birger Persson thought this a good thing as it hid us from view. For myself, I feared an ambush. I think the fact that it was at night when we travelled made it less likely that any would be watching for us. I was glad that our horses had had food, shelter and rest. The cold sapped energy just as much as the heat had in the Holy Land.

I rode next to William and Edward. Each day I saw a difference in William. He was now more confident. He had shown great skill in the battles we had fought. I noticed even my more experienced men at arms respected the young squire. We talked of Stockton. Now that he helped William Edward had opened up to me even more.

Edward told me how life had changed dramatically after my father had died. "It was not just that he had died but the other knights. It was as if there was no one left to take charge. When the Scots raided and took captives it was the last straw. We sought help from the bishop and he betrayed us by claiming the land. Had he done anything to stop the Scots then we could have lived with that. We were forced to ride forth and stop them." He shook his head, "None of us had the skill of your father or grandfather. We ride behind you and you make it look easy. As we discovered it is not. We defeated the Scots but we lost more men than we should. That is why you have so few to lead."

Each day I rued my father's decision to go to the Holy Land. Nothing good had come of it. The handful of men we had found and the treasure we had earned could not compensate for the loss of so many loyal men and the valley itself. I knew that my father would have said the same. "I am sorry, Edward. I can see now that my father made a mistake when we followed King Richard's banner. I just pray that it is not too late."

"It is not, lord, I feel it in my water." Edward, like all of my men, had a positive attitude to this war. They had more confidence than I did.

When the scouts spotted the settlement, we had to wait longer for it was men on foot who were making their way around to await our attack. The scouts told us that they thought there were fifty or so warriors there. And, once again, there were captives. We also had the knowledge that their herd of reindeer were on the far side. Our men could use them for cover.

We waited. This time there would be no signal. We would not alert the enemy. They would hear our hooves and the rattle of metal on metal but they would not know what it was. As the jarl had said, they had never experienced this type of war before. They would learn but we had the chance to make decisive victories. We waited on a frozen stream. The bank hid us and we had men at the top watching the village. One of them, Eystein, came slithering down, "Jarl, they are all collecting in the middle. It looks like they are having some form of gathering."

"This is too good an opportunity to shun. Even if the men on the other side are not in position, we will attack. Mount." He looked at me, "And remember that we have a duty to protect Brother Harald and his men." He had been listening when I had spoken.

Our horses struggled to get up the snow-covered bank. Once we reached the top I saw the huts and the people. They were less than three hundred paces from us. I saw a man, bare from the waist up. He was being pulled onto a cross. I had a feeling I knew what they intended to do to him. We quickly formed into a long line. There was nothing between us and the huts. I think it was an area they used for grazing. We had spears but this would be the last time we would have enough for all of us. It was another lesson for the jarl. He needed to bring more weapons on these raids.

They had some men watching and they gave the alarm. The women scattered and the men ran for weapons. We were heading for them at a steady speed. I had impressed on the jarl the need to keep boot to boot if we could and, so far, he and his men were heeding my advice. The Estonians grabbed their weapons but they came at us piecemeal. It was easier than the battle we had previously fought. We had more men facing us but there was no attempt to form one line.

We hit them as one. I pulled back my arm and I saw, as I struck, that the other spears came forward as mine did. Even the ones which hit shields were effective. The force of the blow, the mail and our horses knocked the warriors to the ground and they were trampled. I then saw arrows falling amongst the Estonians. David and the archers were in position. Then I heard a cry, "God and Bishop Albert!" Brother Harald, belying his years led the men to fall upon the rear of the Estonians. This time they did beg for quarter. We had unleashed a hell on them they had not expected. We looked around for any more foes and there were none. I sheathed my sword and looked to see if any of my men had been hurt. I could not see the archers but my men at arms were wiping blood from weapons. They lived.

Chapter 12

Petr ran to the man who had been hung between two trees. I could now see that he was a youth. Brother Harald was looking around for more men to slay and then I heard him shout to his men to free the captives. The two jarls had the warriors, as well as the women and children, herded in the middle. My men were slipping amongst them to remove weapons. I smiled. We had become one army. It might be the smallest army in which I had ever fought but that did not matter.

I dismounted and handed my reins to William. "Lord, you still have your spear!"

I nodded, "I am learning the best place to strike at these heathens."

Petr shouted, "Sir Thomas, I need assistance."

When I reached him, I saw that the young man, he was little more than a boy and I put his age at no more than fourteen summers, was not just tied to the two trees, a nail had been driven through each palm. Petr was supporting him so that the weight did not tear the nail through his hand. He was, mercifully unconscious. I turned and shouted, "William, fetch Skuld and be quick!"

Petr said, "I know him. His father, Folke the Quiet, is the jarl of a settlement twenty miles west of here. This is his son, Fótr. They are Norse."

William arrived and I opened the saddlebag. I had a pair of pincers I had made by a blacksmith in the Holy Land. I knew how to shoe a horse. Often you could not find a farrier in the desert. It was a skill of which I was proud. The pincers were used to remove old nails. Now I saw a medical use. "Petr, put your hand flat against his palm and leave a gap between your fingers."

"Aye lord."

I knew that I had to be quick. He was bleeding heavily. The cold had slowed down the bleeding, perhaps it had even saved his life. I put the pincers around the head and pulled. I did so firmly. I had learned to do so on horses. One swift jerk was better than a series of tugs. The youth gave a sort of moan.

"William, fetch the healer and fire. Petr, the other hand."

I pulled the other one out and then we laid him down on his back. The two jarls and Brother Harald rushed over, "Dear God, what have the heathens done to this poor boy!" The priest quickly used vinegar to cleanse the wound. He rammed some honey in to stem the bleeding and then he grabbed the brand. He nodded to me, "Quick thinking, lord. You may have saved this youth's hands."

There was a hiss and the boy spasmed and his eyes flew open. He looked terrified. Brother Harald did the same with the other hand. Laying down the brand, Brother Harald put his arms around him and said, "You are safe now, boy! Your ordeal is over!"

The Jarl Birger Brosa was grim-faced as he asked, "Where is your family?"

The youth looked in shock but he appeared to recognise the jarl. He shook his head, "I am not certain. They attacked our home three days since. The warband split up and I was brought here. My father and mother were taken by the others."

Jarl Birger Persson asked Birger Brosa, "Others? It sounds to me like two clans combined for a raid. Folke the Quiet had a well-made hall with a ditch and a palisade. It would not have fallen easily."

"Your brothers, Folki and Magnus, what of them?"

"They were slain. My father was hurt. I tried to defend my mother but I was struck from behind."

Brother Harald turned the youth around and looked at the back of his head. "Fetch water he has another hurt." He glared at The Jarl Birger Brosa, "He needs food, jarl and rest not questions."

"You are right and we know enough already." We walked away. The Estonians were being closely watched. There were fewer captives here but when David of Wales came over he said, "Lord, there is a charnel house yonder. I found many bones. There were pieces of flesh there. Do these heathens just throw their dead away?"

The jarl looked at the captives. "No, archer, they do not. The bones are of the captives they took and who were of no use to them. They kept the women and the girls. They are the men and boys. When they would have finished with Fótr he would have been disposed of in the same way."

He strode over to the Estonians. He grabbed an old man and hauled him up. He began to speak with him. The man did not appear to understand. Suddenly he spat at the jarl and then pulled a wicked skinning knife from his sealskin boot. He would have succeeded in his assassination attempt had not Will son of Robin sent an arrow into his back. The treachery had an immediate effect. We had only taken a handful of men and about six boys. The jarl's men dragged them from the captives and summarily executed them. It happened so fast that we could not stop it. Their blood was hot. As they searched the bodies, they pulled out knives from their boots. Now we saw why these had surrendered. The women wailed until the jarl, now recovered from the shock of almost dying, shouted and there was a sullen silence. He spoke again and this time one woman spoke. It was a brief conversation.

The jarl turned to us, "I thank your archer, Sir Thomas. Once again, I give thanks to God that you were sent to us. The clan joined with another to raid Folki. This village took the boy and the animals, the other had the captives. We need to get there quickly."

I asked, "How far is it?"

"Twenty miles."

"If you travel now you will hurt the horses and we have captives and freed slaves to care for."

"I know Sir Thomas but these are cruel people. They have Fótr's mother."

I nodded. He was right. I looked at the sky. I was new to the land but the clouds looked to be snow laden to me. "And if it snows?"

Brother Harald had come over to join us, "It will snow. I have stitched his head and given him a sleeping draught. He cannot be moved yet."

I saw the dilemma which the jarl faced. He walked to the horses and began to stroke his animal. When he turned he was smiling, "Brother Harald, I leave you here with the prisoners and the captives. We will take men who are mounted and those of my men who are unhurt. They can use skis. The Estonians have great quantities of them. We will go with a smaller number and hope that the blizzard can help us. We will go in on foot and silently. If God is with us then we will emerge victorious."

It was not the best plan in the world but I could also see that it was the only plan. I left six archers with the priest. They were the ones without horses. I took just David and Will. In all, we had forty-six men. The jarl knew that we would be outnumbered but he hoped that our armour and our skill would help us. I had seen skis before but this was the first time I had seen them used in war. As the snow began to fall we left. Amazingly the skiers moved faster than the horses. They flanked us and moved easily across country.

The jarl had heeded my words and we went steadily rather than fast. We had grabbed food and were eating even as we rode. I had grain in my saddlebags for Skuld and water in my skin. With all the snow around, we could melt it and make water if we had to. The blizzard meant that we could not see far ahead and we relied upon The Jarl Birger Brosa's scouts. I had my spare cloak tied around my saddle to afford some protection for Skuld. My hood hung over my face so that the snow did not continually drive into my flesh. I had never endured like this before. It was like being in a cocoon. I could hear little and see less. Old Crusaders had told me of sandstorms which were as bad. I had never had to ride in one. I had been lucky and watched them from the safety of Acre's walls.

It was hard to estimate time but I saw the sky growing darker. Night was falling. It seemed to have lasted but a short time. The snow-laden clouds had not helped. We had stopped twice to feed and rest the horses. The skiers did not seem to need the rest and they had ranged ahead before returning to report on the terrain we would encounter.

I found myself almost dozing off as darkness fell. Skuld stopped and I looked out of my cloak. Jarl Birger Persson had stopped. He turned. He mimed dismounting. We had reached the village although, as I peered beyond him I could see nothing. I could smell nothing. It was as though we were in a white hell. I dismounted. We were close to a forest of spindly pines. We led our horses there and tied them to the trees. They would have some shelter from the snow. I saw the others take off their cloaks and I did the same. We would be colder but we needed the freedom to swing.

This time David and Will would be under the command of the Swedes. This was their sort of war. Sverge, their leader tapped them on their shoulders and they headed through the snow. The dismounted warriors seemed a tiny number to do what we had to do. My men naturally formed up behind me. We made up almost half of the number of warriors who would attack the village. The jarls had made their plans before we had left. We would spread out in a long line and work our way in to the village. The archers we had taken would be on the far side. We hoped that our enemy would be confused. The blizzard would keep most of the Estonians inside their huts. Had we been in England I would have sent a scout in to find out where the captives were being kept. We would not be doing that. We would have to enter each hut and identify the occupants.

Leading my men, I waved my sword to the left and the right and my men spread out. Edward was on my left and William on my right. We started to walk. There was a gap between each man. I could not see anything at first and I relied on the skill of the scouts. The blizzard began to abate, even as we walked through the virgin snow. It was hard going, walking in snow which came up above our ankles. You had to lift your foot higher than normal. As the snow stopped I saw the shadows of huts ahead and the glow, through an open door of a fire. I could also smell animals. There were reindeer. I glanced to my right and saw The Jarl Birger Brosa and his men. We were still in one line.

Suddenly, ahead of me was a line of spears and on top of each one was a skull. Three of them were fresh. I saw their gory faces and knew that one of them had to be Folki the Quiet. I pulled my shield around a little closer. The silence of the night was broken from my right. One of the Estonian sentries had been slain. I raised my sword and we began to move faster.

There was a hut just twenty paces from us. A warrior ran out with an axe in his hand. As he glanced around he saw us and shouted something. Henry Youngblood ran up to him and talking the axe blow on his shield hacked his sword across his middle. My men followed him into the hut. I turned as William shouted. Four warriors had emerged from a hut to our right and were running at us. Hugh of Bath and William turned to face them. They locked their shields.

"Edward, with me!" Leaving the rest of our men to deal with the warriors in the hut we ran to the aid of William and Hugh. I saw Hugh's shield shivered by an Estonian axe and I brought my sword overhand to strike down on the axeman's head. Even if his hide cap stopped my edge cutting too deeply the weight of the sword would crush his skull. Edward rammed his sword into the neck of a second Estonian. Hugh headbutted the warrior who faced him. The nasal on Hugh's helmet broke the Estonian's nose and, as he reeled, he hacked him across the middle. William kept punching his enemy in the face with his shield until the man's guard dropped and William's sword sliced through his throat.

Henry led my men from the hut. Their swords were bloody. I saw the two jarls surrounded by warriors. Arrows flew from the dark and whittled down the Estonians but there were many of them. Even as I watch an Estonian axe sliced through the shield of one of The Jarl Birger Brosa's men at arms and a second eviscerated him with a curved skinning knife. I led my men towards the fray. The snow had stopped but it was still deep. We could not reach them quickly. I saw one of the squires hit on the side of his helmet by the flat of an axe he fell.

Before the Estonian could finish him off William had reached the Estonian and hacked through his thigh. The artery was severed and blood sprayed on the white snow. I lunged at an Estonian whose arm was raised to bring his axe down. Had the blow connected then Jarl Birger Persson's man at arms would have been killed. My sword went under his arm and into the soft flesh of his armpit. Striking through his neck it came out at the other side. I used my foot to push his body from my blade.

The sheer weight of numbers was helping the Estonians to win. Each of our men was being attacked by two of theirs. The battles and the journey had taken their toll on the men of the two jarls. Things might have gone against us had David not led the archers to close with the Estonians. From a range of twenty paces, they poured arrow after arrow into them. Even their hide jerkins could not save them. With the rest of us hacking and stabbing at their front we ground them down.

The Jarl Birger Brosa shouted, "No, quarter!"

I did not disagree. I had seen the skulls of the dead jarl and his men. By the time dawn broke, we had finished the last of the men. Some of the women and children had escaped. That could not be helped. Eight of the Swedes we had brought with us lay dead including two squires. The knights they had served were distraught.

"Find Folki the Quiet!"

I shook my head, "Look over there. I spied some spears with freshly hewn skulls upon them."

The jarl himself went and when he returned, his face was grim. "It is he. But where is his wife? Gather the captives together and ask where she is. Have the prisoners guarded."

Hugh of Bath had a bad wound in his leg. An axe had sliced through his chausse and laid open his calf. Our healer was back at the other camp. Will son of Robin said, "I will see to it. I am handy with a needle."

"William, take Petr and the squires who remain, fetch our horses."

I joined the other two jarls and the two knights as we sought the lady. It was Birger Persson who found her. She was in one of the huts along with two other

121

women. They had been used by the Estonians. They were dead. My friend turned and drew his sword. I knew what he intended. I stood in the doorway. "Do not do this, Birger, you will regret it. There are just women, children and the old out there." I said it quietly and in a calm voice in the hope that it would calm him. He tried to push past me. I said, over my shoulder, "Ridley, I need you."

Birger said, "Did you see what those animals did to those women! They were gentle ladies. Those girls were her daughters!"

Ridley appeared behind me. Birger was going nowhere in a hurry. "And those men are dead. We slew them. Perhaps the Brother can save their souls. The women did not do this. The children did not do this. Men behaved like animals and they have paid. If you hurt them then you are no better than the beasts we slew."

I saw his shoulders slump. He nodded, "You are right but I just want to hit out at something."

"I know." I turned to Ridley, "Thank you."

He grinned, "Any time, lord."

We stayed at the camp for the night. We were tired and we wanted a whole day to take the Estonians and the captives we had recovered back to the Brother and the rest of our men. The Jarl Birger Brosa also wanted as many of their animals as we could drive. "If we have them then any survivors will starve. We will find their bones come spring." They fought their wars in a different way here on this northern border.

We knew that some had escaped. The archers had deserted their post. It had been the right decision. If they had not then we might have lost. I comforted the jarls, "This may be better. They will return home and the survivors will tell of what we did here. They will choose easier places to raid and to roam."

We had bodies to bury and huts to search. With slow-moving captives, it took some time to return to our camp.

When we reached Brother Harald I saw that Fótr was watching for us and ran towards us. His face was full of hope. That hope was dashed when he saw our faces. "Your family has been avenged, Fótr Folkisson. Brother Harald will offer words of comfort."

His face became a mask of anger, "I want no comfort. I want the arms and the skills to do as you did. I would go amongst our enemies and I would slaughter them."

Jarl Birger Persson said, "Then you had better serve Sir Thomas of Stockton." He pointed to me. "He needs a squire and there is none better to train you."

He nodded, "Would you have me, lord? I know little but I swear that I will learn."

I saw William's face. He was willing me to agree. It was a great responsibility but I knew I had to do as they asked, "Aye, you will be my squire until you are ready to be knighted. That will be the decision of The Jarl Birger Brosa."

The jarl smiled, "This is good. When spring comes we will visit your home and see what can be salvaged."

Sverre said, "We recovered the jarl's mail, lord, his sword and his shield. They were in the hut of the chief."

Birger nodded his approval, "Then you have made a good start to becoming a knight. Now let us make the journey back to Stock Holm for I have had enough of this debatable land."

It took four days to reach home. We had more snow and six of the rescued captives died. They had been ill-treated and despite the best efforts of Brother Harald, they could not be saved. Our horses had also suffered. Skuld's ribs showed through.

As we neared Stock Holm I said, "We will not ride again this winter."

My friend said, "Probably not."

"No, that was not a question. We will not ride again this winter for if we do we will kill our animals and the horses we have are the best in this land until Gonfanon can sire colts and fillies. We have lost too many men." I waved a hand behind me. "You and The Jarl Birger Brosa have lost more men than you bring back. You have paid for me to advise you. Defend what you have! Spend the next year, perhaps two, building up your armies and a castle. You rely too much on the water. The water can only defend you so far. The rest depends upon men of steel on good horses."

"You are right. It is just that I feel I wasted all those years in the Holy land. I could have been here."

"I thought that too but they were not wasted. They helped to prepare us for this. And for me it is important that my men and I learn while we are here for when I return home, to England, I have an equally daunting task facing me. I have to save England! My great grandfather did so. I had thought that we would never need to repeat his feats. I can see that I am wrong. When knights are no longer vigilant then it is the people and the land which suffer. My father made one mistake in his life. He went to the Holy Land. My grandfather went to the Holy Land and it was the best of decisions. I hope that I have made a good one by coming here."

Birger looked back to Fótr chatting easily to William. "Of that, there is no doubt."

The Stone Walls of Kastelholm

Chapter 13

Lady Brigida was one of the kindest women I had ever met. By the time we returned to Stock Holm the freed captives had all been housed and clothed, and, even though it was winter, she had had her men erect halls. The converts were also housed. I am sure that one reason why they became truly Christian was because of the jarl's wife's kindness. She had had the snow cleared around the halls and was there to greet us when we arrived. There was genuine relief that we had survived and true sadness for our losses. When she heard of the deaths of Fótr's family she ordered a mass to be said for them and she found some of her son, Phillipus', clothes and gave them to him.

That evening as we ate, courtesy of the Estonians for we slaughtered some of their animals, we told the jarl's wife of the battles we had fought. We sanitized them for her but she needed to know why we had not brought any male prisoners back.

"They fought to the death and those that did surrender intended to do us harm. I believe that the only hope for them is to be converted."

I saw the two brothers nodding.

Jarl Birger Persson asked, "Have we had word from the king yet?"

Lady Brigida shook her head, "The Queen is still close to death. Our daughter is a great comfort to him."

I had discovered, whilst we had campaigned, that, unlike England and France, the king was elected. Sverker was the second such named and he had replaced Knut Eriksson. Apparently, Knut Eriksson had a son but the Swedes, upon the advice of The Jarl Birger Brosa had chosen Sverker. It was no wonder that he was contemplating marrying as soon as his wife died. The daughter of The Jarl Birger Brosa would ensure that he would rule without fear of revolt or dissension.

Over the next few months, we and our horses recovered. Our beards had fully regrown and that was a comfort in the cold climate of Sweden. I had no more letters from home. Henry would only return when all threat of ice had abated. They had iron in abundance and good smiths. I helped them to design and make betters swords, mail and helmets for the men who would be campaigning with us when next we raided. I enjoyed it. There was an urgent need for such armaments.

My new squire had mail but his father had been bigger than he and it had to be fitted for him. He needed a new helmet and his was the first which I designed. It was based upon mine. The open helmet with the nasal had some benefits but a full-face helmet gave more protection.

Fótr proved to be a good squire. He listened and he remembered. He watched William. William was anxious for Fótr to become skilled for he would be able to share some of the duties. I knew that we needed more horses. Fótr did not have one. When Henry returned I would use some of my coin to buy more. I needed all of my men mounted. I had been surprised at just how much we had made from the sacked villages. The oil, skins and furs yielded a great deal of coin from the markets of Brabant and Brugge. I made sure that all of my men benefitted from the raids. They deserved to be in profit too. It was not totally altruistic. They were already loyal and the money they had in their purses made them keen to follow me even more.

I also spent time with Birger Persson. The island we had found would be his new home. He had already named it, Kastelholm. His money and further advances from the Jarl Birger Brosa had gone on hiring two masons and buying the stone that he would need. The building season in Sweden was a short one. Everything had to be ready. Work would begin as soon as the ground thawed enough for a spade. I sat with the masons and Birger talking through the features we would need. The island's position meant that he did not need a high curtain wall. He could build a hall that was both high and could be seen from a long way away. Deterrence was as important as defence. The single gatehouse could be like a small castle. Birger and I liked the idea that the gatehouse could be defended by a small number of men.

The stone would be ready before the snows had melted. We would build the causeway and causeway bridge first. The masons would use slaves to lay the causeway. The bridge would be made of wood and already there were huge trees, felled before winter which were being prepared by being soaked in pine tar. Carrying them and working on them would not be a pleasant task. The slaves would rue the day they were captured.

Work did not stop on Stock Holm. The Jarl Birger Brosa had his own masons. He had a stone hall almost complete and they were now working on his wall. It would dwarf Kastelholm. The new work drew in men who saw an opportunity to serve a lord. Many were crusaders who returned from a land that was now hostile to them. None were English but there were Danes, Norse, Swedes and even Rus. The Jarl Birger Brosa was lucky enough to recruit four former Teutonic Knights. They brought their own squires and sergeants. They became his personal bodyguards. I had discovered that Jarl Birger Brosa was a very rich man. My friend said that he was the richest man in Sweden. His wife's fortune had been added to that of his already wealthy family. It explained both his power and his ability to build imposing structures.

Stock Holm became more of an armed camp. It was a direct contrast to the place I had first seen almost half a year earlier. When Henry arrived at the end of March I was ready for news from home. Soon I would be leaving Stock Holm. I had written a letter to my aunt explaining and outlining my plans. I did not want her to worry about the lack of news. Henry handed me a letter and I gave him coin for more horses. He knew what I wanted.

I asked him about home. He shook his head, "The king needs to be home and not fighting in Normandy. People are suffering. The Welsh and the Scots raid at will. Some sea captains told me that the Irish have started slave raids in the west. Taxes are too high and people are starving. I am afraid that the valley is not a happy place. People talk of the days of the Warlord and his son."

"Not my father?"

"I am sorry, lord. Your father's departure is viewed as the cause of all the woes the people suffer."

"And me?"

He laughed, "You are spoken of like a ghost, a phantom. They speak of the knight who flew into the Bishop of Durham's castle and killed him and all his guards."

"But I did not!"

"It matters not. Each time the story is told then the numbers increase. The fact that no one can find you adds to the legend. Prince John's men and the Bishop's guards ride the valley in tens and twenties for they fear smaller numbers would be slain by you. You are a myth and a legend at the same time. When one of the Prince's men is found dead or one of the bishop's tax collectors die it is laid at your doorstep. I know it is not you and I tell people but they believe what they want to believe. The only one who does not seem to fear you nor search for you is Sir Richard of Stockton."

I hid a smile. It was obvious that Henry did not know of the connection. "I will return one day, Henry, that I swear. The time is not right. When King Richard tires of Normandy then I will come home and join with him to put England back together."

I did not know then that England had another seventeen years or more to suffer the privations of John Lackland.

I took the letter and read it alone.

You know who you are and I hope you know that I think of you every day! Each night you are in my prayers.

I am no longer alone. I have comfort and, after the death of my husband, I never thought that I would. You were the cause of that and I thank you. It is strange the way our lives touch and then move on. The connection is never lost and the memories hold us together.

Know that people in Stockton and the Tees valley speak of you and your return. You have become a mythical, legendary figure for the oppressed people of this land. I encourage it for it gives the people hope. When Prince John's men are robbed or killed then you are given the credit. I know it is not you. I hope and pray that you are still safe. When my messenger returns, if he does not have a missive, I hope at least he knows that you are alive.

xxx

I was touched by the letter. It confirmed that Henry had, indeed, spoken the truth. I had already given my unsigned letter to Henry.

I took my men with Jarl Birger Persson. With so many slaves working he would need plenty of eyes to watch them. He had recruited more men and The Jarl Birger Brosa sent four knights and their men at arms to assist in the construction of the castle and the defence of the workers. The Karelians had used the island for years. They would not take kindly to its loss.

The rest had done the horses good. My men, too, with a healthy diet and plenty of exercise, were in prime condition. I was becoming used to this land. It had been a shock when we had first arrived, especially after the Holy Land, but now I saw its beauty.

I rode with Birger Persson. The knights we had brought with us rode with the two warrior-priests ahead of us. "Tell me, Birger, why have you never married?"

"One of the reasons I was so willing to go on the crusade for Bishop Albert was because I was betrothed to be married and she died in an Estonian raid. They had taken my bride to be for ransom but she tried to flee and fell from her horse. Her skull was crushed." He was silent. I knew that he was trying to compose himself, "I would have paid the ransom. I hunted down her abductors and Petr and I slew them all."

He had revealed more to me in that one sentence than in all the other conversations we had over the years. He said no more about it and I did not intrude. It explained much.

We camped on the mainland side. The plan was to build the causeway and the bridge first. Once our camp was established I took my archers and my squires and we rode long patrols. I wanted to get a feel for the land as well as to discourage any Karelians or Estonians from raiding. We left each morning after we had broken our fast and returned each evening to be greeted by the smell of food being cooked.

On the fifth day, David said, "Lord, we are being paid to ride around the country, eat some of the best food I have ever eaten in my life and yet there are no enemies to fight? It seems almost dishonest."

Fótr had picked up our language quickly. He was both young and clever. Sometimes his idiom was incorrect but the men did not mind. "In this land, David of Wales, when danger comes it does not give you a warning. It leaps from the night and rips your heart out. This appears peaceful but the heathens are watching us."

"You are certain?"

He nodded, "My father had spotted the tracks of the Estonians who slew my family. He thought they would not risk such a target. He was wrong. Keep your wits about you, lord."

David laughed, "To be truthful, young master, I know that we have passed close by Estonians. I have smelled them. The grease and the food they eat make them stink. But he is right lord, I have yet to see one. They are good at hiding."

William said, "Perhaps they fear us."

"They do not know you, William. My father and his men did not use horses. It is your use of horses that confuses them. My father's people would ride to war on horses and then dismount to fight. They fear the fact that you and the horse appear to be one." He smiled shyly at me, "You, my lord, particularly so. I have watched you. She turns before you command her to."

"Skuld is special but William here understands his horse too. A knight who does not like horses is doomed to an early death. You will learn. You are my squire and it is our duty to teach you."

It took half a month to raise the causeway and then build the wooden bridge. At first, it was a simple affair. It was just rough-cut planks that were raised and lowered by hand but it allowed us to move onto the island where we were more secure. We stayed to help the others clear the trees and to begin to build the castle. The slaves would be needed until midsummer. By then the sun would barely set and the masons wanted the slaves to work in shifts so that we could keep going all the time. We were given the task of digging the well. My great grandfather had been besieged and he never underestimated the effect of a good well. I enjoyed the challenge. I joined my men, stripped to the waist, and helped to dig.

We had just struck water when one of the scouts we had sent out reported a fleet of Karelian ships approaching. He said he had spied them ten miles away. That gave us two hours at the most. Jarl Birger Persson was not surprised. He was just annoyed with the timing. We had our wooden wall erected. That had been easy. We had used the cleared trees and split them into four. Using sand and soil we had buried them around the island so that we had a barrier. The foundations for the curtain wall had been dug and the first layer of stones laid. Another month and we would have been defensible. As it was there was a danger that we could be driven from the island and the raiders would have a better base, thanks to us.

Jarl Birger Persson knew our enemies better than I did. He sent a rider to head back to Stock Holm. He then had a guard created to watch the slave pen. He enlisted the masons and their assistants to help him. That left fifty of us to fight the Karelians. Once our rider had gone for help we raised the bridge to the mainland and we prepared for war.

"We have fifteen archers. They have over a thousand arrows between them. If we can keep the enemy ships at bay we have a chance."

I shook my head, "Wrong, my friend. We let them come close."

"Are you mad? They pack their ships with warriors. We would be overwhelmed."

"The greatest fear of any sailor is fire. Their ships are made of timber. They have oiled ropes and hulls. They have canvas. We burn them!"

"How?"

"By letting them get close. We use two methods. The empty pots from the food we brought can be packed with burning coals. We tie a cord around the neck. We use our biggest warriors to hurl them like a war hammer into the ships. We make fire arrows and send them into their sails. Let them come close, for the closer they are then the more will die." I pointed to the causeway. "They cannot come that way, can they?"

"No."

"Then they have to come from the sea, the east. We have a wooden wall there. Array your men behind it. They will come to the shore to land. We hold them while Ridley the Giant and other strong warriors send our fire pots into their ships. We use our shields and our spears and we hold them."

He could not think of a better solution and he agreed.

"Jarl, I see their sails. We do not have much time."

The pots were easy to fill with burning coals and to keep fed. It was the fire arrows that took time. We used seal oil-impregnated cloths wrapped around arrow heads. David of Wales had made them before and he supervised. The rest of us took all of our spears and planted ourselves behind the wall. There was no fighting platform. The wall was the height of a man. The curtain wall which would be built would be more substantial. It would be much taller than a man. If they had come a year later they would have climbed the wooden wall and then been trapped in the ditch we had begun to build.

I turned to Fótr. He had not fought with us before. "We want no heroes. When I look around after this battle I expect to see you standing behind me without wounds! These are barbarians. They are wild. Use your shield and your spear. Strike at flesh. If I shout for you to fall back then do so. We head for the foundations of the curtain wall. They will have to climb our new ditch."

He nodded. "Are you afraid, lord?"

"A man who says he is not afraid before he goes into battle is lying and you do not trust him but that is not the question you mean. What you wish to ask me is do you think we will die?" He nodded. "Not this day. The enemy you fear is the one armed and mailed like you. The enemy who rides a horse as good as you and the one who has been trained as well as you. On that day, there is a chance that you may die."

William laughed, "But as Sir Thomas has trained you there would need to be four such men facing you."

I stared out to sea. The four Karelian ships were heavily laden with men and they were now less than a thousand paces from us. I smelled smoke as the pot throwers and the archers arrived. David used stones to make an improvised hearth and then a pot of coal was dropped upon it. He put more kindling on it and the flames leapt up. That would be the fire for the arrows.

I looked at Birger Persson, "Sir Thomas, this is your plan. You give the command."

I nodded and turned to the ten men with the pots. "You are big men. You are strong men. What you are not are stupid men! There are four ships out there. Two pots to a boat and then two in case any do not fire their ships."

They nodded.

"Spread yourselves out. Listen for my command!"

"Aye, lord!"

The ships were now approaching the shore. They had seen our spears and they had moved apart to attack us along the length of the wall. I glanced over my shoulder and saw the pot throwers hurrying closer to where they thought the targets would be. I heard David giving orders to the archers. We were ready. I saw that the enemy had their shields up. They expected arrows. The four ships were just paces from the shore. Two were close to me.

"Now!" I shouted in Swedish and the Karelians heard. They knew that something was coming and they hesitated. Hesitation can be fatal. Eight pots soared. Six ignited and the other two flew to follow the first eight. Fifteen fire arrows flew overhead. The ships were less than fifty paces from us. They all hit and another fifteen soared. We only had thirty-five fire arrows but we would not need any more. Our archers changed to man killers and they released arrow after arrow.

The Karelian's choices were to fight the fire, to flee or to get at us. They did not flee. Some ran at us and some tried to fight the fires. I watched twelve warriors run at us. We were spread thinly. I had eight men with which to face them and one was untried, Fótr. I held my spear so that it angled up. The wooden wall was not hard to climb. The difficulty lay in descending safely. A young warrior with a small shield and a curved short sword climbed up and stood on the top of the wall. I noticed that, as he grinned, he had no front teeth. I rammed my spear up into his groin. His grin turned to a scream and, as he fell backwards, his guts were left on my spear. I did not remove them. I just pulled my arm back and awaited the next one.

I had time to look down the line and see that three of the ships were firmly ablaze. The one at the southern end was the one with the least damage and their sail had been furled so that it was not afire.

More men tried to come over our wall. The next man had seen what I had done and his shield covered his middle. I stabbed him in the calf and twisted my spear. The head tore through muscle and tendon. Screaming he fell backwards. Then someone took charge and arrows began to fall. They had to release them vertically to avoid hitting their own men. I shouted, "Shields!"

One hit my shield. I heard them rattling like hail on our shields. It allowed some men to climb over. I watched as Fótr killed his first man. He had been listening to me. He feinted at the Karelian's middle and the warrior pulled his shield down. Fótr thrust at the unprotected neck and his spear pierced the sallow and greasy skin of the warrior.

"Well done Fótr! Your first kill!"

Further down the line, I saw that others were not having the same success. "Robert and Hugh go to the aid of Petr."

"Aye lord."

The two gaps left by my men meant we had to expand slightly. Then the Estonians tried a new tactic. Instead of climbing the wall, they began to run at the wall and two warriors held their shield so that they could spring over the walls using the bodies of their dead which lay before the wall to do so. They flew!

"David!"

The flying warriors were a distraction. We had to look up to watch them and that allowed others to gain purchase on the walls. I speared one as he descended. He impaled himself upon my spear but his fall and his weight took the spear from my hand. I drew my sword as Dick and the archers behind switched targets. They began to hit the Karelians as they descended.

The damage had been done. There were half a dozen Karelians who were inside the wooden wall. They were, however, wary. They did not rush at us. They were trying to hold the wall and allow their comrades to clamber over.

"William, Fótr! To me!"

I ran at the knot of warriors who were trying to enlarge the toehold they had gained. With my sword held over my shield, I ran at the middle of them. Some had short, curved swords and some had short axes. William and Fótr reached me. They both had their spears. We hit the five warriors together. Our shields were larger and covered our bodies. As two axes struck my shield and a sword rang off my helmet I rammed my sword into the screaming open mouth of the nearest warrior. Knowing he would be dead I began to pull the sword out sideways and I used the edge to rip into the neck of the warrior next to him. His head turned and he spat at me. I saw the wound widen. The man was dead, he simply did not know it. My two squire's spears pinned their men to the wall. I punched the last man in the side of the head with my shield. He was held in place by the body of the man William had pinned. My sword entered his side and he died with a soft sigh.

I stepped back to survey the scene. We had held. Further down Jarl Birger Persson and his men were despatching the ones who remained on our side of the wall and I saw the last Estonian smoking, but afloat, as she began to edge away. The surviving Karelians were hurling themselves into the sea. Their shields and weapons lay on the beach where they had discarded them. It was soon clear that the only ones who remained were the dead and the dying. Even the wounded had tried to flee.

"Despatch those who remain."

"Aye lord."

"Edward, come with me."

Using some of the bodies as stepping stones we climbed to the top of the wall and jumped down. The three ships had burned to the water line and lay in the shallows with smoking, blackened hulls. A Karelian, his middle laid open, had crawled closer to the water and he groaned as we passed him and Edward slid his sword across the man's throat to end his suffering. There had to be thirty or forty bodies on the sea side of the wall. I knew that there had to be at least fifty on the wall or on our side. Jarl Birger Persson had hurt the Karelians. If nothing else the building of the stone walls of Kastelholm would discourage the heathens from raiding this coastline further.

Having ensured that none were feigning death we returned inside our walls. The two priests were seeing to the wounded. Already Birger Persson was having the Karelian dead stripped of anything we could use. I said, "If we put their bodies on the beach we can burn them. The island is free from vermin. Let us keep it that way."

He nodded. "And we will make a cemetery on the mainland." We had already decided that would be where the church would be. There were no farmers nor families here yet. No fishermen used the anchorage. Up until now, it had been too dangerous. There were simply too many raiders. The jarl intended to encourage families to come but they would have to use the Kastelholm in times of war.

Riders arrived from Stock Holm. They were not needed and we sent them back, escorting our wounded.

In the days following the attack, there was a renewed effort on the part of everyone. Even the slaves worked harder. They were The Jarl Birger Brosa's slaves and Stock Holm was safer than the wild frontier that was Kastelholm. If the Karelians had won they would not have had freedom. They would have exchanged one master for another and the Karelians were known to be cruel to their slaves. The weather became more benign and that allowed the building to proceed faster.

The two priests began to build the church. Now that we had the cemetery its position was decided. Bishop Albert would have to consecrate the ground but if the church was erected then it would be a marker. Ships sailing these waters would know that it was Christian.

By Midsummer Day, when there was almost no night, we had the curtain wall in place and the gatehouse. The first floor of the keep was built and the tread mill crane creaked and groaned as it lifted stones. Settlers arrived. We had sent a constant stream of messengers back to Stock Holm so that The Jarl Birger Brosa and Bishop Albert knew of our progress. Bishop Albert came with the settlers. These were the ones who had lived at Sigtuna. Their new home would be further east but they would have security. The ceremony of consecration was a symbolic act. For the new farmers and fishermen, it was confirmation that God was on their side and for Bishop Albert and the jarl, it was a sign that this part of the coast was now secure.

Birger Persson also chose that moment to have his brother knighted. Petr had shown that he was a good knight and I had spoken to Birger many times about his status. He did not see himself as the castellan at Kastelholm, he wanted to join Bishop Albert on the crusade which would bring Christianity to the Baltic. Petr was knighted and his title was confirmed by Bishop Albert. There was a real sense of relief for Birger Persson. His young brother would rule this part of the coast. He would find a wife and marry. The family name would continue.

In the months that followed I thought of my own future. I was the last of a noble line. It went back to before the time of the Conquest. If I had no offspring I would be letting them down. I could not, however, marry while England was in the hands of Prince John. I would have to wait until King Richard returned.

King John of England

Chapter 14

Stock Holm 1199

My men and I had lived at the new castle built by The Jarl Birger Brosa for well over a year. After we had made sure that Kastelholm was almost finished and Petr and his new bride happy, Jarl Birger Persson and I headed south. The old queen had died and The Jarl Birger Brosa's daughter, Ingegerd was now Queen of Sweden. The Jarl Birger Brosa now had almost total power in Sweden. Bishop Albert had almost gathered his army to invade the lands of the heathen. It was no surprise to me that Bishop Albert used Stock Holm as the place from which he would launch his invasion. Stock Holm had changed dramatically since I had first arrived. Now with strong walls and a healthy garrison, it was the strongest city in the whole of the Kingdom.

We had seen changes too. William was courting the daughter of one of the knights who now served The Jarl Birger Brosa. Margarite was younger than William but they seemed well suited. We were just waiting for an opportunity to knight my squire. William had money. We all did. Our raids and attacks on the Karelians and Estonians over the years had yielded more than one might have thought. All of my men had fine armour, helmets and weapons. Three of them had married local girls. All of us wished to return to England.

Skuld had produced a mare from Gonfanon. I had named her Skuldsdotter in the manner of the Swedes. It seemed to suit. Already as big as her mother, when full-grown she would be three hands taller and I would have a war horse I could use. Gonfanon had been busy. He would never ride to war again but his colts and fillies would. His offspring brought me more money than all of the raids and battles fought thus far.

We were in a state of limbo for we were waiting for news of the invasion of the eastern Baltic. Bishop Albert had an alliance with Philip of Swabia as well as the new Pope Innocent. Our religious leader had told me that when he had a church built there then my penance would be over. The winter had been a hard one. As we waited for the first ship to come from England I sat with my men at arms watching the young horses being schooled.

"This is a good country, lord, and I have enjoyed my time here but I long for an English winter. You know, lord, snow that lasts a month at most and rivers which rarely freeze."

I nodded, "I know what you mean, Edward."

Fótr had become as English as any of my men. "Aye lord and William wishes to be back in England so that he can be knighted, wed and lord of a manor."

My other men laughed at William's discomfort. William had grown considerably and he turned the conversation back to me, "And what of you lord? What of a bride for you?"

"You were lucky with Margarite. She is well suited to you. I will continue to look for one. In truth, I seek an English bride and they are rarer than hen's teeth in these parts."

"And this crusade lord, when do we leave?" David of Wales had never had as much coin and yet he too yearned for home.

"Bishop Albert has twenty-three ships ready to sail. When last I spoke with him he had more than six hundred crusaders ready to sail." I pointed to the snow which could still be seen in places. "I have never seen the land to which we sail but I have heard that the snow lies there longer. It will be summer when we sail. I fear that we will have a harsh winter of campaigning but as soon as a church has been built then we sail home with Bishop Albert's blessing."

Will son of Robin said, "And when I get home then I shall be married and have children. My father waited a long time." He waved an arm down his body, "And as you can see I was worth it!"

Jack son of Harold laughed, "Not from where I am looking. No, I will buy an inn and marry an ale wife. My father's dream was to be an innkeeper. I will fulfil his dream."

His words made my other men think of their own fathers. Most had come from Stockton. Their fathers had fought for my great grandfather and grandfather. They would never have thought that their families would be exiled from England. Surely King Richard would return soon and see the disaster that his young brother had wrought on the land.

I saw Lady Brigida and some of her ladies coming toward us. She was like my aunt. She surrounded herself with the widows of dead warriors. They were a convent without religious restrictions. She looked serious as she approached. I wondered if something had happened to her son. He was fighting for King Sverre, Lady Brigida's brother and the King of Norway. He was an earl and a doughty warrior. Inevitably that meant he would be in constant danger.

She smiled sadly, "I am here with news of your land. I would give it to Sir Thomas, alone, but I know that he is close to you all and he would tell you himself." She sighed, "King Richard has been killed in Normandy. He was struck by the bolt from a crossbow." I saw the look on my archers' faces. They hated all crossbows with a vengeance. This had just fuelled their hatred. "Prince John has been crowned king." She knew what that meant. I had no secrets from the jarl and his wife. "I am sorry, Sir Thomas. I fear you will be trapped here for a little while longer."

They left us and our faces were a sea of despair. Although King Richard had shown no sign of wishing to return home, while he had been alive it had been a hope. What use was the money, the horses and the armour if we had no home to return to? All of our dreams were gone. Our hopes were shattered. If we returned then we were outlaws and everyman's hand would be turned against us.

I was their leader and it was time that I acted as one. I stood, "William, marry Margarite. I will speak with Jarl Birger Persson. I will see if we cannot get you a manor here. Will, son of Robin, the rest of you, do not wait to take a wife who is English. There are comely lasses here who would take any one of you as a husband. You speak their language. I say this for when we sail to war we all know that not all of us may return."

Edward stood. He was the unofficial leader of the men. It had been David of Wales who still led the archers but even David deferred to Edward. "His lordship is right but I say that we make a covenant this day. If any of us fall in battle then their goods and coin are divided between the ones who are unmarried."

Jack son of Harold said, "No, Edward for those who are married need their families caring for. The coin and the goods of those who fall will be shared by all of the survivors equally; including the families. His lordship is right. Gertha, who serves ale by the port, has flashed her eyes at me often enough. I would marry her if she will have me." He shrugged, "Perhaps someone will tire of the new king and kill him. He has enemies enough but I would live and not wait for a life."

"What say you Edward son of Edgar?"

"I like the proposal."

Fótr said, "Would you like me to draw up an agreement for you to sign?"

Jack son of Harold shook his head, "We are brothers in arms. We are like our lord. None of us would be foresworn. If we swear it then it will be so. We need no cleric to scratch marks on a piece of parchment. Let us do so now. Will is right. Today we begin to live. We waited long enough for a king who disappointed us."

And so they swore. A month later, as we were preparing our equipment, for the fleet had arrived, Henry sailed in from England. We almost did not recognise him for he had a new ship. At its prow was a swan and I saw after she had tied up, her name, '*Swan of Stockton*'. He had a letter for me. I handed him mine.

"I see you have a new ship."

He nodded, "Aye lord. I have made much in this trade and the old one had the worm."

"A little like England then. A pity we cannot build a new king as easily as a ship!"

He said, "I take it, Sir Thomas, that you have heard the news?"

"King John?" He nodded. "I have. What is the mood in England?"

"There is talk of rebellion. However, the king is clever. He has the land preparing for war in Normandy. He talks of it as a crusade to recover the lands stolen by the King of France. The Earl of Pembroke is seen as the only hope for England."

"What of Arthur, Geoffrey of Anjou's son?"

"He is backed by the King of France, Phillip. It is he who leads the rebellion in Normandy and Anjou."

I knew that my grandfather had never been happy with the actions of Geoffrey of Anjou. Now that brother was, once again, dividing England.

"Thank you, Henry. We sail on crusade. It may be some time before I see you again."

"Will you not return home, lord? There are many in the north who would support you if you fought King John."

"And who would we put on the throne? I would not and could not support Arthur. I am afraid that, until God shows me the way, I will have to stay here and serve him and my men."

I went somewhere quiet to read the letter from home.

You know who you are and I hope you know that I think of you every day! Each night you are in my prayers.

I am afraid that the first news I must deliver is not the best. King Richard is dead and King John is now ruling our land. We hear that there has been an outbreak in banditry close to the castles of Bolsover and Nottingham. Some knights have left England to join with the Duke of Brittany. The country is split and divided once more. I am pleased that you are not here for I fear your life would be at risk. However, I do miss you. I wonder if I will ever see you again.

There is hope for my benefactor feared for my safety. He has friends further south and he discovered that King John knows that I am alive. I did not think that he would dare to harm a lady and the widow of a knight but my benefactor decided not to take that chance. We were married in the church in Stockton. I now live in a fine hall. It feels strange to see the castle without a gatehouse, walls and towers. The castle I knew as a child felt more protective than this. It feels exposed, as though we are naked.

There is another reason he brought me here. The Scots are using the discord in England to raid along the border. Billingham, Cowpen and Newton were all raided. Cattle were stolen and folk taken. My father and his father would be appalled. We need a knight who can protect the people. My benefactor would but he has so little coin; the new Bishop of Durham is just as greedy as de Puiset.

Take care but do not even think of returning home. You do have friends. I will not name them lest this letter falls into the wrong hands.

xxx

I read it a number of times. Perhaps this was as close to home as I would be getting for some time. I was pleased that Sir Richard had married her. I wondered at the amount of information she had put in the letter. King John was unpleasant and he was sly but he was no fool. He would have been able to work out that she was in touch with me if the letter had not reached me. I was pleased that I had added a post script to my own letter telling her that I would not be able to write for some time.

We threw ourselves into the business of preparing for war. Skuldsdotter was not ready for war. She would stay in the stables. For Skuld, this might be her last war. She was getting old. We now had chests that contained our weapons and our surcoats. We had a new banner, sewn by Lady Brigida and blessed by Bishop Albert himself. We were able to be selective about what we took. We did not skimp on furs and cold weather war gear. We were veterans now. Hugh of Bath had a mark on his face where he had been frostbitten. Henry Youngblood had lost his little finger in the same bad winter.

I sought Lady Brigida on the day before we sailed. The horses and chests were being loaded. I took Edward with me.

"My lady we have a boon to ask."

She smiled, "You know that we will refuse you nothing. You came here at our darkest time and you have never forsaken us. Others promised much but did not deliver what they said. Ask."

"My men and I have chests with our treasure. It seems foolish to take it with us. We would leave it here." She nodded. "When we return we will divide it up between the survivors."

She looked surprised, "You all agreed to this?"

I smiled, "It was Edward's idea. We all agreed."

She paused, "And if God forbid, you all perish what then?"

"Then the money is divided up between the families of Hugh of Bath, Henry Youngblood, Rafe son of Roger, Gertha, the servant and Lady Margarite."

"The last two are not married to your men, are they?"

"No, but both have an arrangement. My men would see it honoured. It will be something to remember William and Will son of Harold."

"I think your band are the most suited and qualified to take part in a crusade, for your hearts are true. Go with God."

The ships were more crowded than we would have liked. We had one which we shared with Jarl Birger Persson. Fortunately, our men got on and they made the best of it. As things turned out the distance was not great. Jarl Birger Persson estimated it to be no more than one hundred and eighty miles. We would be landing at the mouth of the River Daugava. The Vikings had used it. There was a port there and we would be able to land our men. We had been selected as part of the first five hundred men to land there. Our task was to hold the town and clear any danger away from the area to allow others to land. More crusaders were gathering and they would be sent for if they were needed.

In the end, the journey took just over a day for the winds were with us. What the people who lived at the mouth of the Daugava thought I have no idea but most fled upstream as soon as they spied our mighty fleet. We rested rather than slept on the voyage for the ship was too crowded for comfort. Jarl Birger Persson told me about the area and it became clear why Bishop Albert had chosen it.

"Vikings have used the river since, well since before Folki the Fat. When this river ends there is a ridge they hauled their ships over and then they could sail down the Volga river. Eventually, they reached the city we called, Miklagård."

"Constantinople."

"Exactly. If we can make it Christian and establish trading links then there will be a direct link across the Baltic. That link will extend to the Empire. Our waters will be safe and our people more prosperous. God will win. Bishop Albert is a clever man."

We arrived at the mouth of the river. There was a fort there but it was made of wood. Those who had lived within fled at the sight of the fleet. The ships pulled into the wooden quay. We all had our shields ready in case we received a flurry of arrows but there was nothing. Bishop Albert had twenty knights who bore his emblem and had sergeants. They were fanatical zealots and they raced ashore followed by Brother Magnus and Brother Harald with the holy banner. It was something of an anti-climax. All that they found were the very old and the very young: the ones unable to flee. They advanced towards the fort and confirmed it was also abandoned. I was quite happy. We had time to take the horses from the ships. We had somewhere safe to sleep and we had food. I took it as a sign that God was with us.

We stayed in the port while the Livonian Brothers of the Sword took up residence in the fort. Bishop Albert took great delight in baptising the old and the young who remained. I saw, in their eyes, that they were being pragmatic. They wished to avoid death!

Our horses had not been on the ship long enough for them to have suffered. Nonetheless, we made sure that they were exercised, watered and fed before night fell.

Bishop Albert was leading this crusade. He was no fool. He called together the senior knights and he included me in that number. "God has shown us that this land is ours for the taking. This is Mary's Land, as the Pope has told us. Tomorrow I will send out my Livonian Brothers of the Sword and they will find our foes. We have but begun to make this land of heathens Christian."

I was not convinced. I had seen many heathens pay lip service to priests. I had watched as they feigned conversion. So long as they kept their amulets around their necks then they were pagans and I, for one, would not trust them. It took four days for the knights of the Holy Order to find the enemy. They were twenty miles south of us. It seems their leader, we knew not his title, Ylle, had sent far and wide for warriors to fight us. We gave him the title of king for that seemed easiest. The knights told us that there were ten thousand men heading for us. I did not believe them. I said so when we held our counsel of war but I was overruled. I realised that for most of the men with whom I fought, I was a mercenary. I was a sword for hire. They thought because they followed the cross, that they were, somehow, better than me and my men. It was at that meeting that I made the decision to return home. If I had neither honour nor standing then what was I doing here? Better to join the men of the forests close to Bolsover and fight King John. First, I had to make sure that Bishop Albert could build his church in this land.

Leaving enough men to guard the fort, port and ships, we set off south to meet the enemy. Bishop Albert came with us. I did not like the fact that we had no one with a military mind who was making these decisions. Bishop Albert was a good man but he knew nothing of tactics. As we headed south, along the river I kept my men together.

"What is wrong, lord?"

"We have ships. We should be sailing them up the river to give us support. The further south we go then the further we are from food and the shelter of the fort. I do not believe the numbers the knights of the Holy Orders have given but I do believe that we will be outnumbered."

I feared another Hattin. We kept in a tight column. We had few scouts out and no lighter troops. More than half of our number were horsemen. There were knights, men and sergeants at arms. But we also had two hundred and twenty men on foot. Many were archers. Mine were the only mounted ones in the whole army. When we camped, close by the river, I made sure that my archers protected my camp.

Jarl Birger Persson and The Jarl Birger Brosa camped on either side of me. I took it as a compliment that they thought I knew what I was doing. I made sure that we kept a good watch. The next morning, we discovered that four of the knights of the Livonian Brothers of the Sword had been slain. Their throats had been cut. Worse, ten warhorses had been driven off. It felt like a defeat. Sadly, the knights of the Holy Order became angry and I feared for their reaction when we fought. You needed a cool head to defeat barbarians. They fought with their hearts.

Sword For Hire

The next day we headed south. This time the scouts did their job. The enemy had formed up two miles away with their flank on the river. The other flank was protected by a forest. Their leader knew his business. We did not have enough light troops to flank them. That left only one option; a direct charge. We had been told that they had archers and they would make a killing ground of the space before them. They had few horsemen and even fewer mailed men, but they had over two thousand men. We had less than four hundred and forty. It was not yet noon. We would have to fight them or risk a knife in the night and more valuable war horses being taken.

The more dangerous flank was our left and the woods. Even as we gathered to hear Bishop Albert's dispositions I knew that our task would be to guard the left flank. Bishop Albert used every inflexion and invective to exhort us to win. He sought to make us believe that we could defeat odds of four to one.

"Today we face a huge barbarian army but I am not afeard. They are Godless and we have God on our side. The Pope, Christ's representative on this earth, has sanctioned our actions. If any are to die today, then they are guaranteed to sup with Christ in heaven." He looked at me, "No matter what sins they have committed." There was a huge cheer at that.

"We will have the Knights of the sword in the right by the river. In the centre will be The Jarl Birger Brosa and the warriors of Sweden and, on the left will be our stalwart crusader, Thomas of Stockton. The enemy think we fear their numbers; we do not. Brother Magnus and Brother Harald will take the holy banner with The Jarl Birger Brosa. They will break the enemy line!"

There were even more cheers. That was when I wished that my men did not have the language. Jack son of Harold shook his head, "Bleeding death sentence. Those woods will be packed with hairy arsed barbarians who are keen to get my bollocks!"

Will son of Robin shouted, "If they are the same size as your dick you are safe. They will never find them!"

My men were in good mood. However, Jack was right. There would be enemies waiting for us. When we reached our starting positions, I turned Skuld and faced them. "I take it as an honour that we have been chosen. Look down the line. Are there any with our experience? The answer is no. The only men who could do what we have been asked are us!"

Alf Smithson shouted, "Bloody right too, my lord!"

The rest all laughed. "David of Wales you and our archers will leave your horses at the edge of the woods. You will hunt our foes and you will slay them. The rest of us will dismount and ready our shields for the attack of the barbarians. We will not risk our horses."

Fótr said, "But Bishop Albert wants an attack all the way down the line."

William said, quietly, "And if we do so then the enemy will fall upon our flanks. We will die."

"We will mount and we will charge but we do so when our flank is secure. Obey me. I want no heroes!"

Rafe shouted, "Never fear, lord, you will get none!"

They all laughed.

While the rest rode their horses to the start line we walked ours. I ignored the strange looks from the men of Jarl Birger Persson. They knew our reputation. They could not understand why we did what we did.

We had four servants now. They had hide jerkins and short swords. We left them guarding the horses as my archers slipped silently into the forest. I shouted, "Shield wall!"

We stood in a single line with spears braced and shields held close to us. We were level with Jarl Birger Persson. The horn signalled the charge and over two hundred knights and sergeants galloped to strike at the Estonians. The two hundred men on foot waited with shields at the ready and spears braced. They were in two lines.

For the first few moments of the battle, we had a good view and were able to watch. The knights kept a good line. The sergeants behind were a little ragged but they were doing their best. When the arrows fell then the horses and the men began to fall. We were forced to turn and to look to our left. We heard men dying in the forest. Our archers were good. They had lived over here for enough years to know the woods and forests. The Estonians had thought to use the woods to gain an advantage. When it became clear that they had not done so then their right flank began to advance. Over two hundred men advanced towards us. The rest of our army was engaged and this force of two hundred men could sweep through us and fall on the flanks of Jarl Birger Persson. Any sane man would have fled but my men were not sane. They believed in me.

"Brace and trust to the man on your right!"

"Aye, lord!"

David and my archers had cleared the ambush and, as the barbarians ran at us the arrows fell from the forest. They fell not upon us but the Estonians. They had not expected this. Every arrow found flesh. The Estonian right slowed. They turned their shields to the arrows. When they hit us, they would be an oblique line and their right flank would be threatened. As they struck us they would be looking over their right shoulders and seeking the arrows that would bring death. The Estonians were wild warriors. They fought in clans and they fought for the men in their villages. They sought glory by being the first to reach our line. They struck us piecemeal. It was like the battle of Kastelholm all over again.

The first four warriors ran into our spears. They looked for our faces and not our spears. I flicked my spear to the side to discard the body and awaited the next one. A warrior had to focus on his own battle. He had to trust to his comrades to do as he was doing. A glance to the side could bring disaster. The body dropped off. I saw the next warrior run at me. I knew what he would do. He used the body of the dead man as a springboard. He leapt up into the air with an axe held above his head in two hands. I lifted my spear and his chest struck the spear. It went through his body and, as it struck his spine, it snapped. I drew my sword.

The Estonians would soon have the weight of numbers on their side. We would be locked together; shield to shield. I took the opportunity to slip my dagger into my left hand. The next thirty warriors hit us together. A spear struck my helmet. I had seen it coming and lowered my head. The spear slid over the top. I stabbed blindly and was rewarded with a scream as it slid into flesh. I pulled back and lifted my head, the dying warrior slipped to the ground. My sword was held before me still and I took a chance. I swung it to the right and down. I felt it strike something and I pulled my sword towards me. It ripped across the throat of the warrior fighting William. I was aware that while those on my right were being forced back the ones to my left were not. David and his archers were eating into the enemy flank.

I shouted, "Hold them! Hold them!"

My men on the right took heart. I lowered my sword and thrust up and under the shield of the man whose axe smashed into my shield. His face thought he had the better of me but as I found flesh, pushed and twisted, his eyes rolled in agony. The sword had ripped through his groin and he sought to escape the pain. He could not. The fact there were six bodies before me, made the next warriors hesitate. In a battle, hesitation can be disastrous. I stepped forward and brought my sword down on the next Estonian who was advancing too cautiously. I hit his leather cap and smashed my blade into his skull. He fell back and I took another step. I was now fighting men who thought they had time to measure their blow, to time their attack and to find a weak spot. They found death! The archers had cleared the woods and now they had thinned those on the far right of the Estonian line. There had been two hundred men charging us and now less than eighty remained. They ran.

Now was our chance. "To your horses!"

As I turned I saw that Rafe, son of Roger had left a widow. He was dead. I was angry. As I mounted Skuld I said, "Fetch Rafe's body here and make sure he is not further harmed."

"Aye lord."

I picked up another spear and rode back to our starting line. I surveyed the battle. The two jarls and their men had held the enemy but the knights of the Holy Order, closer to the river, were being forced back. The ground was muddier there and their horses did not have firm ground on which to gallop. I saw that some Estonians had swum the river and were sending arrows into the flanks of the knights. They did not hurt the knights but slew their horses.

I pointed to the standard of the Estonians. It was a hundred and eighty paces from us. Their attention was on the knights of the Holy Order. They looked to have just half a dozen horses tethered there. It was a small piece of slightly higher ground. It looked like a rocky pimple but it afforded a fine view across the battlefield. I counted eight banners including the battle flag of their king. The clan banners were adorned with skulls and bones. There were seven clans in this warband.

"There is our target! We take the banner. David, follow us and give us cover!"

"Aye, lord!"

It was a risk but it seemed to me that it was our only choice. The men who had attacked us had fled and left a gap. We simply followed them. The Estonians gathered around their banners and their lords had their attention on the river where the swampy ground had allowed their men to push back the knights of the Holy Order. The enemy lords were ignoring the two jarls for they knew that once they had broken the knights they could roll up the line.

When we were eighty paces from them I spurred Skuld and lowered my spear. We were seen and pandemonium ensued. The lords and their king had bodyguards. Each set of bodyguards protected their own. That was a mistake. Some had but two body guards. If they had banded together then they might have held my line. Fótr and William had now become as skilled as any knight and the three of us, in the centre of my line, would punch a hole through their centre. The Estonians sounded their horns. They were recalling their clans to defend their chiefs.

The bodyguards wore no mail. The chiefs had helmets and mail byrnies. I aimed my spear at the broad, bearded warrior with tattoos. He held a long, curved sword. His shield was a large round one. I had seen one in Stockton. They were the type of shields used by the Varangians. Studded with metal they would blunt a blade and resist the blow of an axe. I lowered my spear when I was twenty paces from the man and he mirrored me with his shield. I spurred Skuld and lifted the tip. I was too close for him to react and my spear rammed deep into his tattooed chest. He was a tough man and he wrenched the spear from my grip as he fell dying, to the ground. I let it go and drew my sword. I saw bodyguards falling to arrows. David and his men were being selective. They dared not risk a volley for fear of hitting us. Instead, they used the gaps between my men to kill our enemies. The lord behind the warrior I had killed had thought his bodyguards would protect him and he was slow to react. I swung my sword sideways and bit through his mail and into his neck.

Fótr and William had enlarged the hole which I had made. Edward and Robert of La Flèche also had driven deep into the pockets of bodyguards. I spied the king and his bodyguards grabbing the six horses which remained and they ran. I spurred Skuld but she was tiring. I saw that they would not be caught. I whipped Skuld's head around and rode to the battle standard. Swinging my sword, I hacked through the staff. It fell to the ground. I then continued my turn and rode, with Fótr and William, to attack the rear of the men fighting my men at arms. The first three we slew knew nothing about it. They were busy fighting Henry and Hugh. Leaning from the saddle I brought my sword across the mailed back of one of their chiefs. My blade broke the mail, his flesh and his spine.

And then there were none left alive on the small pimple of land. We had won. We had not escaped unscathed. I saw Ridley the Giant cradling Walther son of Wilson. He had been gutted by one of the curved blades.

"Form a defensive position!"

David shouted to his men to mount. They galloped over to us and threw themselves from their horses, tying their horses to the banners. We dismounted and held our weapons ready to fend off the barbarians who streamed up the slope to us. I heard The Jarl Birger Brosa's horn and saw a line of horsemen charging across the field to get at the Estonians. It was an uneven race. The horses gained with every stride they took. When they hit the mob of wild men it was as though a farmer had taken a scythe to reap wheat. They fell, not in ones and twos but in their tens and twenties. Those who were not stabbed, speared or slashed were crushed by hooves.

The Estonians veered away from the small rise and took the easier course down towards the river. The two jarls hurtled after them. They were in full cry. They could win the war in this single charge. Edward asked, "Do we follow them, lord?"

I shook my head. "We have their banners and their dead lords. We hold these for Bishop Albert." I smiled, "But you may search the dead and reap the reward for being the finest of horsemen. We may be exiled from our home but today we showed the rest what a handful of men from Stockton can do!"

Chapter 15

Bishop Albert, his bodyguards and the two brothers made their way across the body littered field to us. The battle by the river still raged although the Holy Order had triumphed. The Estonians were trying to flee across the river. Our foot had joined us and archers were reaping a bloody harvest. Bishop Albert beamed, "Sir Thomas, today you have atoned for any sin you might have committed in the past. God truly smiles upon you for you have laid low the leaders of these heathens."

I smiled my thanks, "I am just sorry that their king escaped."

He shook his head, "That is no matter. Today we have broken their grip on this river and we can begin to build." He turned to the two brothers, "Gather the standards from their staffs, we will take them back to our camp. They are a symbol of our victory."

William came to me, "There is an irony here, lord. We are now absolved and can return home yet we have no home to which we can return. We are stuck here."

"Perhaps, William, the Lord has not yet forgiven me and there are other tasks I must perform." I saw that Ridley still cradled the body of his friend. "Come we will bury Walther here. Edward, take the broken staff from the king's standard. Fashion it into a cross. Fetch the body of Rafe, we shall bury them together."

We buried Walther and Rafe on the small mound which overlooked the river. We buried them in their mail with helmets and swords. Walter's surcoat and cloak covered the terrible wound which had killed him. Rafe was given Jack son of Harold's surcoat for his was bloody and torn. We lined the grave with the shields of the dead Estonians and laid his shield over his face. After covering the bodies with soil Edward planted the cross. There was no name but this was the only Christian burial on that field. They were a symbol. They had died far from their homes but, as we stood around the grave and spoke of their lives then it was as though we were in the Tees Valley.

"We say farewell to our friend, Walther son of Wilson, and Rafe son of Roger. Loyal to the end they died as warriors should, facing foes and fighting until they were slain. We will remember them. When we return to Stockton we will tell those who knew them of their courage and how, on this holy crusade, they helped to defeat the heathen."

Sword For Hire

We raised our swords and as one shouted, "Walther son of Wilson! Rafe son of Roger!"

Perhaps I imagined it but I saw a pair of hawks rise from the woods to the north of us. They spiralled up into the air and seemed to hover above us. I was not the only one to see it. Edward, son of Edgar said, "My father would have said that Walther and Rafe's spirits were in those hawks, lord. Not a Christian thing to think but I take comfort from that. If I died I should like to be a bird flying on the air. The Bible and the priests can't explain everything, can they lord?"

"No, Edward, they cannot. Come let us follow Bishop Albert to our camp."

My men's saddlebags were filled with that which they had collected. The Estonians were barbarians but they liked their gold and their silver. Rings, torcs, necklaces and battle bands had been taken from their dead. Their lords had had jewels. They were now in our possession. As we headed back an idea began to form in my mind. We were swords for hire. There would be others. If we had enough coin and treasure we could buy an army. Perhaps we could wrest the crown from King John's slimy grip. Just as suddenly as it had come the idea evaporated like morning mist in the summer sun. Who would rule if we deposed John? I had an idea but it was not a solution.

We camped at our starting point for the battle. Men and horses were weary. The river was filled with Estonian bodies floating to the sea and the battlefield was littered with the dead of both sides. Bishop Albert had our dead collected and they were buried close by the river. I wondered at that. When the river flooded the soil would be washed from the bones and exposed. It was the Swedish dead we buried. Our two dead men lay on high ground.

Petr and the jarls had survived the battle. We camped together. Our men were comrades and they spoke of the dead as we ate our rations. The dried food was augmented by the horses killed in the battle. We had not lost any but the Knights of the Holy Order had. They did not wish to eat their mounts. We did not mind.

"We thought you had gone mad, Thomas, when you dismounted."

"The trees which were close by were too much of a temptation for our enemies. I wished to retain our horses." I smiled, "And I trusted to David of Wales and my archers. If the trees were a threat to us then if I held them they were a threat to the enemy. So it proved. Besides, as you know Jarl Birger Persson, a good shield wall can defeat a rabble every time. You just need discipline."

"I had expected more of Bishop Albert's knights."

I looked over to where they were knelt, in their camp, praying before Bishop Albert, the brothers and the standard. "They will learn but they need a leader. We saw that, Birger, in the Holy Land. The knights today lacked order. They did not fight as one but they will learn. They will have to for I do not think they will be so lucky the next time."

The Jarl Birger Brosa's squire, Sverre, asked, "Is it not over, lord? We slew many of their men."

I looked at The Jarl Birger Brosa, "You know the Estonians. Do they have more than seven clans? That is all that we fought today."

"You are right Thomas. There are many more clans. The next time their king, Ylle, will not underestimate us. He will have seen our numbers and thought he had enough to defeat us. He has now seen our horses. He knows what knights can do. However, it will take him time to gather them. We will have one more battle before we return home for the winter."

Sverre asked, "But we have only just got here. Will we not stay until the job is done?"

"We have little shelter here and our horses need fodder and grazing. Some may stay but not all. We will see what Bishop Albert says."

The next day we headed back to the fleet. Bishop Albert ordered the Estonian fort to be burned and the houses of the town torn down. He left the warehouses which lined the river. He intended to make Riga a centre of trade. He thought that merchants would hire men to protect their goods. "We will build a city here. Riga is a good enough name to retain. The men who will man the castle I shall build will be the knights of my order. The name they have used hitherto is a propitious one. They shall be known throughout Christendom as the Livonian Brothers of the Sword!"

While the men at arms obeyed his orders, Bishop Albert approached the three of us. "You three have ever been at the forefront of our fight against the heathen and yet you are not members of the order."

I remembered that, in the Holy Land, Birger had spoken of joining the order. He had obviously changed his mind but I knew not why. We looked at each other. There had been an implied question but we had all ignored it.

Bishop Albert sighed, "Let me speak plainly, I would have the three of you join my order. More than that I would have Sir Thomas of Stockton as the first Master of the order. You have atoned for your sin. You showed today that you are a master of tactics and a brave knight. Every knight would gladly follow you."

I was stunned at the offer. I knew, from the Templars and Hospitallers, that such a title brought with it immeasurable wealth and power. I could use the order to invade England and wrest the crown from John. I hesitated but a heartbeat, "I am flattered, your grace but I cannot accept. My fate is in England. I will fight for you. I will join with the Livonian Brothers of the Sword but I will not be deflected from my course."

He nodded, "You have ever been honest with me. And you?"

The Jarl Birger Brosa shook his head, "The Master will have to live here in the conquered lands and that is not for me."

Birger Persson said, "Nor for me. I thought when I was in the Holy Land that it was. When we built Kastelholm I saw that as a base for the order but since Petr has become a knight and has begun a family I yearn to be a father and a husband. Your Brothers of the Sword need to be dedicated to the order and I cannot do so."

Bishop Albert sighed, "I hoped that one of you would choose the way of the cross but it was not meant to be. I will speak with Hermann Balk. He fought well today and the other knights respect him." He stood and walked over to the knights.

After he had gone I laughed. "What is funny Sir Thomas?"

"It is just that I killed a bishop and yet another bishop begged me to lead knights on a holy crusade. Can you not see the irony, Petr?"

He smiled, "I can but although I never met this Hugh de Puiset you slew he must have deserved it for you are as noble and as true a knight as I have ever met."

Bishop Albert began his mission with the building of a church. As The Jarl Birger Brosa commented, "A wall to keep out the barbarians might have been a better idea!"

Although we had less than five hundred men, our zealous leader insisted upon us riding each day to watch for danger and to explore the land. The warriors on foot were left to build the church and, somewhat belatedly, dig the ditch and begin the building of the walls. His new master, Hermann Balk, showed that he was no fool by insisting that they had a castle built at the same time as the church. I did not envy him wintering in such a hostile environment.

As I was preparing my men to ride he came over to me. "Bishop Albert said that you were offered master first and you refused. For that I am grateful but I want you to know that if you had been master then I would have gladly followed you. I heard how you captured the standards and slew the chiefs. Like me you are young but I can see that you have both skill and experience. If you ever see me doing something which is foolish then I beg you to tell me."

"I will and I think that you are right to have your castle built sooner rather than later. I do not think that the crusade will be over any time soon."

We were given the task of riding along the coast. Mordaf and Gruffyd, the twin sons of Tomas, had proved to be our best scouts. The fact that they were twins seemed to help them understand each other without words. Silence was a prerequisite for a scout. They rode ahead of us. A few miles north of our base we found another river. The locals had names for them but we did not. There was no bridge and rather than risking losing horses we followed it as it wound eastwards. We were about to turn back, for it was already past noon when Mordaf returned to us. "Sir Thomas, I have found a bridge but there is a small fort there. They have a wall."

"Then let us scout in force."

149

We followed the path which ran along the river until we reached Gruffyd. He was hiding beneath the trees which lined the river. "It is just a thousand paces yonder, lord. You can see the wooden bridge."

"I think we will test them. Have your weapons ready. David of Wales, when we halt have your men dismount and ready their bows."

"Lord."

I donned my helmet and said, "Fótr, unfurl the banner."

As we climbed the bank and emerged from the shelter of the trees we were seen. I had intended this to happen. They had a watch of sorts. There were people tending fields. Others were herding animals. I saw men at the fish nets in the river. As soon as we were seen a horn sounded and everyone fled within the walls. They abandoned tools and animals. We moved to within four hundred paces and then I stopped as a few arrows were sent in our direction. These were not the bows that had been used against us at Kastelholm. These arrows fell woefully short. I saw one, just thirty paces from us. That was the closest they came to hitting us.

"Edward, take four men and drive a few of those cattle and animals over here. Let us see what they do. David of Wales, have your archers ready."

The cattle were not as big as the ones we had at home and were grazing with goats and sheep. They were over three hundred paces from the walls of the settlement. Would they try to stop us from taking them? I was testing their defences and, more importantly, their reaction. Edward and his men began to nudge the animals towards us. It evoked a flurry of arrows. None of them came close. There were shouts from the walls and then the gates opened and thirty or forty men raced out towards us.

I raised my arm and, when the band was a hundred and fifty paces from us, dropped it. Eight arrows soared followed by another eight and another eight. My archers' arrows hit raised shields and flesh. I saw one man struck in the head. He lay prone. The others who were struck, six of them, were just wounded. When Edward reached us I shouted, "Save your arrows." The Estonians had stopped. A fifth or more of their men had been hit and they saw my knights, mailed and helmeted, waiting. They let us take their animals.

We drove the animals back to Riga. The journey back was quicker for we were travelling across country and going the shortest route. We passed a small lake not far from Riga. I had not spotted it before. We rode close to it and I saw that it teemed with fish. The Livonian Brothers of the Sword would have a good supply of fish close to hand. The forests lay some way inland. Hunting was a more dangerous occupation than catching fish from a lake.

While my men took the animals to be penned I rode to Bishop Albert who was in deep discussion with the master. I saw that they had foundations dug for the church and that it was going to be of stone and wood construction. Bishop Albert was making a statement.

I pointed behind me to the animals. "There is another river to the north of us. A settlement guards the bridge. If we held it then this town would be easier to defend. When we leave in the autumn then the Estonians could use it to attack."

Hermann nodded, "Could we take it?"

"Easily. They have a wooden wall but I do not think they have sufficient warriors to threaten us but it is a different clan to the ones we fought. We bloodied their nose today. Perhaps if you spoke with them Bishop Albert then they might decide to become allies and convert. If they did not fight with their king there must be a reason."

Hermann nodded his agreement. "It is worth a try, my lord. We can take Sir Thomas' men and my knights. That would be a sufficient force to cow them."

"And bring the captured banners with us."

The Livonian Brothers of the Sword numbered forty knights and twenty mounted sergeants. They would be the ones who would winter in Riga. I could understand why he wished to have allies rather than enemies.

We slaughtered a couple of the older beasts we had found. Ridley the Giant was pleased. He liked his meat, "I could get used to this lord. Meat every day! Was it like this in the Holy Land when you and Master William were there?"

William laughed, "They eat a lot of chicken and grain. Sometimes we played hunt the flesh in the grain. We were not well-fed Ridley."

Bishop Albert took his banner and his priests with us the next day. They all rode the sumpters. Most were poor riders and clung to the backs of their beasts. It made my men smile. We were spotted as we approached. They must have had sentries. The result was that the animals had been driven inside by the time we reached the settlement and the walls were manned. I joined Bishop Albert and the Master.

"I see what you mean, Sir Thomas. This could be used to attack us while we wintered. If this was in our hands then twenty or so sergeants and brothers could hold it."

I nodded and said, "Would you be willing to risk something, Master?"

"Of course. I told you that I am happy to take your advice."

"Do any of your men speak their language? I have a few words but, for what we have in mind, I need precision."

"Goswin von Spanheim does. His lands bordered Estonia until his family were slaughtered. That is why he follows the cross."

"Then I would have the three of us ride, mailed and with helmets to within bow range. Let us try to speak with them."

"That is a risk."

"To our horses, yes, to us? I think not. As I said we throw the bones and see how they fall. If you are worried about your war horse then ride one of the sumpters."

151

In the end, he and Goswin chose to ride the two largest sumpters. I had a feeling that Skuld would be safe. We rode towards the walls. It was nerve-wracking. Had I thought that the Estonians would have understood or accepted the convention of riding bare headed and with open palms then I would have done so. This was all that I could think of.

This time they did not waste their arrows. They waited until we were a hundred paces from the walls. I had intended to stop there in any case. They unleashed a volley of arrows at us. They aimed them at us rather than our horses. Perhaps they thought the horses too valuable. If they killed us then they could take the horses. I raised my shield and four hit it. One stuck in my cantle. Another struck the mask on my helmet. The head barely came through but it struck there. Another hit my shoulder but my mail held it. I looked to my left. The other two had been similarly struck.

"You are a madman Sir Thomas but I see a method in your madness. How did you know that we would be safe?"

"I saw, yesterday, that they used hunting arrows with barbs. The barbs are made of bone. I have yet to hear of a bone headed arrow penetrating mail. When they stop have Sir Goswin ask for their surrender."

The arrows soon stopped. They were not hurting us. One had nicked Skuld when it hit her leg and she whinnied but she did not appear hurt. I risked taking off my helmet. I contemptuously pulled the arrow from my face mask, spat upon it, broke it in two and threw it to the ground. The other two, seeing my actions did the same.

Sir Goswin shouted. There was a reply. "They say why should they surrender? Their walls are strong."

"Tell them that just as our God protects us from their arrows so he will smite their walls and break them asunder. Tell him that we have defeated their king and the other clans." I had the banners behind me and, as Sir Goswin translated my words I threw the banners, one by one to the ground.

This time, after Sir Goswin's words, there was no reply but I could see hurried conference. After what seemed like an age one of the older men shouted something. Sir Goswin was grinning from ear to ear as he said, "They have agreed. They are surrendering. Our God must be stronger than theirs, they say."

Hermann Balk said, "Remind me never to fight you, Sir Thomas."

Bishop Albert was quick-witted. When we told him how we had affected the surrender he played it up when he and the priests were allowed in. He warned them that our God was far more powerful than theirs. We made sure that we had plenty of armed warriors in case of treachery but our little act had planted the seeds of doubt about their gods. Leaving the two brothers and twenty sergeants under the command of Goswin von Spanheim to manage the bridge and the settlement, we returned to Riga.

Bishop Albert was ebullient. He could not shut up all the way back. "We have our first converts! I can see that there are hidden depths to you, Master, and you Sir Thomas! God has sent you both to me."

I did not like to disillusion him but that trick would only work once. Had they been iron tipped arrows then it would have been a different story. That evening I dined with the master and the two jarls. We had taken over one of the warehouses. Birger Persson complained, "He could have left the houses up! I know he wished to let the Estonians know that we brought change but a little comfort is not too much to ask!"

Hermann said, "Bishop Albert has great plans. Sometimes you have to be dramatic." Birger nodded. The warehouse was cool and it was insect free. The fire we had built just outside the entrance saw to that. The river attracted biting insects which were huge.

Birger Persson's men had slaughtered some sheep that they had discovered grazing close by and we ate well.

Hermann said, "That was clever, using the banners. It gave the impression that we had taken their king."

"I know the effect a banner can have. My great grandfather fought in England at a battle led by an Archbishop. It is now called the Battle of the Standards for men defended the holy standards and those of their lords against the Scots. It was a complete victory. If you do not learn from the past then you will never progress."

Birger laughed, "I served with this warrior in the Holy Land. He is a deep one. He thinks!"

Three days later our ships returned. Following the conversion of the small town which we had discovered was called Ādaži, Bishop Albert had sent three quarters of the ships back for more men. He was keen to exploit our success and it would be not only warriors who would be coming but more priests and merchants. We had driven out the Estonians and Bishop Albert intended to replace them with Swedes and Danes. When they arrived, three days later, I felt happier for we now had eight hundred men. Only two hundred were mounted but I hoped that would be enough

We spent a week making short forays into the countryside. It was some of the Livonian Brothers of the Sword who spotted the approach of the Estonian army. I had wondered how long it would take for the king to gather all of the forces at his disposal. They were coming to drive us from their land. The wisdom of securing our base was now obvious. We had a ditch and a wooden wall around Riga. We had a fleet of ships and we intended to use them to attack the Estonians from the river, using archers.

The scouts gave us a day's warning of their attack and that was ample. Stakes were driven into the ground before the men who would fight on foot. The knights and mounted sergeants were in two blocks. One was led by Hermann Balk and consisted of the Livonian Brothers of the Sword. The other was led by The Jarl Birger Brosa and was made up of the rest of our knights and mounted men. The archers were arrayed in the ships. I felt it was a mistake for they could only attack from the river. It left the Estonians with the opportunity to put more men against our left flank. That was where we stood beneath the gryphon banners.

We had our two wings of horsemen on the slightly higher ground. For that I was grateful. We would have the slope with us. The enemy had shown no subtlety. They had almost three thousand men in ten lines. The centre of the front rank was made up of their lords. They had mail. They had helmets with mail coifs. They had spears and they had shields. The rest of their front rank was made up of men with spears, helmets and shields. The ones behind were the wild barbarians. They had a variety of weapons. They had helmets which ranged from leather skull caps to helmets with nasals. Some had shields with metal studs, others had simple willow boards. The most common weapon that I could see was an axe. Some were two handed Danish axes while the majority had a wood cutting axe. If the edge was sharp it would make no difference.

They had brought a drummer with them. He banged out the beat as they advanced. They chanted. The words were lost on us but they were deafening and they added to the fear of the approaching horde. My grandfather had told me how the housecarls of King Harold had chanted and sang as they marched. It had helped to keep the rhythm and it had bolstered their spirits. I could see the heads of some of the men, waiting to meet these barbarians, drop.

We could not learn a song that quickly and so I just began to bang my shield and shout, 'Albert!' The men around me took it up and soon it rippled and then echoed down our ranks. Heads that had drooped now rose. Fear is infectious; so is hope!

Bishop Albert was no coward. He and his priests stood with his banner behind the men on foot. I knew that they would not run. It was not in his nature. If our line of warriors on foot broke then they would fight to the death. I had brought the banner of King Ylle with me. Handing my spear to Fótr I took the standard from my saddlebag and galloped towards the advancing Estonians. Stopping a hundred paces from their front line I stood in my stirrups and, taking my dagger, ripped the banner in two. I spat upon it and then dropped it behind Skuld. Skuld was a clever horse. She had senses and skills which a witch would envy but I know not how she knew to do what I willed her to. She lifted her tail and dropped a pile of dung upon the banner. Our men roared and banged their shields so hard that I thought my ears would break. The Estonians forgot their drum. They ignored their orders. They lost their temper. They charged at me. Patting Skuld on the neck I galloped back to our lines.

The effect of my desecration of the standard was to draw every Estonian towards our left flank.

I reached the line and The Jarl Birger Brosa was laughing like a madman. "Sir Thomas each time I think that I know you, you surprise me! Men of the Gryphon! Charge!"

These were not our orders but they were the right ones. The Estonians had lost cohesion. By turning and charging at us they were coming up the hill. As I took my spear from Fótr, I spurred Skuld and we headed down the slope. I heard Hermann Balk roar, "Brothers of the Sword, charge!"

The Estonians were charging uphill and we were galloping down. The difference was that we were holding our line. They were a mob of barbarians intent upon getting to me and killing the man who had dishonoured their standard. I rested my spear on my cantle. I had time to choose my target. The Estonians were spreading out as they flooded up the hill. The younger, eager warriors forgot what their king had commanded. They sought glory. They ignored the energy-sapping slope up which they ran.

We kept a steady line. I was flanked by William and Fótr. There might have been a time when I would have been worried but no longer. Hermann Balk did not have such good warriors with him. I was aware that my feet were touching those of William and Fótr. When we met the Estonians, we would be a single, solid line.

I was the one they wanted to kill. Skuld was a devil they wished to destroy and so they came at me. The first warrior I slew was young. He must have been a good warrior for he had mail. He was fit and had outstripped the others. He had a war axe in his hand and he screamed. I guessed he was cursing me but I cared not. I moved my spear so that I held it halfway down its shaft. I moved it behind me. As I saw him swing I thrust forward with my spear. It smashed into his face. The spear head pulverised flesh, bone and brain. He seemed frozen and then he dropped like a stone. The weight of his body dragged it from my spear. Fótr and William had an easier task. The two men they slew were trying to get at me and did not even see the two spears which killed them.

There was a clash like thunder as our spears met their mail, their shields and their bodies. Spears have a longer range than swords and axes. Few had spears. These were the warriors who wore mail. A sword was seen as the weapon of a noble. They died. Horses were hurt. Warriors were wounded but it was the Estonians who died and as the ones with mail fell the others, the ones who followed without mail were like ripe plums, ready for the plucking.

The slope helped us. We did not need to ride fast. The Estonians were already beginning to become out of breath. Their king had known what he was doing. A steady march would have brought six hundred men to strike at our lines. His wild men had shattered that plan. He would be hoping now that the sheer weight of numbers would destroy us. I pulled my arm back and struck at the Estonian with a tree felling axe. My spear struck him above his breastbone. I felt it grate off the bone. I was already twisting the head to shake him from it when the next

155

barbarian appeared. I twisted my reins so that Skuld's head went to his right and his axe swing struck air. I could not bring around my spear quickly enough to spear him and as I smacked him hard across the face with the haft of my spear. He went down and William's horse pounded his face to a pulp.

Fótr's spear had broken and he was leaning out with his sword to take heads as he galloped through men without mail. I knew not how the battle went for The Jarl Birger Brosa or the Livonian Brothers of the Sword. I was in a battle that was as wide as my men and as deep as the enemy. I could not afford to glance to the side. I was the point of the sword and I had to drive as deep into the enemy lines as I could. Skuld was in her stride. She was not over stretching and I was not spurring her. At this speed, I could ride for miles.

Ahead of me, I heard horns. The King of the Estonians was reorganizing his men. I saw that the ones ahead of me no longer tried to get at me. They stood. They were trying to obey their king. The Battle of Arsuf had been decided because a band of knights ignored their orders and charged for the enemy. This was just such a moment. If I had reined in and led my men back then I would have been praised for my adherence to orders. I saw the chance to break the enemy once and for all. Ahead of me were warriors without mail. From the sunlight glinting on mail to my left and right I knew that this was not the case across the battlefield but here, before me, it was.

I stood in my stirrups and raised my spear, "Stockton, we ride to glory!"

I slowed Skuld down to allow Fótr and William to join me. My men at arms spurred their horses to form a solid line and we moved down the slope. The Estonians tried to make a shield wall to face our line. We, however, were still heading obliquely down the line. We were approaching from their sword side. We had few shields facing us. I hit the first warrior in the right shoulder and my spear went through his body. My spear broke. Even as I drew my sword Skuld had knocked over and trampled the next man in the line. The ones before us were desperately trying to adjust their line to face us but Bishop Albert must have ordered an advance for I heard the drums and horns as our warriors advanced. I swung my sword and my blade bit through the upper arm and into the chest of an Estonian who was torn between obeying orders and saving his life.

I was now riding freely. There was a gap between me and my squires but it did not matter for we had broken this line. I could see the river ahead. Someone had ordered the ships to close with the northern bank and the archers had disembarked and were loosing arrows into the rear of the Estonian line. I wheeled Skuld to the right. If I could lead my men to break their line where the archers were attacking we would have one secure flank. My move took some of my warriors unawares but most managed to follow me. We were now charging directly through the Estonian lines. Their shields were on their left side and as they turned they were struck in the rear by arrows and on their shield side by the spears of the men on foot. No matter how brave the warrior he cannot fight on three fronts. My sword was now almost blunted. I wielded an iron bar. It was an effective iron bar. I smashed it across the face of a helmeted warrior. The speed of my horse and the power of the blow made his skull disintegrate as though struck by a war machine. Skuld was tiring and so I slowed her down. The point of my sword had not been used and so I rammed it, point first, into the faces of the next two warriors.

When I saw the grinning face of Will son of Robin then I knew we were close to the river. I wheeled Skuld around and looked back up the slope. My charge had taken the two blocks of horsemen obliquely through the Estonian line. A large part of the Estonian army was surrounded. Men on foot attacked one side while horsemen attacked on two sides and my archers on a third. Even as I gathered my breath I saw the Estonian king taking the remnants of his army, less than a thousand of them, east. He was beaten. It took us the rest of the day but we worked our way through the heathens. We hacked slashed and stabbed until they were all dead. The sun was setting and I could barely raise my arm but we had won. Bishop Albert had his own state of Livonia. The Battle of Riga had decided that.

Chapter 16

As I saw the coast of Sweden appear, it felt like I was coming home and yet this was not home. This was exile. This was just another halt on our journey to our real home; England. Rafe's wife would be waiting on the shore for us. They had only been married for a few months when we had left and now she would be a widow. She would be a rich widow for we had Rafe's share of the new treasure and there would be more which Lady Brigida was storing. Walther had had no wife. All of my men would benefit from his death. None was overjoyed at that. They would have forgone the money to have the man alive still.

We had more room on the ships returning. With the garrisons left to watch the two captured settlements, we had a whole ship to ourselves. Petr and his men would return directly to Kastelholm. He was anxious to see his wife.

Bishop Albert had insisted that we stay as long as possible to deter the Estonians from becoming restless. Their king had agreed to peace but as we had found at Ādaži, not all the Estonians supported their king. Rivals might see this as an opportunity to become king. Our late departure meant we beat winter home by days rather than weeks. As we would be returning in spring none of us would enjoy much of the land. We would be surrounded by a sea of white and ice. That was the winter when I began to become increasingly restless. Knowing that I could not return home made my valley in England even more attractive and winter in Sweden was not a pleasant prospect.

Rafe's wife had a surprise for us. She was about to give birth. She had been hoping that her husband would arrive home to see their son born. The despair on her face was heartbreaking. Surprisingly it was my gentle giant, Ridley who came to her and offered her counsel. "Your husband was a good man and like a brother to us. You are not alone. You are not without a man to defend you and your bairns. You and your child will want for nothing."

The baby was born a week after our return and was a boy. He was named Rafe after his father. Ridley the Giant, a man who could hold a shield wall together on his own, became almost maternal. He held the young babe in the palm of one hand and made plaintive noises. Jack son of Harold had said, "The baby is too young to know what you do, Ridley."

Ridley handed the baby back to Anya, the mother and said, "He knows. He will remember me."

Sword For Hire

Over the next month, Ridley spent more and more time with Anya and Rafe. It came as no surprise when they were wed. I think that they married for different reasons. Anya was a young and frightened woman and she needed a man. Ridley was just smitten with the baby. It was a better arrangement than many marriages.

William and Margarite were also married and he was knighted at Christmas. It brightened the gloom of perpetual night. We still had no manor for William but Lady Brigida had had a home built for them. She was kind. The Swedes knew how to celebrate. I suspect it was their Viking past and the feast which followed was a lively one. William and Margarite retired early and I slipped away too. I was happy for William and his bride. I was delighted that my men were enjoying the celebrations but something nagged within me. I went, wrapped in my cloak, to the gatehouse. It was a clear cold night and my breath appeared before me as I walked. The sentries knew me and moved so that I could stand, alone, in the right-hand guard tower. I stared south and west as though I could see all the way to England.

I was aware of the smell of roses behind me and Lady Brigida appeared, "Lady, it is cold and the steps are slippery."

She laughed, "I am not an old woman yet, Thomas, and I saw that you were troubled. You have much to celebrate and yet you are here alone. I know that you are happy for William. What ails your heart?"

I pointed, "England. Two of my men died and I am here instead of there. King John is doing great harm to my land and I am helpless to stop it."

"Precisely. You are helpless. Take my advice and bide your time. You are young. I know, from my husband, that you have great skills as a warrior and a leader. He told me that you are actually improving day by day. You are not yet the leader you will become. Bishop Albert did not offer you the Brothers of the Swords out of sympathy. It was because you, despite your youth, were the best man to lead it. This king of yours cannot last long. Tyrants never do. Return when the time is right. Return with men behind you and with the knowledge that you can defeat him."

She was right. If I went back now I would lose and our time here would have been wasted.

"Come, rejoin the feast. Your men look for you." She took my arm and we descended.

The winter passed slowly. There would be no ship from England until the ice had gone. We were trapped in a sea of ice and white. William was besotted with his new bride and that just exacerbated my malaise. Skuldsdotter gave me my only relief. I groomed her and began to school her as well as I could. It would be a year or two before I could ride her to war. It was in my mind that I would do so in England. A warhorse was needed when you fought other knights or men mounted in mail. The heathens we fought here were just as likely to kill a horse as a man. The Livonian Brothers of the Sword had discovered that. In the first

159

battle, the Estonians who had swum over the river had used viciously sharp knives to hamstring the horses.

Hugh and Henry became fathers too. I wondered if my married men would be tempted to stay here in Sweden. They had roots. I noticed that many of my men did not seem concerned about our extended sojourn in Sweden. I had expected to return to England before now. I could not foresee a time when I would return. I would not return as a young man.

'Swan of Stockton' arrived when there was still a sheen of ice on the water. The sails and shrouds had a film of ice upon them as she tied up at the empty quay. Half a dozen men carrying chests followed Henry down the gangplank. Its unexpected arrival drew my men from the warmth of their hall and homes. The exception was William!

"This is unexpected, Henry."

He nodded, "Aye lord. I was sent." He handed me a letter and gestured behind him. "These are men who have asked to join you. Your friend in England vouches for them." He lowered his voice. "Things are bad in England, lord. King John has almost lost Normandy. The land which remains to him cannot last o'er long. All that King Richard recovered is gone."

I nodded and put the letter in my belt. "I have no letter ready yet. Will you be staying long?"

"Aye lord. I have to arrange a cargo. It will take some days to do that."

"Good." I turned to the men. "I am Sir Thomas of Stockton and these," I waved a hand at my men behind me, "are my men. You wish to join us?"

One man, slightly older than the others nodded and, after looking at their faces to see that he had their approval, he began to speak, "All of us have been called outlaw by King John. None of us is an outlaw, lord but we have been branded thus. Hunted from our homes we all found our way north. We heard of a sanctuary called Wulfestun. There, noble ladies with kind hearts sheltered and hid us. All of us had heard of your family. We had heard of your deeds and we wished to join you. I am Harry Longsword. I served under King Richard in Normandy. When I returned after the wars the Sherriff of Gloucester had taken my lands and declared me outlaw and traitor."

A younger man stepped forward, "I am Peter son of Richard. I was a warrior too. I fought against the Welsh. After the war, I returned to find a new lord had been given the manor of Barton. He had had my father executed for hunting. I killed him, lord." He said it simply but I knew that there had to be more to that story. To kill a lord of the manor was not an easy thing.

The next two men stepped forward together to give me their stories, "I am Hamlin the Archer and this is John Wayfarer. Our families needed food and we hunted the deer in Sherwood. The Sherriff could not get to us and so he took our families and imprisoned them. They died of starvation."

I looked at the last two who had remained silent, "And you two?"

"My story is much the same as the others, lord. I am Godfrey of Lancaster. I came back from the wars and there was nothing for me. I can use a sword but I do not know how to farm. I served some lords but there was no honour in what we did. I left."

"I cannot promise you honour here."

"No, that is true but you offer the hope of some and that is enough. We all heard of your heroism at Arsuf. The warrior who defended his father, his squire and his standard, is a man to follow."

The last warrior nodded. He was a huge man and almost the size of Ridley. "I am Godwin of Battle. I come from a long line of warriors. One of my forebears fought at Hastings with King Harold. We had served the lord of the manor at Battle since then. I was with our lord in Normandy when he fell fighting for King Richard. When we returned home King John had given the manor to another and we were thrown out. There were five of us. I am the last left alive. Drink, disease, hunger, they are not the death a warrior should endure. If I am to die I would do it serving a lord such as you."

"Then I welcome you all. My men have a pact. We share equally in the treasure we take. If a man dies then his wealth is shared by the others. What say you to that?"

Harry Longsword smiled, "We came not for coin but if there is some then this seems an amicable arrangement. Aye."

I turned, "Edward, get them surcoats, mail and helmets. We have new warriors, it seems."

I returned to my chamber to read the letter. It had been almost a year since I had received such a missive.

You know who you are and I hope you know that I think of you every day! Each night you are in my prayers.

The men that have come are all good men. There were more of them originally but their journey north was hard and some succumbed to hunger and disease. Many suffer such deaths in this land. Our valley used to be prosperous but no longer. The Bishop of Durham extracts every coin that he can. It is little better in the lands ruled by King John. He uses the excuse of the disastrous war in Normandy. He needs to address the war here. The Scots have grown bold. Our home has not suffered but Gainford was sacked as was Piercebridge. My father will not be sleeping easy in his grave.

There is some good news. A ship came from La Flèche. Your manor there is still loyal to you. Sir Phillip, the grandson of Sir Leofric, holds it for you. I sent a message back, telling him that you are still alive. Have you not thought of returning to Anjou? There you could start again. King John holds no sway there.

I am always here for you.

Xxx

I did wonder at that. I had forgotten the manor which had been given to my great grandfather. There was another in the Welsh Marches too. If the situation in England did not improve then I would take a ship to Anjou. My aunt was right. A new start might be the answer. I wrote a letter informing my aunt of our success and of the offer made by the bishop. I told her that I had atoned for my crime.

The arrival of *'Swan of Stockton'* heralded the arrival of other ships. As soon as she left for England her berth was taken by one of the many ships which would take the crusaders back to Estonia. With more men and the need to find horses for them all, I was too busy to brood.

Sir William now had a squire. Margarite's younger brother, Harald, was keen to serve. He was thirteen years old and could ride. That was his only skill. William would have his work cut out training him. Fótr helped. My squire seemed to have put his family's manor from his mind. We had visited once to bring back anything which the raiders had left. There was little. The Jarl Birger Brosa told Fótr that the manor would be his whenever he chose to return. I think that my squire wanted to be a better knight and be able to defend his own land before he took on that responsibility. I hoped that he might stay with me and return to England. He had developed into a good knight with many skills. The new men fitted in well. Their stories were so similar to those of my veterans that it was an easy adjustment to make.

We sailed on Easter Day. It was seen as propitious and, certainly, the voyage was trouble free. As we approached Riga I saw that they had not been idle in the winter. There was still little evidence of stonework but the church was finished and there were wooden towers ringing the wooden wall. The quays were also full. We later learned that Bishop Albert had opened a market. Goods still came down the river from deep in the land of the Rus and from as far afield as Constantinople. Our ship was the first to dock. My men disembarked with the horses and led them to the stables. I went with Sir William to meet with the Master and Bishop Albert.

"Ah, the hero of Ādaži is here! I hope you are ready to smite the heathen!"

I smiled, "I am, Bishop Albert. I have knighted William and we have new men who are fresh and wish to strike a blow for God."

Hermann Balk said, "And we shall need them. As you can see Bishop Albert now has a market."

Bishop Albert shook his head, "We have ships arriving with goods to trade but the journey down the river is still fraught with danger. It was not much of a problem in the winter. The river was frozen and there was little travel. Now we need to discourage the heathens from attacking the traders."

"Their king has broken the peace?"

Hermann shook his head, "He says he has not and that it is the work of rogue clans. I do not believe him. When our army arrives, we will drive down the two rivers in two columns. The rivers are the lifeblood of this land. Our mission this battle season is to secure the rivers. We will build castles to guard strategic points."

"And I will have stone brought to make Riga the strongest castle this side of the Baltic!"

There was a great deal of enthusiasm. I hoped it was justified. The Jarl Birger Brosa and Jarl Birger Persson were also optimistic. The winter had seen their retinues increased. Only Petr was less happy. He had left a pregnant wife at Kastelholm. The thought of a summer fighting heathens did not appeal. One evening I found him by the river looking wistfully west. I knew what he was thinking. I sat next to him on the wooden mooring bollard.

"Sir Thomas, may I speak with you in confidence?"

"Of course. You and I have been through much together. You are as much a brother to me as any man."

"And I, you. Would it be dishonourable if I made this my last raiding season? I know that my brother will stay until this is Christian land but each time I leave I worry about my wife at home. I do not want my child growing up not knowing his father."

"Bishop Albert has said that his Brothers of the Sword are the ones who will rule this land. The rest of us are here for a season. If we return then that is good and if not then we have each done our part to bring God to this Godless country. Your brother would understand. When he has a wife he too will wish to stay home. I know William does."

"And you, Sir Thomas, will you take a wife?"

"Perhaps. However, I would marry an English woman and there are precious few of those here." I saw the worry in the young knight's face. He did not wish to let his brother down. "Your brother will understand. You have done more than enough already for the bishop."

As the week passed and more men had arrived, we headed south in two columns. Hermann Balk led one and The Jarl Birger Brosa the other. I had my new men each paired up with an old hand. The new ones did not know the language and they did not know the country. The first two days were easy. The Estonians were not expecting us and the few warriors that we found, fled. This time we had no infantry with us. Hermann Balk wished to move quickly. It appeared to be a good strategy for we made seventy miles in two days. We had riders keeping us in touch with each other. It was unlikely that the Estonians would be able to mobilise great numbers but if they did then we would join up to face them.

Spring and early summer were the best times to campaign. As soon as it neared autumn then we would be plagued with flies and flying insects. Those of us who had been here for some time appreciated the cooler mornings.

We received a message from Hermann Balk that the Estonians had gathered an army before the town of Preiļi. I say town but it was just a smattering of huts around which many of the Estonians had settled with their animals. As we discovered it had little structure. However, their king had chosen it to be a rallying point for his people. During the winter Bishop Albert had converted some of the smaller settlements which were close to Riga. Some of the Estonians regarded Bishop Albert as some sort of wizard. Consequently, many had fled south. They had gathered, to make a stand, at Preiļi.

The Jarl Birger Brosa led our company of two hundred mounted men to join the Livonian Brothers of the Sword. Hermann Balk now had over a hundred knights and almost eighty sergeants at arms. The only archers were my handful of mounted ones. When we reached his camp, he took the three of us with him to survey the enemy lines and defences.

"As you can see they have made it difficult for us. They have used their wagons and carts as barriers to our horses and filled the gaps with stakes. If we charge them then they will slaughter our horses."

Jarl Birger Persson said, "Sir Thomas has shown you the way."

"How?"

"Do as he did last year. Fight on foot."

"But we are knights!"

"And knights can fight just as well on foot, lord." I pointed to the enemy wagons. "They are a barrier to us but they could be a weapon we use against them."

"How?"

"They are made of wood. They have, in them, men defending them. We burn them. Have your sergeants make pots of fire. Get close and they can whirl around and throw them. We used them against ships at Kastelholm and they worked there. They can work here too. I have seen them thrown thirty, even forty paces. I have two men who could throw them fifty paces. We advance with our knights. You and I know how poor their arrows are against shields and mail. We stop thirty paces from them."

"Suppose they attack us?"

The Jarl Birger Brosa laughed, "Then we will have won for that is exactly what we wish them to do. They are strongest in a defensive line where we have to attack. It costs us a hundred pots of fire. If it does not work then we try something else."

We had him convinced. That night he sent his sergeant to scour the area for pots. His men gathered more than a hundred. They tied ropes around the necks of the pots. As they were doing it David of Wales said, "Lord, when we were in the Holy Land the Saracens often used oil and pig fat to burn us when we attacked their castles. If we used the spare pots to hold oil then they would make the fires burn faster." He waved an arm. "They eat pig around here and use seal oil."

"Take the archers and find as much as you can."

My men were eager to try this out and they rode further afield than the sergeant of the order of the Brothers of the Sword did.

I think the Estonians expected a night attack for they stood to all night. They would be exhausted when we did attack. It was our knights who first moved into position. We wanted them to believe that we would attack in the way they expected. The sergeants who would be throwing the pots walked behind, leading their horses. I was confident that Ridley and Godwin of Battle would be able to send their pots further than the others. For that reason, they had the pots of seal oil and pig fat ready to launch.

We had with us the two brothers and Bishop Albert's standard. We marched behind them for we had learned that the Estonians feared their magic. Goswin von Spanheim gave them a chance to surrender, reminding them that their king had broken the peace. His words were met by jeers. We knew that our words would fall on deaf ears. As soon as Goswin and Hermann returned then we dismounted and handed our reins to our squires. We had a line of one hundred and twenty knights. Behind us were a hundred and twenty squires. They were still mounted. I saw that we had confused the Estonians. What were we doing? We began to march and, as we did so, we banged our spears against our shields. Each bang took us a step closer. It was important that they concentrated on us and not the sergeant and men at arms who trudged behind. Tendrils of smoke rose from their hot projectiles.

The Estonians sent their arrows towards us. Our shields stopped them. Those that did not hit our shields either bounced from our helmets or stuck in our cloaks, surcoats or mail. They stopped wasting them. When we were forty paces from them we stopped. Brother Harald and Brother Magnus began singing. We all joined in. Once again, the enemy soldiers were confused. As soon as it stopped we took another ten paces forward. It was then that we broke ranks and the sergeants and men at arms ran and hurled their pots. Some of the Estonians had their wits about them. They sent a few desultory arrows and spears towards them. One sergeant fell with an arrow in his chest another was struck in the leg but gamely carried on. The pots flew. Those who had oil and fat threw theirs too. Another two sergeants fell: one with an axe embedded in his chest and a second with a spear. As they turned and ran for the protection of our ranks another three were hit. Then there was the roar of flames and fire as the pots struck the tinder-dry wood and ignited it. Some of those within the wagons were set on fire. The ones who were not, fled. We stood and watched as the smell of burning wood and then flesh filled the air. Smoke began to billow towards the huts and the bulk of the enemy army.

Hermann Balk had a horn sounded and we began to advance through the stakes. The Estonians had counted on being able to attack us from their mobile castles. They were now crematoria. We could not attack with a continuous line. The stakes prevented that but the enemy warriors were shaken. I stepped between the stakes and rammed my spear at a shocked Estonian. It was a powerful blow and he was knocked backwards. He stumbled and, as he began to fall I speared his thigh. The bright arcing blood told me that he had been mortally wounded and I stepped over him and took the axe blow from the next warrior on my shield. Sir William's spear penetrated the warrior's ear and then his skull. I thrust again at the next man, aware that we had moved ten more paces closer to the enemy town. The Estonian took the blow on his shield and his curved sword hacked through my spear. Holding it overhand I jabbed the broken wooden end at him. He had an open helmet and the broken end took his eye. As he screamed I punched him with my shield while drawing my sword. I ended his pain as I stepped over him and stabbed him in the neck.

I was through the wooden stakes and so I halted. Now we could use our superior training, mail and swords. I waited for Sir William to join me on one side and Eystein, one of Birger Brosa's men, on the other. As soon as their shields touched mine I raised my sword and our long line of knights moved forward. David and the handful of archers closed behind us. They would help to both thin and clear the men from ahead of us. Even as we stepped forward their arrows found flesh. They were not bone barbed missiles. These were long steel bodkins. They would tear through mail and, at this close range, rip through flesh and out of the back. They might even strike those behind.

David and the archers were just clearing a line ten men wide. Behind us my men at arms, having thrown their pots, were now armed and advancing to give us support. We would be three ranks deep and ten men wide. The smoke from the fires was now adding to our attack for it drifted into the faces of our foes. The smell of burning flesh filled the air. This must be what it would be like in hell. I had atoned. I had been forgiven. Hell did not await me. We stepped over bodies stuck with arrows. The Estonians ahead held their shields up to save them from an aerial death. I rammed my sword into the guts of one such warrior. He did not even see the blow coming for he was hiding behind his shield. I used my sword to pull him from my path and then I stepped onto his body and, raising my sword brought it down on the skull of the next Estonian. He had a helmet. It was poorly made.

I saw that the Estonians had stiffened their ranks with Slavs. The Margraviate of Brandenburg had been ordered by the Emperor to drive the Slavs from his land. They had become hired swords themselves. Some of their nobles had mail and helmets. They liked war axes and they were fond of gold. I saw one such noble ahead of me. He had his bodyguard with him. Dressed in a variety of helmets and pieces of mail they would present us with a more rigorous test than the Estonians. I saw that they did not hold their shield on their arms for they were smaller than ours but on their fists. They would punch. They had not been in the front line for behind them I saw King Ylle and his men. He had hired mercenaries. The Slavs love of gold meant he had more chance of protection than countrymen with dubious motives.

"Stockton, to me!"

I did not mind fighting with Birger Brosa and his men. They were good warriors but if I had a choice then it would be men who followed me.

"Form a wedge!"

Sir William and Edward tucked in behind me. Ridley the Giant and Godwin of Battle flanked Phillip of Poitiers. The rest formed behind them. None of us had spears and so we held our swords before us. We had a chant, a sing song, we had developed. It was in English and it was unique to us. It was simply to help us march in step.

Stockton men are big and brave
Send a Scot to an early grave
Stockton men fear no foe
Fight us and to hell you go
Stockton
Stockton
Stockton men fear no one
Stockton men are big and brave
Send a Scot to an early grave
Stockton men fear no foe
Fight us and to hell you go
Stockton
Stockton
Stockton men fear no one

I knew without looking that my men were grinning as we marched. Ahead I could see, for he wore an open helmet, doubt appear on the face of the Slav lord. They were used to fighting man on man. They were wild and they were unpredictable. They had never met us before and I could see he was confused. His eyes flickered to the side. Would his men cope with this wedge of steel that was coming for them?

I knew he would use his shield offensively and punch at me. I suddenly lowered my sword and, sure enough, his shield came at my face at the same time as his axe swung at my shield. My shield was bigger than his and it covered my

167

body and half of my face. I did not need to move it. I lowered my head so that his shield hit the top of my helmet. At the same time, I lunged with my sword. It ripped and tore through his leg. It snagged on his thigh bone and I twisted it. His axe had struck the top of my head. I had a padded cap and a coif beneath mine. It did not hurt. As I looked up I saw the look of pain on his face. I pulled out my sword. It slurped as it came out. I must have severed a tendon for he dropped to one knee. I swung my own shield at his face as it drew level. He fell unconscious. He would bleed to death. I shouted, "Victory!"

Sir William and Edward hacked and slashed at their opponents and I flicked my sword to the side to score a deep wound against the leg of Sir William's foe. When Edward gutted his foe, their line was broken and, once again, King Ylle ran. He had paid for what he had thought were the best of bodyguards and we had sliced through them as though they were butter. We turned and slaughtered the other Slavs. There was no way we could catch the Estonian king. They had been mounted on horses. However, a flurry of arrows flew and I saw two bodyguards fall and an arrow strike the king in the shoulder. This time he had not escaped unscathed.

"Lord, we have outstripped the rest!"

"Then we hold here. Shield wall!" We turned and made a circle. It was ironic for the bodies we protected were the Slavs. The Estonians and the other Slave mercenaries gave us a wide berth. They fell back, keeping their front to face the knights who hacked, slashed and chopped their way through them. I think they must have known this was their last battle. Their king had no idea how to defeat us and their warriors just bled on our swords.

The battle passed us and our squires brought our horses and my banner. While the rest of the army finished off the wounded my men found the treasure that the king had left and the Slavs had carried with them. Unlike us, they did not have a lady to watch over their coin and every Slav carried his payment about him.

I heard Harry Longsword shout, "Who needs England with rewards like this! Thank you, Sir Thomas."

I took off my helmet and lowered my coif. We had lost no men and that was a good thing but Harry was wrong. We needed England. I was an English knight and while I fought here I was letting down my country. I had to get home!

The German Widow

Chapter 17

This time King Ylle returned to the field to sue for peace. David's arrow had hurt him. He would live but our victory, the second such monumental one, had made him realise that he ought to convert and then our God would fight for him. He surrendered Estonia to Hermann Balk and Bishop Albert. Birger Persson was not happy, "This was your victory, Thomas! You should have had the credit!"

"I am a sword for hire. If I had wanted glory then I would have accepted Bishop Albert's offer. This is good. We have treasure and our share from this victory will make it easier when I return home."

"You will still return home?"

"I like your country, Birger. I feel a kinship to it as though some part of it is in my blood but it is not England and can never be. This may well be my last season here. If I cannot go to England then I will return to my estate in Anjou."

"We will miss you."

I shook my head, "Hermann Balk has learned. His plan was a good one. You and Birger Brosa have wise heads." I ruffled his hair, "Do not look downhearted. We have a whole summer yet! Estonia is ours but there are more barbarians yet to conquer."

It took almost a month to totally pacify the area and to begin to build a castle. We used the conquered Estonians to dig the ditch and build the mound. In English terms, it was an old fashioned and primitive castle but it would suffice. The master left twenty knights and twenty sergeants in command and then we headed back to Riga. We had animals, hostages and treasure to escort. There were no enemies between the rivers. To the west of the river, the Danes were busy converting heathens of their own. I knew that to the east lay hordes of enemies. I doubted that would be my task. I had finished with the winter war and the northern crusade.

Of course, I was wrong. Those women Birger had spoken of, the Norns, determined that I would not go quietly into the night.

Bishop Albert, after speaking with Hermann Balk, was fulsome in his praise of me. I was given a chest of gold and offered more titles than I had ever heard of. There was just one title I wished for, Lord of the Manor of Stockton. I had long ago given up on Earl of Cleveland. We spent the next month riding long forays into lands we had conquered. My banner was known and Bishop Albert used it to cow his foes. We captured or killed many small bands of warriors who had escaped the battle and sought to fight on.

We had just returned to Riga at the end of summer when I was summoned to the Bishop's hall. It was almost a keep and it was made of stone. The bishop valued his safety. "Sir Thomas, I understand that this will be your last season of fighting alongside us."

I sensed the censure in his tone. I had not spoken of this to him. The Jarl Birger Brosa must have broached the subject. I did not feel honour bound to fight more. I had never made a commitment. Bishop Albert had told me that I had done my penance. It had come to me that he might have done that in the hope that I would have taken the position of master. Bishop Albert was a good man but he was driven and he had a single aim; he would bring God to the godless.

"It will, your grace. The Estonians are beaten and most are converted to Christianity. The Livonian Brothers of the Sword can hold this land. Hermann Balk knows how to fight them."

"You know that I am disappointed."

"And I am flattered that you need me."

"I do for Jarl Birger Persson and his brother have also said that they will not take the cross next year. That is your doing."

He was now trying to make me feel guilty. "A man makes his own choices, Bishop Albert. If he does something because of another then that is his weakness. You will not bend nor will I. I have served you well. My men have died for your cause. It is enough."

"It can never be enough for there are still heathens who do not believe in God!"

This was a circular argument. I would not get into it and so I remained silent.

He smiled, "You too are strong. I have one more task for you. A column of Teutonic Knights, led by Burchard von Bruggeneye have been pushing from the land south of Lithuania. They are driving Slavs northwards. I would have you take your men and meet them where we stopped our advance." He handed me a parchment. "Give him this." I took it. I saw that it was sealed with wax. I just nodded as I took it. "You do not ask what is in it?"

"I am a messenger. I am guessing it is important and that it should not fall into the hands of any other than Burchard von Bruggeneye."

He laughed, "You are a deep one, Englishman. Yes, you are right. I wish the two orders to join together next year and drive towards the Prussians and the Lithuanians. King Canute is heading east to Estonia. He will subdue that land. It is why I wished you to be with us. You are not only a good general, the men like to follow you, but you also inspire confidence. You are seen as important as my holy banner."

"I am sorry, your grace. I have been fighting the enemies of Christ for most of my life. I have enemies who are closer to my home I should war against."

"You are still outlawed in England."

"I know. I will take my chances." I had confided in no one yet what my real plans were. I had felt guilty keeping the information from my men. When we wintered in Stock Holm I would tell them.

We took spare horses with us. These were not horses for riding. They were the small ponies and horses we had taken from Estonians. They would carry supplies. The twins led us as we headed south. Although Bishop Albert and the Swedes called all of these people Estonians they were, in fact, made up of different tribes. We had spoken to some of those who had converted and it explained why we had been able to defeat them despite their superiority of numbers. Those to the east of the river were the Latgalians. It was their king we had defeated. To the west of the river were the Selonians and Semigallians. They had fought alongside King Ylle in the last battle. They were largely undefeated. The fact that we had not crossed the Daugava was the only reason we had not had to fight a major battle with these people. That battle would come. Bishop Albert had used the river as a natural boundary. So long as trade came down the river then he and the merchants would be happy. So far, that was the case. What would happen when King Canute pressed their borders on one side and then the Holy Orders on the other was unknown. And then there were the people of Poland. That had been a strong country of pagans until the leader, Prince Bolesław III Wrymouth had divided the land between his sons. Bishop Albert had set himself a mighty task.

My twins scouted ahead of us as we headed for the scene of the last battle. The place we would meet the Teutonic knights was forty miles south of there. When we reached the battlefield the bones of the dead still littered it. The town had been abandoned. The walls had been burned and destroyed after the battle and they must have moved on. It was a good site and one day someone would rebuild but I would not see it.

Gruffyd ap Tomas signalled to us. He and his brother were riding the ruins to see if any remained. He led us to what had been the centre of the town. There we found the body of King Ylle. He had been impaled upon a spear. His eyes had been eaten already and rats had gnawed at his flesh but I recognised him by his clothes. He had paid the price of defeat.

We continued the next day. The king had promised peace and he was dead. I had been cautious before and now I was even more so. I needed to get back to Bishop Albert with the news. He was making great plans assuming that the land was at peace. That was not the case.

We found the Teutonic Knights towards dusk. I had been considering making camp when Mordaf spied them. They were easy to spot in their distinctive surcoats. I was pleased to see that they had built a camp with stakes around it. There were twenty knights and forty sergeants. We rode in and dismounted.

"I am Sir Thomas of Stockton and I have been sent by Bishop Albert of Riga. I seek Burchard von Bruggeneye."

A man of about my age stepped forward, "I am he. You are a brave man to venture forth with just two knights."

I handed him the document, "This is for you. I need no knights. My men and I have fought together many times. They are good warriors."

We sat. "I have heard of you. You are the hero of Arsuf. I was a squire myself in the Holy Land but I was not at the battle. I envied you that glory."

"It has not yielded me much save the loss of my father and the knights who trained me."

"Their deaths were glorious! They defended their king."

"And what did it avail us? We now have a tyrant ruling our land with an iron fist."

He nodded, "You are not of a Holy Order. We have a higher purpose. We serve God."

"No, I am not a brother knight. I am now forced to be a sword for hire."

"This life suits us. Any we find we fight and we slay for they are heathens. We have travelled hundreds of miles to reach this place. The bones of many pagans litter our route. When we return, we will slay more."

I shook my head. "Tell me why I was sent here. This missive could have been sent by ship and then across land which was safe."

He smiled, "We have scouted the land. When we come next season then I will lead the vanguard for I know the land. This is preparation. Our master wishes me to find out the calibre of the enemies we will fight. Will we be fighting alongside you, Sir Thomas?"

"No, this is my last journey in the east. I will return to Stock Holm in the autumn."

"A pity. This will be the only chance I have to speak with you. I will use it well."

I was assaulted by questions about Arsuf, England, the Baltic and the campaign thus far. He seemed a professional warrior. He would do well.

We parted the next day. Burchard von Bruggeneye was an adventurer. This life would suit him. We went back a different way. Now that I knew their king was dead this land was less safe. We had left a trail south. I wanted no ambushes as we headed north. We followed the river downstream. The grass was lush there and afforded good grazing. The trees which lined it gave shelter and shade and the river meant our horses could be watered. It made camping easier. We made thirty miles that first day. My men put lines in the river to catch fish and we built our camp. The main channel of the river here was both narrow and shallow. There were many smaller branches. We camped by the main branch protected on two sides by water. I was looking forward to a trouble-free journey home. The man in the river prevented that. It was Skuld who found him. Skuld whinnied and we drew our weapons. My men had learned to trust his instincts.

It was getting on to dusk. Mordaf had good eyes and it was he who spotted him. There was a wounded man clinging on to an overhanging branch of the river. He looked barely alive. Mordaf looked at me. I nodded. I had no idea if this was an enemy or not. He looked to be alone and I took the chance. Gruffyd helped his brother to drag the wounded man to the fire. Edward used his knife to cut away the cloth of his tunic. The man was not an Estonian. His clothes were too well made. As the torn material fell away we saw the wooden cross around his neck. Crudely made it still identified him as Christian.

"Lord, he has a bad wound along his side. He has lost blood."

"Clean it with vinegar and then have him stitched. Will the son of Robin, you are handy with a needle."

"Aye lord."

"He is unconscious. Do it quickly." I turned, "Have some honeyed ale prepared."

Jack son of Harold said, "He is more dead than alive lord. It is a waste of good ale if you ask me." We had a limited amount of ale and Jack was like his father in that respect. He liked a drink.

"Nonetheless he will have the honeyed ale. What is a Christian doing here deep in the land of the pagan?"

I sat and watched as the man was stitched. He did not look either Slavic or Estonian. His skin was not tanned nor was it as pale as those who lived in these parts. He was not Swede or Dane. I put his age to be older than me. He looked to have seen more than thirty summers. His hands were gnarled and showed evidence of hard work. He was not well fed but his body was muscled. He was an enigma. No matter how hard I thought I could not come up with an explanation.

We ate while he slept. The ale was kept warm in a metal pot by the fire. We kept a good guard. I was about to retire when he moved. David of Wales and Edward were on watch and we all went to the man's side, "Edward, fetch the ale."

Edward put a good glug of honey into the warm ale and stirred it. He had put in some dried rosemary. We believed it helped to heal but, even if it did not, we liked the smell. David held the man's head while Edward poured the warmed ale into his mouth. He coughed a little.

"Don't waste it, my friend."

Suddenly the man's eyes opened wide, "You are English!"

The enigma had become even more confusing. What was an Englishman doing here in the middle of this wild and pagan land? "I am Sir Thomas. We are English warriors serving Bishop Albert of Riga. Who are you and what are you doing here?"

Edward said, "Lord, let him drink some more. He is weak."

I nodded, "You are right to chastise me, Edward. Drink friend. We can wait a few moments for your story."

The man drank deeply and then shook his head, "You are wrong, lord. We have no time to waste. My lady is in trouble and she needs your help." He struggled to sit up.

"Be careful, my friend, you have a wound which we have stitched."

"I am John of Derby and I serve Lady Margaret the daughter of Sir William Mowbray. My lady recently married a German knight, Diderick von der Borch. We were on our way to Riga for he wished to speak with his cousin who serves with the Livonian Brothers of the Swords. We were ambushed yesterday." He looked around to orientate himself. "Where is the river?"

Edward pointed to the west, "Yonder. It is where we found you."

"We were west of the river. It was a band of Slavs, or so Sir Diderick's squire, young Johann said. The baron's men fought hard, we all did. I was told to flee with Lady Margaret, her two ladies and Johann. We headed for the river. They chased us and I was hit and fell into the water. I must have lost consciousness for I did not wake until…"

"Until just now." I stood. "David, wake the men, we ride."

"But it is nighttime, lord."

I nodded, "And there may be English women out there. They too may have fallen from their horses or, even worse, taken by the Slavs."

"There may be Slavs waiting too, lord."

"I am counting on that for if there are they will have a fire and we will be able to see them."

The men were roused.

"John of Derby, how many men were there in this band?"

"They had twenty on horses but there were two score or more who rose from the grass when they ambushed us."

That meant that there had been sixty Slavs. I had to hope that this baron had killed some or we would struggle to overcome them. This was their land and they would have friends nearby. We were now in a land that was unconquered.

We used one of the ponies for John of Derby and we forded the rivers. It was not easy. I feared for John of Derby as the river was swift and I prayed he would not be swept towards the sea. We made it. After we had adjusted our girths I pointed south. We would go upstream. I had worked out that John would have been swept downstream when he had been knocked from his horse and the ambush had to have taken place upstream. We backtracked up the river. Skuld whinnied. Our weapons were in our hands. I saw the horse grazing. John said, "That is Tom, my horse. This must be where I fell."

I shook my head, John was not a warrior that much was obvious, "No, John, your horse would have been taken if this was where you were struck. Your horse ran on after you had fallen. We have a way to go yet."

The moon was out, making it easier to see. We found where John had fallen. The grass was flattened. There had been horses and we saw that the tracks led west. Of the ladies and the German, there was no sign. I took that as hopeful. If they had been killed we would have seen their bodies.

We heard the foxes fighting and knew that we had found where the battle had been. We approached cautiously. The carrion fled and we found Baron Diderick and his men. After they had been killed their heads had been placed on spears and their bodies dismembered. There were ten bodies.

"Is Johann amongst these?"

"No lord. These were the sergeants the Baron had with him."

"Which is the baron?"

He pointed to a grey-bearded man. He looked old although a skull was not a good indicator of age. "Is Lady Margaret old?"

He shook his head. "She has seen eighteen summers. Her mother and father died of the plague. King John took her lands and Baron Diderick was an old friend of the family and he married her to keep her safe." He hesitated. "He did not lie with her lord. He was a true gentleman. It is why he sought to visit with Bishop Albert. It was to give thanks to God for his bride."

"Lord, I can see their tracks and, unless I am mistaken, I can smell wood smoke in the wind." Mordaf and Gruffyd had noses like hounds and I trusted them.

"Lead on. Be ready, all of you, to fight. Give John of Derby a weapon."

We followed the trail which soon became so obvious that even I could see it. They were not attempting to hide their tracks by spreading out. They had cut a swathe through the grass. The wind was from the west and soon I smelled wood smoke and food. Their camp was close but I could not see it. Behind us, I saw a lightening of the sky. Dawn was not far away.

Mordaf held up his hand and we stopped. Faintly, in the distance I could hear noises. It could have been another band of Slavs but I did not think so. We had not lost the trail and had just passed a pile of warm horse manure. This was the band we sought. Moving until we saw the glow from their campfire and the murmur of voices could be heard we dismounted. We hobbled our horses. I could not afford to leave men to guard them. I would have charged in on horses if I had thought that the ladies and this Johann were dead. Then it would have been a vengeance raid. So long as there was a chance that they were alive we had to be precise. We had to save the captives and then slaughter the rest. The problem was that I did not know the numbers we would be facing.

I spoke quietly to Fótr, Harald and John of Derby. "Your task is to ensure that the captives if they are still alive, remain so. Leave the killing to us." They nodded, "David, I rely on you and your archers to take out the sentries. As for the rest, stay together and kill as quickly as you can. We have seen what these men do to captives."

We did not wear our helmets. They were dangerous in the dark. We would have to hope that our mail coifs would give us enough protection. Taking off my spurs I also left my cloak on Skuld too. I wanted the freedom to swing. We moved in a loose line. I took them to approach the camp from the south. If the sun came up I did not wish to be silhouetted against the light. The thin light of dawn was sufficient for us to see shapes.

My archers led. The glow from the fires was a good indicator of the camp. The smell of their horses and the neighing told us where they were. As we neared the camp I saw the sentries. There were pairs of them. I counted three sets. I had told David of Wales what to do. I waited. My archers had worked together for long enough so that they did not need words. The ten arrows flew and six sentries dropped. Inevitably the falling bodies made a noise. Even as I heard a question in the dark we were moving forward. More voices shouted. I did not know their words but I worked out they were asking the sentries what the problem was.

The sun began to peep over the horizon to our right. By the glow of the fire ahead I saw Slavs grabbing weapons. Dawn's light would soon illuminate them. I could see no captives. I ran, with William and Edward, towards the nearest Slav warrior. He roared in the dark and I saw sleeping men rise. Arrows flew from behind us as David and his archers slew the ones they deemed to be the most dangerous of our opponents. They were hampered by our bodies. It was still poor light and we were in the way. I ripped my sword across the body of a half-naked Slav. His guts tumbled from his middle and I was already punching my shield at another who had risen from beneath my feet. As he fell backwards, stunned, I rammed my sword through his chest. It was a confused battle. All that I knew was anyone in mail was one of my men. Those who ran at me with weapons were enemies.

The sun was now rising like a red glow in the east. I saw the captives. Six warriors stood before them. There were, however, another thirty warriors who had yet to be killed. We had woken them and they had grabbed whatever weapons were to hand. Few had shields and the ones they had were smaller than ours. We hacked, slashed, stabbed and chopped our way through them. Suddenly I saw two men break from the ones around the captives and run to their horses.

"David!"

Arrows flew and one Slav fell but the other made his horse and he galloped off. He would have gone for help. Time was no longer on our side. The Slavs fought hard and they died hard. None even thought of running. The only place they ran was at us. One used the bodies lying before me to jump high into the air. I held my sword up and he impaled himself on my sword. The weight of his body knocked me to the ground. I rolled him off me and stood. It was now light enough to see clearly and the majority of the enemy were dead or dying. The four who remained, five paces from us, could now be seen standing behind the four captives: three women and a bloodied body that had to be Johann. They held sharp knives to their throats. Two of the women were weeping but the third looked at me and I swear she smiled.

One of them shouted something. I did not understand his words but I knew what he wanted. I said, "David have you a target?"

"A risky one, lord. Your bodies are in the way."

I shouted, "The rest of you sheathe your weapons." We all sheathed our weapons. "On my command, I want you to sit. David, the lives of those four are the hands of you and my archers."

"And God, lord." I heard him take a breath to calm himself. "Ready lord."

"Now!"

It happened so suddenly that it surprised even me. As we sat ten arrows flew towards the four Slavs. My men were just ten paces from them. They did not miss. The four Slavs fell and, as they did so, Johann also fell.

Chapter 18

"Edward, John of Derby, see to the captives. Philip of Poitiers, see to the wounded."

Sir William said sadly, "He is dead lord as is Hugh of Bath. I will see to the wounded."

Ridley the Giant said, "I will see to them, lord." It was as I saw him trudge away that I remembered how close the two had been. Philip the small chatterbox and Ridley the silent giant.

I would grieve for the dead later. Right now, we had more pressing business. One Slav had escaped. He was riding for help. I did not think that help would be close at hand. If it was then they would have ridden there instead of making a camp. We had to use that time well.

"Mordaf and Gruffyd, fetch their horses. Will the son of Robin and Thomas son of Tom fetch our horses."

I hurried over to the captives. The two women were still wailing. The one who had smiled snapped, "Hilda and Bertha, pull yourselves together. We are not dead. It is poor Johann who is hurt." She took my hand and kissed it, "Thank you, lord. God must have sent you!"

"I am Sir Thomas of Stockton, Lady Margaret, we will talk later. Right now, we need to get out as soon as we can. What is wrong with the youth?"

"He received a blow to his head. They broke the bones in his feet and a couple of his ribs. I think they intended to do to him what they did to my husband and his men."

There was the hint of a tear in her eye. It was understandable. "We will protect you. We have a long way to go but my men are the best."

Mordaf shouted, "They have six horses lord."

"Put Philip and Hugh on two of them. As soon as Edward has attended to Johann we leave."

Sir William approached, "Which way do we go, lord? Back across the river?"

I shook my head. "We will head for the river but ride down this bank. There are ships which use the river. They can give us protection. I am not risking the ladies and an injured man to ford a river." John of Derby had struggled and the three women looked to be even more of a liability.

Sword For Hire

It was not the solution I wanted but events had forced my hand. As soon as our horses arrived we mounted. We left the Slavs where they had fallen. Everything of value was taken. Most of it now belonged to the German's widow. The sun was climbing in the sky when we eventually left. We had had to tie Johann onto the back of a horse. Edward had rigged up support for his back and he was tied to that and the saddle. Edward led the horse by a length of rope. I was not certain if he would survive but we had no choice. We rode steadily north and east. I wished to take the most direct route to Riga. I was not sure if there were any bridges but that did not matter. Bishop Albert could use ships to ferry us across. What we had to do was to avoid capture. We spied the river just afternoon. Gruffyd was sure that he spied the mast of a ship as we approached but by the time we had reached the river, if there had been one, then it had gone. The river was too wide and deep for us to ford. I had made our bed and we would have to lie in it.

The two weeping ladies proved to be the problem and not Johann. They complained the whole way. I knew that it was difficult for them but Lady Margaret was bearing herself stoically. Having said that she was a competent rider. She rode as a man did. She had control and mastery of her horse. The two ladies clung on for dear life. We stopped only for the horses. My men had dried meat and we shared that with the four captives. Johann remained unconscious. Edward forced water into his lips each time we stopped.

By evening I estimated that we had travelled thirty miles and we had twenty left to go. We camped by the river. "We will light no fire. I do not wish to give our pursuers a beacon."

I sat with Lady Margaret and her women. Edward, Fótr and Harald were designated as nurses for Johann. He was of an age with the two squires. As we ate more dried meat and drank the last of our ale I spoke with the young Lady Margaret. Her two ladies cuddled close together and slept.

"I am sorry for your loss, my lady."

She smiled, "Diderick was a kind, old man. He married me so that I would not be married off to one of King John's cronies. Diderick was an old man. He and my father had fought together in the Holy Land. He said that when he died then I would inherit his estates. It was pure luck that he arrived when he did. He was on his way back from the Holy Land and intended to join Bishop Albert's crusade. When he saw my predicament he acted swiftly. He was a true knight." Tears streamed silently down her face. I think she had only just realised that he was not coming back. "He said that he was old and would not live long. Then I could choose a husband. I would not be chosen."

"He sounds like a brave man but why come to Riga? Why risk the journey through such hostile lands?"

"His cousin is Reimar von Tork. His father was the eldest child and the manors all belonged to him. My husband had been in the Holy Land for twenty years. Reimar von Tork had promised the Livonian Brothers of the Sword his estates.

179

He had dedicated his life to God. He had given away Diderick's too. My husband was sure that it was a mistake. He said that if he explained in person why he wanted them then they would be returned to him."

"I do not understand. I thought you said that the estates belonged to Diderick."

"They did but he had spent twenty years in the Holy Land. The Emperor allowed Reimar to manage them. As I said, my husband was certain that it was a mistake. He had not been concerned when it was just him but he wanted me to have the means to choose my own husband."

I remembered Reimar. He had struck me as an ambitious knight. I was not so certain that it was a mistake. He was now second in command to Hermann. Hermann's motives were honourable. I wondered if this Reimar von Tork saw the gift of estates which were not his as a way of gaining control of the order.

I had been silent for a few moments. "Do you think we will reach Riga?" Her voice seemed somewhat shaky. Perhaps the enormity of her task was coming home to her. She might have to fight for her husband's lands. She had just had to fight for her life.

I felt sorry for her. I noticed she was shaking. I put my arm and my cloak around her, "I believe that we will."

She put her head on my shoulder and began to sob. I let her do so. I saw some of my men looking at me strangely. Edward smiled. "That is what she needs lord. My mother was a wise woman and she told us that a good cry helped a woman. She will be stronger for it."

When she stopped sobbing I waited for her to speak. Then I heard her breathing deeply. She was asleep. I did not have the heart to leave her alone and so I sat up with her all night. Her steady breathing was comforting.

"And now the sleep will finish the job. Nature is a wondrous thing, lord, wondrous." Edward was wise.

It was almost dawn when she awoke. She appeared startled, "Why did you not lay me down? I am not a child!"

I said, softly, "I did not want you to wake. Edward said it would help you to heal."

She smiled, "Forgive my waspish tongue, lord. I was startled that was all. I dreamed I was at home and, as I woke I remembered the nightmare through which we live."

"With luck, the ordeal will be over by nightfall. We are not far from Riga, it is just that we are on the wrong side of the river."

The two women carped and moaned as they were woken. Lady Margaret and I joined my squires by the unconscious Johann. He appeared to be breathing easier. My squires and Edward had given him water during the night. "What was he to the baron?"

"He was the son of a knight who died in the Holy Land. I think he was going to train him as a squire. He was my companion. He was made of sterner stuff than the two flowers I inherited from my mother."

I smiled. The sleep had helped her regain her resilience.

She stroked his hair and, amazingly, his eyes opened. He recognised her. He spoke English but it was heavily accented, "My lady! You are alive! When that savage struck me, I thought I was dead like poor John."

John of Derby had been making water. He had just returned to hear Johann's words. He smiled, "No, young master, poor John is alive, thanks to Sir Thomas and his men. We have a chance of life."

He tried to stand and he winced with the pain. Edward shook his head, "I am afraid that they have hurt you, master. The ride will be painful but at least we will not have to tie you on the horse."

"Are we not safe yet?"

Lady Margaret shook her head, "No, but we are in good hands. These warriors will protect us. They are my countrymen."

It took time to get Johann to the horse. My men and John of Derby were as gentle as they could be but he was badly hurt. The rest of us mounted and left before dawn. I had Mordaf and Gruffyd to our rear and David of Wales led the scouts.

As we rode lady Margaret looked at my surcoat and then at me, "My lord, if you do not mind my impertinence, may I ask you a question?"

"Of course." I was not looking at her. My eyes scanned the horizon for danger.

"Are you the Sir Thomas of Stockton who murdered the Bishop of Durham?"

I had known that I would be called a murderer despite the fact that it had been an execution. I answered anyway. "Bluntly put but yes, I killed him for hurts he had done my family."

"I heard you were a savage monster."

"Don't tell me, you heard I drank baby's blood and consorted with the devil."

She laughed, "Something like that."

"Well, now you can judge for yourself."

As the river broadened to our right I began to hope that we would soon reach Riga and safety. My hopes were dashed when first Mordaf and then David galloped towards us, "Lord there are riders ahead. They are Slavs."

David pointed behind, "And more men come from that direction."

"Then they appear to have us." I looked around. The only hope I spied was a sandspit in the river. It meant that they could not gallop at us. The shallow water would slow them down. If we had not had the women and an injured man with us I might have risked fording the river but that was out of the question. "To the sandspit!"

I waited with Sir William and the two squires as my men led the women and Johann to the island. My archers dismounted and prepared their bows. I heard

Robert of La Fiche shout, "Bury the spears in the river. Let them try to get through that!"

It was a clever idea. We all had three spears. By using the spares and burying them haft down we would have a hedgehog of steel. I turned to Fótr, "Fetch us a spear each. We will try to discourage them!" I saw that the two groups had moved closer to us. I estimated there to be about forty or so horsemen. The Slavs used mounted archers. I hoped these had none or that could be a quick end to what I had in mind. I put on my helmet and readied my spear. "What we do is to charge together. Stay close. We hit their leading riders. They will be the bravest and the best. If you cannot hit the men then hit their horses. Turn and ride for the river as soon as you have struck flesh. Slip your shield around your back and trust to God!"

The three raised their spears and shouted, "Aye lord!"

The nearest Slavs were eighty paces from us and wondering what we were doing. I spurred Skuld and she leapt forward. I knew that I was risking Harald and Fótr but I had little choice. They had the best mail and the best helmets. I saw that the leading Slav had mail. They all wore helmets and they all had the small round shield which they held in their fist. Most had spears but they were shorter than ours. More importantly, they rode in a loose formation. Most barbarians did.

I lowered my spear and they copied me. Holding my shield tight and at an angle, I leaned forward whilst holding my spear behind me. I rammed my spear forward and it struck the Slav's shield. Skuld was a bigger horse than the Slav's and I wore mail and was heavier. The spearhead skidded off the shield and hit his shoulder. He fell into the path of the man who was following. My three companions had faced men without mail. They had all been clever enough to strike at flesh rather than the shield and all three men that they had hit were wounded. Sir William's fell from the saddle holding the spear which had killed him.

"Back!" As I turned Skuld I threw the spear at the Slav who launched himself at me. I hit him in the shoulder and he too fell from the horse. Five men were down and the men and the horses made the others swerve to avoid them. Edward and Robert had left a gap through which we were able to ride. David and the archers sent a volley of arrows into the air as we splashed through the water to reach the sandspit. As soon as we turned Henry Youngblood plugged the gap with spears.

Although the spears faced the shore we could still attempt to cross the river. I was reluctant to do so for it would probably mean the deaths of those we had rescued. It was a last resort. Maddeningly we were just six miles from Riga. Had we been on the other shore we would have been almost able to see the cross on the tower of the church.

I drew my sword and dismounted. As I did so I saw that David of Wales had made sure that the five we had rescued were safe behind horses. It did not guarantee that they would survive but they would be the last to die!

The Slavs did have horse archers. There were eight of them. The leader of the second band was more cautious than the man I had slain. He had his men rein in while his archers began sending arrows towards us. We held up our shields and arrows rattled and rained into them. Then David and his men began to target the archers. As the rain of arrows slowed I risked a look. There were just two of their archers left alive. I heard the screams of one of our horses which had been injured. The screams ended when one of my men slit its throat.

Suddenly the Slavs galloped at us. We had hurt almost a quarter of their men. I had hoped that by making them bleed they would reconsider and let us go. Then I heard Robert of La Flèche, "Lord there are more barbarians coming down the river bank. They are on foot and there are forty of them."

"How far away are they?"

"I would say a mile."

I turned to Sir William. "Then that is why these are charging! They wish to hold us here."

The river slowed them up, as I knew it would, David and his archers had hit more of them. The Slavs hurled spears at us. Their horses were struggling to keep their footing in the river. It was not deep but it was muddy.

"Men at arms! At them!"

I slipped between the spears and ran into the shallows. The Slavs thought I had gone mad. I was leaving the safety of the sandspit to get close to them. I had no intention of fighting a horseman on equal terms. I was a knight and I knew that the greatest danger lay in losing your horse. I ducked beneath the spear and plunged my sword into the throat of the nearest horse. In its death throes, it reared and threw the rider into the river. The next horse trampled him. Edward swung his sword and hacked through the leg of a Slav and then into his horse. Ridley the Giant and Godwin of Battle had slung their shields over their backs and swung two mighty axes into the heads of two horses. The survivors had had enough and they turned to head to the safety of the advancing men on foot. As they turned David and his archers sent arrows into their backs.

We waded back to the sandspit. David of Wales said, "Lord, we are down to our last ten flights each. After that, we will be joining you to fight with sword and shield."

I nodded, "Is anyone hurt?"

"Henry Youngblood is wounded; John of Derby and Lady Margaret are tending to him."

"Clear the dead horse, put it into the river. Use it as a barrier to the enemy."

I watched the next warband as they approached. Robert had been wrong. There were nearer seventy of them. They would be able to move through our spears.

We had beaten their horsemen. We could not expect to beat so many men on foot. My grandfather had always told me that a man never gave up until someone took his sword from his dead hand. I shouted, "Lock shields. We will make a shield wall."

We faced west and the thirteen men at arms, knights and squires who remained prepared to fight to the last. Our ten archers stood behind us. I could hear the two women weeping and wailing. Will son of Harold said, "I wish they were more like Lady Margaret lord. Can we not give them to the Slavs?"

It was a tempting thought. "I think not."

The enemy had formed up and they had shields held before them. David and his archers selected targets. They did so judiciously. They aimed at the most dangerous enemies. They sent arrows into the open helmets of the warriors with mail. They targeted the men carrying the standards. Barbarians fell but they still came on. When they reached the water David and his archers slew another four when they clambered over the dead horses. They lost cohesion as they came through the spears. I lunged at them and took one in the neck. Then an order was shouted and the Slavs grabbed the spears and turned them on us. I had doomed us by my attempt to stop horses.

Holding my shield before me I stepped onto my right leg and swung my sword horizontally. A spear hit my helmet and made my head ring. Another struck my mail and went into my side. I felt my sword connect. I swung again.

Sir William shouted, "Back, Sir Thomas." As I stepped back I saw, through my two eye holes that three Slavs lay dead.

David of Wales said, "Four arrows each lord."

"We fight to the end! We are the men of Stockton!"

Stockton men are big and brave
Send a Scot to an early grave
Stockton men fear no foe
Fight us and to hell you go
Stockton
Stockton
Stockton men fear no one
Stockton men are big and brave
Send a Scot to an early grave
Stockton men fear no foe
Fight us and to hell you go
Stockton
Stockton
Stockton men fear no one

It made the enemy hesitate and then I heard John of Derby shout, "Lord, there are men coming up the river. They wear your livery!"

I heard a horn. It was The Jarl Birger Brosa! I did not turn. I watched the Slavs. They turned and they fled. Forty men and horses splashed through the water and, in a ragged line, began to hunt down and spear the Slavs. Had they arrived any later then we would have been dead for we would have died upon our own spears.

We crossed back to the bank. Henry Youngblood was not badly wounded but he would not be fighting for some time. By the time our friends returned we were mounted and ready to return to Riga.

I clasped Jarl Birger Persson's arm, "How did you know to find us?"

"A river captain said that he spied men wearing the gryphon on the wrong side of the river some days since. It had to be you. We left as soon as he told us." He pointed downstream. "There are two boats moored downstream. It is how we crossed. We will ferry you."

I pointed to the women, "We would have risked crossing the river but, as you can see, we have guests."

The Jarl Birger Brosa laughed, "Another fine tale awaits us!"

Chapter 19

It was dark when we reached Riga. We went directly to Bishop Albert. We told him the tale of Lady Margaret. He was sympathetic. "You shall stay with me until Reimar von Tork returns. He is with the Master. They are dealing with a band of Estonians who tried to attack Ādaži. It should only take them a couple of days."

Sir William and I bade farewell to Lady Margaret and the others. She looked unhappy, "Will you leave us so quickly, Sir Thomas? I have much to say to you. We owe you our lives!"

"I will be back tomorrow, fear not but your husband's kinsman will look after you now. I return to Stock Holm at the end of the month. I have done my duty and I am pleased that all five of you survived. I did not think that we would. God was with us."

She shook her head, "It was God who watched but it was you and your men who acted." She stood on tiptoe and kissed me. "I will speak with you again when you are less tired."

I did not understand what she meant. But she was right, I was tired. I had had two nights without sleep. As we headed back to our hall Sir William said, "Lord, I know I am young and know little."

"You are learning."

"Aye lord, but you are not!"

"What?"

"Could you not see that the lady is smitten by you? She did not wish to be parted from you."

"But she is a widow and…"

"And therefore, free and available or do you find her unattractive lord?"

We had reached our hall and Jarl Birger Persson had heard his words, "Who, Lady Margaret?"

Sir William said, "I cannot talk sense to him, perhaps you can. The lady kissed him and all but begged for him to stay and speak with her."

"She is attractive, Thomas, and I confess that she only had eyes for you when we returned."

"It cannot be, Birger," I told him her story and explained her situation. "So you see. It would be dishonourable to woo her. I would be seen as someone after her

186

fortune. If I had land and a future then I might consider it for I am not made of stone and she did stir me."

I talked with the two jarls and William for a little while about the Slavs and the attack. Then I felt myself falling asleep while I spoke and, leaving the other three to talk, I retired. My dreams were filled with Lady Margaret. She would be the love I lost for she could never be mine.

The next day, when I went to see Lady Margaret and Bishop Albert I found myself being praised on all sides. All seemed taken with my actions. I was embarrassed. I did not like the attention. Bishop Albert presented me with a silver crown encrusted with jewels. I was flattered. Later I discovered that he had not had it made but it had come into his possession. The fact that he did it so publicly with his priests and the two brothers there meant he did it to enhance his reputation as a generous lord.

When we were dismissed I walked with Lady Margaret. We walked by the river. It was a pleasant late summer's day and I enjoyed walking and talking with someone from England. We spoke of English weather and food. We talked of rain in summer and sun in winter. We touched on King John and then she began to ask me about my family. It was logical for she knew that my family, in the shape of my great grandfather, had been responsible for King John's father gaining the throne.

"It seems ungrateful! And your father died saving his brother!"

"I do not think he liked his brother. I believe that King Henry was ill-served by his children." I laughed, "However, as I am no parent, I cannot judge, can I? I have no brothers or sisters what do I know of families?"

"And I am without brothers or sisters. It was lonely growing up alone. The two weeping ladies were the only companions I had."

I laughed, "Then you have my sympathy!"

"You have your men. I know, from speaking with them, that they think more of you than any man alive. That is something of which you can be proud."

"And I am!"

It was easy talking to her and, for the next three days, we spent every moment we could in each other's company. I was actually disappointed when I heard of the return of the Brothers of the Sword. I had known it would have to come to an end but I had prayed it would not. We were at the quay when we heard the trumpets and horns announce the arrival of the victorious warriors.

"You had best go. Your kinsman will wish to speak with you."

"I beg you to come with me. I know him not. You have met him. Please."

"Of course. I would do anything for you."

"You have already done more than enough, lord."

By the time we reached Bishop Albert, I could see that the news had already been given to the second in command of the order. Hermann Balk smiled and came over to clasp my arm, "You are the true embodiment of knighthood. I wish you were a Brother of the Sword."

I shrugged, "I am in spirit but I cannot commit to a venture like this. I warn you, Master, that the Slavs will be a harder enemy to defeat than the Estonians."

Reimar had kept back a little and, having seen Hermann welcome me, he stepped forward. "I have to thank you, Sir Thomas. You have avenged my uncle. He was my father's younger brother and I loved him dearly. It pained me when I heard of the manner of his death."

"I was just grateful to save his widow. At least her life and future will be assured with the manor of your uncle."

I suddenly realised that he had not looked in Lady Margaret's direction. His next words were delivered with neither compassion nor kindness, "I have given the manor of my uncle to the order. It cannot be undone. I am afraid that even had my uncle asked me to return it to him I could not."

Lady Margaret said, incredulously, "You would have had your father's brother homeless?"

"Of course not. He could have stayed in the castle of the order."

I stared at the German, "But not his wife, of course."

"Of course not! We are a holy order." Lady Margaret ran from the room. Reimar just shrugged, "Women!"

If he expected others to laugh with him he was wrong. They were as shocked as I was. I was also angry. I walked up to him and said, "You are a villain. You have no honour. If you are a man then face me sword to sword."

He laughed, "You are distraught!"

I backhanded him across the mouth so hard that he fell over. "Face me or all the world shall know you for a coward!"

Hermann Balk stepped between us although his knight made no effort to rise. I saw, in his eyes, fear. In that moment, I saw all the battles of the order. I had never seen him in the front rank. "Sir Thomas, we cannot fight amongst ourselves."

"Master, I believe in honour. Lady Margaret was made a promise by this snake's kinsman. He is honour bound to fulfil that promise."

Reimar stood, "And I will not! She bewitched the old man. Why else would he marry her?" He suddenly seized upon the idea, "That is it. She is a witch. We should have a trial!"

That was the point at which he lost Bishop Albert and the Master. Bishop Albert shook his head, "There will be no combat, Sir Thomas! I forbid it. Unless you wish to quarrel with the church then you will withdraw. You have already shown scant regard for priests. Do not undo all of your good work." He paused and I could see the idea forming. "In fact, as you were going home at the end of the fighting season I send you now. I will pay you and your men for their service and thank you for what you have done." He nodded as though agreeing with his own idea, "And you can escort the Lady Margaret back to England. You are both English after all."

"You will not order him to fulfil his uncle's promise?"

Bishop Albert shrugged, "We only have her word that the old man made the promise. Perhaps he was coming here to join the order. Whatever the reason the gift to the order will bring God to the godless and that is worth more than the tears of a young girl. She is young enough to find another man."

I could not help it and my hand went to my sword.

Bishop Albert said, "And you, Sir Thomas are forbidden to ever come to Riga again… on pain of death!" Knights' hands went to their swords. I was alone and although I would kill the Bishop and many of his knights then I would die.

Hermann Balk said, "Go, my friend. I am with you in this but bloodshed only helps the heathen. Go I beg of you. I will do what I can for Lady Margaret."

Ignoring him I pointed to Reimar, "If I were you, I would stay here in the east for if you ever breathe the same air as me then you die. That I swear. And I never break an oath!" I watched as he physically recoiled. He was terrified of me.

I sought Lady Margaret but I could not find her and then Bishop Albert's brothers appeared. They had a chest with our gold but they also had armed men. Brother Harald said, "Sir Thomas, leave. I would not wish to order these men to put you in irons but I will do so unless you leave quietly. There will be two ships ready to take you and your people in the morning. Bishop Albert insists that you leave quickly and quietly. Lady Margaret and her people will join you." He put his hand on my arm. "It is for the best."

I shook my head, "You are a good man but I am afraid there is something rotten here in Riga. I saw this in the Holy Land and I see it here. I will go and I will not return but I fear this venture will end badly."

Word had spread of the confrontation. By the time I reached the hall, there were rumours and exaggerations.

The Jarl Birger Brosa said, "What has happened?"

I took the horn of ale Edward held for me and I told them all, word for word. My men, Petr, Birger Persson were outraged. The Jarl Birger Brosa appeared more pragmatic. "You have been well paid and you can now take the lady to England. Marry her. You were going to leave anyway."

Petr and his brother turned to their leader. Their faces were filled with anger tinged with disappointment. Birger said, "I will not return here. My brother and I will stay in Sweden. I thought you had honour. I can see that you have not if you side with them."

The Jarl Birger Brosa reddened, "You go too far cousin."

"Stop!" My roar silenced them. "I will not have blood brothers fight over me. I will return to Stock Holm and take my leave of your wife. Then we will sail away from Sweden. I will never return. I thought I had come here to find myself. I have but I have also found things about other men that I like not. King John is not the only man to have disappointed me." I put down the horn. "And now I have much to do. We leave this barren land in the morning and I, for one, will be glad to see the back of it."

Epilogue

Herman Balk himself escorted Lady Margaret to the ships. "I have tried, Sir Thomas but Reimar and Bishop Albert will not be moved. Farewell. If you were to take my advice it would be to marry. I think that you have been thrown together for just this purpose." He shrugged, "But what do I know?"

I stood with Lady Margaret as the ships left Sweden. She was stiff with anger. "I am not something to be passed around. I am not helpless! I need no man's sympathy and pity!"

I smiled and put my arm around her. She fought a little but I am strong, "And you will get neither from me. We are both orphans now. Neither of us has a home. I ask you to marry me. I for one do not mind if you do so out of pity for Hermann Balk was right. We were thrown together for a purpose." She looked up at me and there was a hint of a smile. "So what say you? Will you agree to marry a priest killer? An outlaw? Someone who sups with the devil?"

She laughed, "Aye I will. You are the finest man I have ever known. I will be honoured to marry you. We will find a new home together!" She kissed me and, as our lips met, I knew that this was the start of something good. "You have done more than enough already. I want you to live for me, not die for me."

"I am not certain where we shall live."

She had laughed, "I care not. I do not think that it will be dull!"

By the time we reached Stock Holm, I had told her everything about me and we had discussed what we would do next. It was easy for we thought the same. She had been shocked to learn the lengths I would have gone to in order to protect her. She was unconcerned about the estates and more worried that my men and I might have risked our lives for her.

I was honest with Lady Brigida and told her all. I left nothing out including the bad feeling between her husband and Birger Persson. She had smiled, "That will pass. They need each other." She shook her head, "And when my husband returns it will be to the sad news that our son died fighting for my uncle. Perhaps that will put this argument into perspective."

"I am sorry, my lady."

"I know you are for you do not know how to lie." She had put her arms around Lady Margaret and me. "And we shall have you wed before you leave. My son is dead. Perhaps you can live the life I hoped he would lead."

And so we were married in the stone church in Stock Holm. It was my men, the wives of my men and Sir William and Lady Brigida who attended along with Lady Margaret's two ladies, her servant John and Johann. I could not ask for more. When '*Swan of Stockton*' arrived a week later I hired her and the two ships which had brought us from Riga to take us from the Baltic. We had chests of treasure. We had horses. We had family. More importantly, we had each other. We had fought clans and seen the loyalty of such families. We were closer. We were brothers in arms. When we left the Baltic, I had told no one where we were going. No one that is, save for my wife. There would be no secrets from her. I was no longer alone. For the first time since Arsuf, I had a family!

The End

Glossary

Garth- a garth was a farm. Not to be confused with the name Garth
Groat- English coin worth four silver pennies
Herterpol- Hartlepool
Luciaria-Lucerne (Switzerland)
Nissa- Nice (Provence)
Wulfestun- Wolviston (Durham)

Historical Notes

This series of books follow the fortunes of the family of the Warlord begun in the Anarchy. As with that series, the characters in this one are, largely, fictional, but the events are all historically accurate.

Books used in the research:
The Crusades-David Nicholle
Crusader Castles in the Holy Land 1097-1192- David Nicolle
The Normans- David Nicolle
Norman Knight AD 950-1204- Christopher Gravett
The Norman Conquest of the North- William A Kappelle
The Knight in History- Francis Gies
The Norman Achievement- Richard F Cassady
Knights- Constance Brittain Bouchard
Knight Templar 1120-1312 -Helen Nicholson
English Medieval Knight 1200-1300
The Scandinavian Baltic Crusades 1100-1500

For the English maps, I have used the original Ordnance Survey maps. Produced by the army in the 19th century they show England before modern developments and, in most cases, are pre-industrial revolution. Produced by Cassini they are a useful tool for a historian.

Griff Hosker
August 2017

Other books by Griff Hosker

If you enjoyed reading this book, then why not read another one by the author?

Ancient History

The Sword of Cartimandua Series
(Germania and Britannia 50 A.D. – 128 A.D.)
Ulpius Felix- Roman Warrior (prequel)
The Sword of Cartimandua
The Horse Warriors
Invasion Caledonia
Roman Retreat
Revolt of the Red Witch
Druid's Gold
Trajan's Hunters
The Last Frontier
Hero of Rome
Roman Hawk
Roman Treachery
Roman Wall
Roman Courage

The Wolf Warrior series
(Britain in the late 6th Century)
Saxon Dawn
Saxon Revenge
Saxon England
Saxon Blood
Saxon Slayer
Saxon Slaughter
Saxon Bane
Saxon Fall: Rise of the Warlord
Saxon Throne
Saxon Sword

Medieval History

The Dragon Heart Series
Viking Slave
Viking Warrior
Viking Jarl
Viking Kingdom
Viking Wolf
Viking War
Viking Sword
Viking Wrath
Viking Raid
Viking Legend
Viking Vengeance
Viking Dragon
Viking Treasure
Viking Enemy
Viking Witch
Viking Blood
Viking Weregeld
Viking Storm
Viking Warband
Viking Shadow
Viking Legacy
Viking Clan
Viking Bravery

The Norman Genesis Series
Hrolf the Viking
Horseman
The Battle for a Home
Revenge of the Franks
The Land of the Northmen
Ragnvald Hrolfsson
Brothers in Blood
Lord of Rouen
Drekar in the Seine
Duke of Normandy

Sword For Hire

The Duke and the King

Danelaw
(England and Denmark in the 11th Century)
Dragon Sword
Oathsword (October 2021)

New World Series
Blood on the Blade
Across the Seas
The Savage Wilderness
The Bear and the Wolf
Erik The Navigator

The Vengeance Trail

The Reconquista Chronicles
Castilian Knight
El Campeador
The Lord of Valencia

The Aelfraed Series
(Britain and Byzantium 1050 A.D. - 1085 A.D.)
Housecarl
Outlaw
Varangian

**The Anarchy Series England
1120-1180**
English Knight
Knight of the Empress
Northern Knight
Baron of the North
Earl
King Henry's Champion
The King is Dead
Warlord of the North
Enemy at the Gate
The Fallen Crown

4

Warlord's War
Kingmaker
Henry II
Crusader
The Welsh Marches
Irish War
Poisonous Plots
The Princes' Revolt
Earl Marshal

Border Knight
1182-1300
Sword for Hire
Return of the Knight
Baron's War
Magna Carta
Welsh Wars
Henry III
The Bloody Border
Baron's Crusade
Sentinel of the North
War in the West
Debt of Honour

Sir John Hawkwood Series
France and Italy 1339- 1387
Crécy: The Age of the Archer
Man At Arms
The White Company

Lord Edward's Archer
Lord Edward's Archer
King in Waiting
An Archer's Crusade
Targets of Treachery (August 2021)

Struggle for a Crown
1360- 1485
Blood on the Crown

Sword For Hire

To Murder A King
The Throne
King Henry IV
The Road to Agincourt
St Crispin's Day

Tales from the Sword I (Short stories from the Medieval period)

Conquistador
England and America in the 16th Century
Conquistador (November 2021)

Modern History

The Napoleonic Horseman Series
Chasseur à Cheval
Napoleon's Guard
British Light Dragoon
Soldier Spy
1808: The Road to Coruña
Talavera
The Lines of Torres Vedras
Bloody Badajoz
The Road to France
Waterloo

The Lucky Jack American Civil War series
Rebel Raiders
Confederate Rangers
The Road to Gettysburg

The British Ace Series
1914
1915 Fokker Scourge
1916 Angels over the Somme
1917 Eagles Fall
1918 We will remember them
From Arctic Snow to Desert Sand
Wings over Persia

6

Combined Operations series
1940-1945
Commando
Raider
Behind Enemy Lines
Dieppe
Toehold in Europe
Sword Beach
Breakout
The Battle for Antwerp
King Tiger
Beyond the Rhine
Korea
Korean Winter

Tales from the Sword II (Short stories from the Modern period)

Other Books
Great Granny's Ghost (Aimed at 9-14-year-old young people)

For more information on all of the books then please visit the author's website at www.griffhosker.com where there is a link to contact him or visit his Facebook page: GriffHosker at Sword Books

Made in the USA
Las Vegas, NV
07 December 2021

36344110R00115